THE HUNT FOR THE PEGGY C

JOHN WINN MILLER

bancroft press

Cover Design: Christine Van Bree Design
Interior Design: TracyCopesCreative.com
Author Photo: Bill Roughen

978-1-61088-570-6 (HC)
978-1-61088-571-3 (PB)
978-1-61088-572-0 (Ebook)
978-1-61088-573-7 (PDF)
978-1-61088-574-4 (Audio)

Published by Bancroft Press
"Books that Enlighten"
410-358-0658
P.O. Box 65360,
Baltimore, MD 21209
www.bancroftpress.com

Printed in the United States of America

*For my wife Margo,
whose patience and dedicated
editing made this possible,
and for my daughter Allison,
who inspired it*

CHAPTER 1

Captain Jake Rogers' decrepit cargo ship pitched and rolled in a brutal North Sea storm, its engines straining against the churning sea in the middle of a war zone. Mountainous waves crashed into and over the bow in an unrelenting fury.

Rogers had seen plenty of trouble in his years commanding the *Peggy C*, an outdated but usually reliable ship. A three-island tramp steamer, she sailed without a set schedule, the captain going port to port and begging for cargo, and not asking too many questions about what it was or where it was from, only where it was going and how much would he be paid.

Another wave rattled the ship. The *Peggy C* had been through a lot over the years, but the old girl had never let Rogers down.

This time felt different.

Its rusty hull shuddered and moaned every time it plunged from towering crest to trough. The wire rope-stays screeched like violin strings fighting to hold the towering masts aloft. Far too often, the *Peggy C's* propeller raced and whined when a wave thrust the stern out of the water. The North Sea could be treacherous, especially in late autumn when the freezing north winds came howling in from Iceland, chopping up the shallow waters and mudflats around the small islands dotting the Dutch coast. These waters were already troubled by dangerous tides caused when the Atlantic Ocean smashed north through the English Channel into currents rushing south from the Norwegian Sea.

With one hand, Rogers, for balance, clutched the icy railing on the bridge deck outside the three-story high wheelhouse. With the other hand, he struggled to focus his rain-splattered binoculars on something in the murky distance. From his charts, he knew dangerous shoals and shallows were out there somewhere; in his gut, he suspected they were way too close. And his ship couldn't seem to muster enough power to avert the looming disaster.

American flags flapping on the masts and the spotlit ones painted on the hull showed the *Peggy C* to be from a neutral country. But Rogers worried there was little chance a passing warship, in the dreary fog of war, would be able to see the flags before blasting away at another victim. And, if that wasn't bad enough, there were rumors of rogue mines floating into these sea lanes and sinking cargo ships.

For two years since the war started in 1939, the *Peggy C* and her ragtag crew had dodged the mines and torpedoes and random naval duels from Africa to the North Sea, managing to eke out a living while the competition dwindled. Outside the protection of a convoy, fewer and fewer commercial ships dared ply these waters. Though Germany's focus had shifted to the Russian and Mediterranean fronts, too many trigger-happy U-boat captains still lurked about in search of trophies from sunken tonnage.

The situation was truly dire and desperate.

Rogers loved every minute of it.

A ghost of a smile crossed his windburned face, etched with tiny crow's feet around hazel eyes—eyes hardened by years of squinting at threatening storms on the horizon, of staring down edgy sailors with balled-up fists and bad ideas, of calculating the odds in life-or-death situations on an unforgiving sea. All that made Rogers appear older than his thirty-eight years. For captains, sea years were more like dog years.

He was tall and gaunt, with the easy grace of an athlete who'd spent lots of summers on dusty baseball fields, growing strong, quick, and singularly focused on one thing—winning. That penchant had earned him a scholarship to the U.S. Naval Academy, a lucky break for a poor kid from a broken Baltimore family who dreamt and read voraciously about life at sea.

In a raging storm like this, with mast-high spumes of water lashing his ship, the adrenaline, the pounding heartbeat in his ears, the rapid breathing—all exhilarated rather than terrified him. Calm seas were the enemy of the mind, leaving way too much time to dwell on the past, on what-ifs, on terrible things that could never be changed. And nothing so focused the mind as a nearly hopeless challenge.

Rogers glanced over his shoulder at the helmsman in the wheelhouse, a bug-eyed kid standing erect. Though outwardly trying to show fearlessness, he was clasping the large wooden wheel's peg handles so tightly that his fingers had turned white.

"Chief says we've got some power back, but not enough to steer us safely into Amsterdam!" First Mate Ali Nidal shouted into Rogers' ear. "We have to wait out the storm!"

Without taking his attention off the horizon, Rogers handed Nidal the binoculars and pointed off the starboard bow.

"What's that look like?" Rogers asked, hunching forward against the biting ocean spray, holding tight to his white captain's hat.

Nidal pressed the binoculars to his eyes, moving his head left to right and back again before spotting flashing lights. Rogers knew the swarthy Tunisian's pockmarked face, coal-black eyes, and perpetual frown made overworked crew members worry about whether he was staring at them calmly, or menacingly—a quality Rogers actually found useful.

"S-O-S," Nidal said in a slight French accent that sometimes made him hard to understand. But it also was useful for Rogers to have a second-in-command who spoke Arabic, French, Spanish, and English and could more easily deal with a polyglot crew.

"That's what I thought."

"We will pray for their souls," said Nidal, handing back the binoculars, emotionless as always. "Further away from shore."

Rogers peered through the binoculars. "Yeah, that'd be the smart move."

Rogers, Nidal, and three other sailors in oil-skin jackets and rain hats hung over the *Peggy C's* starboard bulwark on the main deck as they tossed roped life rings to six men in a lifeboat bouncing in the angry sea below. Their crippled cargo ship was nearby giving off its last flickering burst of light and steam before being sucked under the water. The men in the lifeboat stretched out their hands as far as they could for the rings, but the gale-force winds kept blowing salvation out of reach. Out of nowhere, a rogue wave crashed over their lifeboat, swallowing it whole like Jonah's whale. One second it was there with its six forlorn passengers; the next, it wasn't.

"Oh my God! Where the hell did they go?" Rogers asked in horror. He shined a hand-held Aldis message lamp on the foaming gray water and moved it in a circle, checking for any sign of movement, any sign of life, hoping against hope that the hungry sea would relent for just a moment and spit out her quarry. Was that a hand? Hands? Rogers focused the light on the apparitions he thought he saw. Three heads popped up. Three men flailed about in the freezing water, shouting in vain to be heard over the crashing waves and howling wind. "There! There!" Rogers shouted, pointing with the lamp. "Throw the rings over there!"

Nidal and the others hurled the roped life rings into the wind; they kept blowing back short of the fading survivors, who eventually managed somehow to fight the current and grab the rings, holding on for dear life as they were dragged through the frigid water toward the ship. Pulling them aboard was an arduous task for Nidal and his men. The survivors, in their soaked winter coats and boots, felt like 300-pound halibuts thrashing and fighting every inch of the way. As the rescuers fought to haul their catch onboard, the slippery rope tore the skin off their frozen hands. One by one, though, they reeled in the three survivors, stretching them out on the deck and pumping their chests to clear their lungs of the saltwater. The men coughed and choked up whatever they had eaten that day, at the same time fighting for breath.

Rogers kept circling the area with his lamp, searching for the other three men, leaning further and further over the rail to get a better angle. Without warning, the *Peggy C* plunged into a trough, and a wave crashed over the bulwark. Rogers, whose hands were on the binoculars and spotlight, was propelled upward. Looking down at his watery grave and cursing his losing hand, he had no smart move to get out of another mess, no way to fix things, and he almost felt regret as his body was being flung overboard.

The plunge stopped with a sharp jerk, shooting pain from Rogers' right ankle up his spine and then to his neck. His head banged on the steel hull, scraping his face as he was dragged up and over the railing and back onto the heaving deck. A brawny African flipped Rogers onto his back, inspecting him for what damage needed repair, and nodded when it was clear his captain was only bruised.

"Thanks, Obasi!" Rogers shouted, gulping in cold saltwater air to catch his breath. "Again!"

Obasi lifted Rogers to his feet as easily as if he were a doll and patted him on the back, grinning. They both rushed over to help the others tend to the drenched survivors huddled on the deck. A crackling bolt of lightning reminded everyone of an ominous threat: the still smoldering cargo ship had not, after all, entirely disappeared beneath the surface. Its jagged bow lurked just yards away, the equivalent of a steel iceberg waiting to shear the *Peggy C* apart.

Through the pouring rain, Rogers glanced up at the wheelhouse for a hopeful sign, but Able Seaman J.J. McAllister, the helmsman, kept spinning the wheel and raising his hands high, indicating there was nothing he could do without more power. The *Peggy C* would drift wherever the heartless sea damn well wanted to send her.

Below deck, in the dimly lit engine room, Chief Engineer Giovanni Turani took a slippery wrench and turned a bolt on a piston. Sweat pouring down his reddened face, he interspersed whispered Italian curses with louder prayers to the Virgin Mary. The problem was that the boilers were only able to engage one of the engine's three pistons that powered the single shaft and screw. Turani should have been frantic, but that wasn't in his nature. A methodical engineer, he always worked step by step to solve a problem, knowing that haste created even more problems.

"Move, damn you!" he finally shouted in frustration. "Give me a larger wrench." Assistant Engineer Nathan Dunawa, a mulatto from St. Vincent, dug through a toolbox and handed what he figured Turani wanted. Clank! Turani smashed the wrench on the bolt and pistons. Clank. The piston moved ever so slightly. Turani did a short jump for joy, wiped his face with a dirty rag, and, with Dunawa's help, turned the bolt until the frozen pistons started pumping again. Picking up speed after a moment, the three pistons rumbled to a glorious roar of metal on metal. Dunawa stepped over to the circular engine order telegraph and jerked the handles left and right, to ring the wheelhouse above with the news. He stopped only when the arrow pointed to "full speed ahead."

In the wheelhouse, McAllister, a young Scot, swung the wheel around and, his ruddy face covered in beads of sweat, focused out the windows. This was his first time alone at the helm, a rare duty for someone so young—he had just turned twenty—and who didn't have many voyages under his belt. Rogers had taken a liking to him. What with his sunny disposition and willingness to learn, McAllister reminded him of himself at the same age.

The fired-up pistons vibrated the deck as Rogers wrapped blankets around the three survivors, all staring in horror at the remains of their ship drawing closer by the second. Looking to the wheelhouse above, Rogers saw McAllister give a thumbs up as he steered the *Peggy C* just clear of the wreck. Rogers caught Nidal's attention and winked. The first mate's blank face made it clear he was not amused.

The trembling survivors were moved to the crew's mess, where they were greeted by Cookie, a portly Brit with molted jowls, tufts of white hair dotting his bald head, and the twinkling eyes of everyone's favorite grandfather. Amiable and a bit daffy, he told everyone he hated his nickname but had learned to live with it because he was, in fact, the ship's cook. He would hasten to add, when introduced, that he was also the ship's chief medical officer, a title he gave himself because he was the only one onboard who knew anything about setting broken bones and patching wounds. By necessity, he was self-taught, having learned anatomy from carcasses, deboning chickens and, for the most part, trial and error.

"Put him on the table and grab him tight," Cookie said, hobbling over on his bad hip. Nidal and Seamus, a timorous red-headed Irishman who always wore both suspenders and a belt, placed one of the survivors on a table and held him down as he moaned and twisted in agony. Cookie leaned over and inspected him from head to toe. "Hold still, mate," Cookie said, nodding for Nidal and Seamus to tighten their grips. "This won't hurt a bit." With a loud snap, Cookie yanked the delirious sailor's right shoulder bone back into its socket. The poor man screamed, then passed out. Nidal did his best to cover him with a ragged blanket.

To the other two survivors, Rogers carried steaming cups of coffee, tins of biscuits, and a slab of butter. Their lips blue, the three survivors sat dazed and shivering at a separate table, clutching blankets.

"Fifteen? For what? I ask you," the larger and younger of the two asked of no one, his face contorted in anguish. "The Old Man said not to worry—"

"Are they all really gone?" the older one interrupted, rising and staggering toward the door. "Let's have a look."

Rogers steered him back to his seat with a gentle arm around his shoulder. "Sorry, old-timer."

"Target practice they made of us," the old timer said. With a wild look in his eye, he snatched Rogers' arm off of him. "We tried to surrender," he said in a shaky voice. "White flag and all. The boarding party said nary a word."

"Bloody Brauer's crew, it was!" his young companion yelled hysterically.

Rogers eyed Nidal and the rest of his crew in the room, grown silent and paying close attention. "Brauer doesn't exist," Rogers said a little too loudly for the benefit of his crew and added: "British propaganda. You need to rest."

"No!" the old-timer screeched, trying to elbow Rogers out of the way. "We have to be ready! U-boats don't care about neutrals no more!" Tears poured down his face. Rogers held onto him, letting him sob while guiding him to sit and drink his coffee. The captain buttered one of the biscuits and offered it to the old timer, but he pushed it away.

"Fifteen mates. All of 'em gone," the younger survivor repeated over and over, unable to grasp the enormity of the loss. Pulling a blanket over his head, he slipped to the floor and curled up into a quivering ball.

Rogers had cargo to drop off in Amsterdam and hopes of picking up another load there, but his heart sank as he watched the survivors and realized life had changed. The war, once remote and avoidable, more often than not, was now all too real, and things were heating up. The sinking of the *SS Robin Moor* off the coast of Sierra Leone by a U-boat in May had been the first reported attack on an American merchant ship, but there had been two others since, the *SS Steel Seafarer* in September in the Gulf of Suez, and the *SS Leigh* off the coast of Africa in October. So far, no U.S. merchant ship had been attacked in the North Atlantic or the North Sea. But, within the last month, U-boat wolfpacks had fired on two American destroyers, sinking one and sparking an international incident that nearly drew America into the war.

Maybe, Rogers thought, he should dock the *Peggy C* for good, but then what? The sea was all he knew. The thirty-year-old ship was well past its life expectancy but had been his home for years. And what about the crew? Was it fair to expose them to the horrors these poor survivors had gone through? Sure, they knew the risks, and they needed the money. Still, Rogers believed their safety was his responsibility. He had always warned his men never to gamble for more than they could afford to lose. Now, despite his concern for his crew, despite all the setbacks, and even despite the war, he decided he still liked his chances.

CHAPTER 2

The *Peggy C* steamed toward the North Sea Canal connecting the ocean to Amsterdam. The sea was calm and the sun shining in a frigid, cloudless sky. It was a welcome sight for the exhausted crew, and it meant less strain on the old hull.

Smallish for its class, the 2,500-gross tonnage, riveted-steel ship stretched about three-quarters the length of a football field and a little over half that width, a size that made it more vulnerable in heavy seas. From a distance, tramp steamers were often indistinguishable from one another, with tall masts known as King posts fore and aft holding two booms each for hoisting cargo. A wire radio antenna stretched from mast to mast. Raised decks or islands, which were at the stern and bow and amidships, held a white, three-story-high, rust-streaked superstructure housing sleeping and eating quarters. The wheelhouse was on top. Towering over everything was a wide-mouth funnel that, in the *Peggy C*'s case, was painted red topped by a black stripe bordered by thin white lines.

As the *Peggy C* approached the harbor entrance at the Port of Ijmuiden, Rogers and Nidal kept a watchful eye on a U-boat—perhaps from training bases at Hamburg to the north—cruising along. It appeared to have a fresh crew, judging from the formal uniforms and clean-shaven faces of the officers in visored caps gathered on the conning tower. That nearly twelve-foot tower looked like a rook from the front and a boot from the side, with the lower platform in the rear, called a *Wintergarten* like a German bandstand, surrounded by open metal railings. It was topped by two periscopes. The shorter of the two, an observation periscope, was used to scan for aircraft and navigational settings. The attack periscope had a smaller head to make it less detectable to planes and enemy ships, and less of a drag on a submerged U-boat in motion.

Running from the tower to the bow and to the stern were thick "jumper wires," lifelines really, that crews hooked onto while working on the deck in rough weather, when otherwise they could easily be dumped in the drink. They also served as a wireless radio antenna. The bow wire was used for transmission; the stern's two wires were for reception.

As was common, no Nazi insignias adorned the submarine's hull. Instead, a large red flag with a swastika and iron cross flew from the Wintergarten. The conning tower was adorned with a bright yellow and green frog, an eerily whimsical emblem (*Wappen*) unique to each U-boat, or sometimes a whole flotilla. The figures replaced identification numbers so as to make it more difficult for the Allies to keep track of which U-boat was where.

Most of the submarine crews thought of themselves as above politics, as carrying out orders for the Fatherland, slaughtering civilians and naval enemies with the same efficient indifference. They were proud sailors of the highly selective U-Bootwaffe, not merely of the Kriegsmarine. After extensive medical and physical evaluations, only one in ten volunteers was considered "fit for U-boats." And like Roman legionnaires, their loyalty was to the officers and men of their U-boat, not to the Navy or even the Third Reich.

The knot in Rogers' stomach eased a bit when the *Peggy C* left the U-boat behind and carefully slipped past the half-submerged remains of the *SS Jan Pieterszoon Coen*. Stuck in the sand of Ijmuiden's shallow harbor, its two gold and black funnels towered over exposed upper decks. To block the canal's entrance, the Royal Netherlands Navy had scuttled the 159-meter-long passenger ship and several smaller ones between the piers in May 1940. It remained closed until the next year when the Germans removed the ship's stern. That fifty-meter-wide gap gave small vessels like the *Peggy C* access to the locks for the sixteen-mile journey past imposing, heavily fortified concrete bunkers and then on to the Port of Amsterdam.

Large ocean-going vessels and warships were still blocked, and ships from non-Axis countries were rarely allowed entry—something that clearly worried the normally stoic Nidal. "Are you sure this is a good idea, Captain?" Nidal asked, standing with Rogers on the starboard end of the flying bridge and nodding discreetly at the trailing German S-Boot, a heavily armed fast-attack craft similar to an American PT boat.

"We have this," Rogers said, pulling out an official-looking German document from his pocket. "Somebody with influence must really want what we're bringing in."

When the *Peggy C* docked, it was already late afternoon, and the crew had to hustle with the cranes to lift the waterproof canvas hatches from the four holds—two forward and two aft—and offload what few crates and bags they had managed to pick up along the way. Crew members were animated, as only someone who escaped death can be, smiling and chatting like giddy old women at afternoon tea. Grunting with exertion, they stepped lively at Nidal's shouted commands, trying to outdo one another with their boasts about who knew the most about the pleasures of Amsterdam.

As soon as the gangplank hit the dock with a loud clang, uniformed port authorities and submachine gun-toting German soldiers streamed aboard to search the *Peggy C* for contraband, collect tariffs, and get a full accounting from the ship's master. Rogers recognized the elderly Chief Inspector De Klerk from previous trips and handed him the manifest and his other papers.

All around them, the ship was in a frenzy of action—the grinding of winches, the rumbling of chains, hatches moaning as they were lifted off the raised steel coamings that protected the hatches from water, shuffling feet and scraping crates on the steel decks. Although a steady, icy wind ripped across the water, the sailors were covered in sweat, and there was a strong odor of oil, grease, and coal dust.

The S-Boot idled nearby, all guns pointed toward *The Peggy C.*

"Good day, Captain Rogers. Pleasant voyage?" the chief inspector asked in perfect English as he sifted through the papers, glancing up on the sly to make sure no one was paying close attention.

"Uneventful," Rogers said. "By the way, there's a load of bananas in Hold Number One. Probably crawling with tarantulas. I'd hate for anybody to get bitten."

"Nice of you to worry about my men, Captain. I'll be sure to warn them away from Hold Number One and check it myself," the chief inspector said, removing several twenty-dollar bills from between the manifest's sheets and stuffing them into his pants' pocket. "I believe you have a package for six-and-a-quarter."

"Pardon?"

"Oh, sorry, Captain," the chief inspector said, leaning in closer and speaking softly. "That's what we call Reichskommissar Arthur Seyss-Inquart." Seeing Rogers' confused face, he continued: "He is the Austrian put in charge of the Netherlands by Hitler. To the Dutch ear, his name sounds like 'six-and-a-quarter.' It is not a joke he finds amusing."

"Yeah, we do have something for, for ..." he pulled out the document from his pocket and read aloud, "for Seyss-Inquart from a Ludwig Clauss at the German Consulate in Spain at Huelva." He handed the paper to the chief inspector, who waved at a German officer on the quay inside a black Opel Admiral Cabriolet, a staff car used by top-ranked officers. The officer strolled onto *The Peggy C* and approached Rogers just as Obasi ran over, holding a suitcase-sized silver metal box with black straps, normally used for shipping delicate photographic equipment.

The officer took the case from Obasi, set it down on the deck, removed the straps, and opened it. Inside, wrapped in blankets, he found a framed painting of angels that, to Rogers, looked very old. Pulling out a large magnifying glass, the officer studied the figures from top to bottom. "Magnificent," he said in English, looking up at Rogers and the chief inspector. "*Der Eiserne* will be thrilled with an authentic Murillo," he said of Bartolomé Esteban Murillo, a seventeenth century baroque painter from Spain. The officer gently returned the painting to the box, stood, and handed Rogers a thick envelope of cash. He waved away the S-Boot and hurried off to deliver the prize to his boss.

The chief inspector shook his head and chuckled. "Six-and-a-quarter will do anything to make Hitler's second-in-command happy."

"Der Eisern?"

"Reichsmarschall Göring calls himself that—the Iron Man. Every January, top German officials go to his hunting lodge for his birthday party and try to outdo one another with elaborate gifts, or so I'm told." The roar of an engine made Rogers and the chief inspector turn around just in time to see the S-boot speed off. "Now, where were we?" he said, glancing down at the papers in his hand.

Satisfied that everything was in order, he took a fountain pen from his shirt pocket and, removing the cap with his teeth, signed several manifest pages with quick strokes, the last one with a flourish. He re-capped the pen and stuffed it in his top pocket, taking a moment to rummage inside it as if to adjust something blocking the way. "Good to see you again. Safe travels," the chief inspector said. "Oh, I almost forgot. I'm to tell you that your usual shipping agent is not available. Afraid you're on your own for supplies and cargo."

Most shipping companies had agents around the world who handled everything from fuel to manifests, and who were essential for cutting through local red tape. The agents Rogers dealt with were almost always cagey about whom they represented; Rogers didn't care. "The Germans won't bother you around the dock area," the inspector said, noticing the concerned look on Rogers' face. "If you need to go elsewhere and get stopped, just show the document from the German consulate. You'll be safe with that."

The chief inspector shook Rogers' hand a little longer than necessary before doffing his cap with a gallant flourish and returning to his men, shooing them away from the bow hold to the "far more important" ones at the stern.

The bored German soldiers fidgeted and shifted their weight from foot to foot with impatience.

Rogers turned his back, opened his right hand, and glanced down at a note the inspector had slipped him during the handshake. Looking up concerned, he tucked the paper into his shirt pocket.

Two of the rescued sailors nodded farewell to Rogers as they carried the third survivor, deathly pale and still unconscious, down the gangplank on a makeshift stretcher, then trudged away without looking back. Rogers had tried to hire them for the next voyage, knowing they were unlikely to accept given their last journey, but he figured it was worth a try. They just shook their battered heads; broken men done with the sea.

Normally, there should have been at least twenty-one crew members aboard. But times were tough, and Rogers could only muster fourteen sailors; a few were veterans, but mostly they were newcomers who owed loyalty to no one, moving from ship to ship for the highest bidder. That often led to onboard misunderstandings and mistakes because it takes quite a while for a crew to gel and work as one.

Once the unloading was completed, Rogers and Nidal stood at the foot of the gangplank handing out pay to departing crew members. Five of them carried kitbags and suitcases containing all their possessions, indicating that they had no intention of ever coming back. "You sure you don't want more work, Henk? You're one of the best bosuns I've ever had," Rogers said, counting out his cash from the envelope the German officer had given him.

The stooped sailor beamed at the compliment. "Too dangerous these days, Cap'n," said Henk, a taciturn Dutchman who wore a curved bosun's whistle on a chain around his neck. The narrow brass pipe marked him as boss of the main deck. Men like him used it to blow high-pitched commands when they couldn't be heard over bad weather or at large ceremonial events.

"Even if the *Peggy C* was in any kind of shape," one of his fellow Dutch sailors said.

"But mates. It's all fixed, right, Mr. Nidal?" Rogers said.

Nidal looked on, stroking his black goatee, silent.

"Ain't no amount of fixin' gonna keep this leaky bucket afloat," Henk said. "The five of us will try our luck here at home. Sorry, Cap'n. You've always been fair." He and his compatriots snatched their money and headed down the quay to town.

Rogers gave Nidal a wide-eyed look of "why the hell didn't you help me?"

"They do have a point," Nidal said, "even if we could find a load."

"I have a lead on one," Rogers said, pulling the note out of his shirt pocket and waving it in Nidal's face. "Once you finish off-loading and get paid, fill out the crew, pick up supplies" He handed him the envelope. "Use whatever you need from this for *special* cargo," Rogers said using code for contraband. "Then get us ready to sail by midnight's ebb tide."

"As you wish, my liege."

Rogers, a little irritated, gave Nidal a double-take but otherwise didn't respond, waving instead at Obasi to follow him off the dock.

Obasi wore a tight-fitting black wool Ozo cap from his native country of Nigeria—something like a watch cap without the folded edges, with a tiny nub on the top. He towered over Rogers as they hustled off the quay together. Nobody knew much about Obasi except that he was one of the Igbo People, and always carried the traditional *abreba*, a seven-inch dagger with a wooden handle decorated with ring-shaped deep cuts and embedded nail heads; its scabbard on his left hip had the same distinctive designs.

Despite broad shoulders and taut biceps that strained whatever shirt he wore, Obasi wasn't much of a sailor. He barely knew bow from stern and was hopeless around knots. But give him something to pull or shove around a heaving deck or hoist from the darkened holds, he was indefatigable, no matter the weather—always cheery, always ready to do more than his share. He rarely spoke, nodding without a word at commands or flashing a broad smile after some impossible feat of strength.

How Obasi ended up as a permanent crew member on the *Peggy C* was a mystery. But one thing everyone learned about Obasi was his loyalty to Rogers. He never let him leave the ship unescorted and could be counted on to be Rogers' avenger for any unlucky crew member who muttered complaints about the good captain, no matter how lame or quietly said.

And Lord help the unfortunate crew member who mistook Rogers' frame and shaggy brown curls and striking face—"pretty boy" was what fools called him behind his back—for weakness. The savvy ones knew the signs of Rogers' simmering anger and obeyed orders without hesitation; the slow ones paid the price: Rogers pummeling them with blinding speed.

Though most European sailors had no idea what baseball was, they soon learned that someone who could throw out a runner at home plate from right field could also throw a devastating punch like Joe Louis, and they'd all heard of The Brown Bomber. Rogers knew the men feared his temper, and it worried him a little, knowing that losing control at the wrong time was dangerous. But he was also aware that it took iron discipline to keep in line a crew of often ill-educated, shiftless vagabonds who became sailors only after failing at everything else, including, in some cases, a life of crime.

⟞➤●⟞⟞

Rogers hadn't visited Amsterdam since the Nazis invaded Holland two years before, and he was eager to talk to some of his oldest customers, hoping they were still active traders despite the war. One had left a note for him with the chief inspector on the off-chance he ever returned. But with a February date, that was cause for concern. Who knew what the situation was now? The damn war was changing everything.

It was a splendid city on a rare sunny day in the fall. Its narrow seventeenth-century homes with ornate gabled facades on cobblestoned streets, and the ring of canals lined with houseboats and graceful elms, a spatter of yellow-brown leaves still clinging to their limbs and glittering like tiny jewels in the still waters below, had always been special to Rogers. "This is where it all began," he said to Obasi, waving his hands around, admiring the scenery. "My first European stop after leaving the States. It's where I joined the crew of the *Peggy C."* He tensed. "Something's off."

They passed groups of sullen-faced people huddled in long lines outside butcher shops and groceries, clutching what looked like ration cards. The normally bustling streets were half-filled with trucks, bicyclists, an occasional car, and even horse-drawn carts. What few pedestrians there were avoided eye contact when Obasi and Rogers passed them. Many of their faces were emaciated, their clothes threadbare, their gait plodding, as if carrying an invisible weight. The festive spirit of the city that Rogers had so much enjoyed for so long was no longer.

As they strolled into Dam Square in the heart of old Amsterdam, Rogers was aghast at the scene. Bands of German soldiers were stopping people in front of the neoclassical Royal Palace, checking their papers, and shoving some into military trucks. Dutch SS soldiers in black uniforms with double lightning bolt patches, and Grüne Polizei, German police in green uniforms, dragged civilians from the electric trams and marched them away, their hands held high. Other Nazi soldiers in BMW sidecars dashed through the nearby streets shouting for people to get out of their way.

Despite the cold, Rogers and Obasi took a seat at an outdoor table on the square and ordered coffee from a young waiter, who apparently was oblivious to the chaos in the street. "What are the Nazis doing?" Rogers asked.

"Arresting Jews," the waiter said mechanically.

"For what?"

"Being Jews." The waiter set down the coffees and returned inside without further explanation.

Obasi looked to Rogers for an answer, but he didn't have one. He, of course, had heard something about the Germans putting restrictions on Jews, but he hadn't paid it much attention. He just assumed that it was because of the war, or was exaggerated by the British. He hadn't heard anything about the food lines or the roundups.

Dam Square had always been one of Rogers' favorite haunts. When he first started out and had no money, he had enjoyed wandering around the six-story De Bijenkorf department store and gawking at all the luxury goods he could never afford, even if he had wanted them. Rogers seemed to recall that "The Beehive" was owned by a Jewish family and wondered what had happened to them. And he always stopped in the nearby Gothic New Church to pay homage to the naval heroes buried there, particularly Lieutenant Admiral Michiel de Ruyter, a seventeenth-century folk hero of the Anglo-Dutch Wars who rose from nothing to be considered one of history's most skilled admirals. When he had time, Rogers browsed the nearby Scheltema bookshop for English-language newspapers and new books, especially first editions. Now, those warm feelings for the square were no more.

"How could people be this stupid over and over? What are they even fighting over?" Rogers said in exasperation. "I blame Napoleon."

"Who was this Napoleon?" Obasi asked, leaning forward for the inevitable history lesson that he always seemed to enjoy so much.

"They may not teach this in Nigeria, but Europeans have been playing the same stupid game for centuries. A lot of historians say the Seven Years' War was the first global war. But in my opinion, it didn't become a never-ending worldwide game until Napoleon became the emperor of France. He conquered almost all of Europe and invaded Russia, and for what? Why did thousands of men willingly fight and die for him? Do you know what Napoleon said?"

"No," Obasi said, hanging on every word.

"He said, 'A soldier will fight long and hard for a bit of colored ribbon.' Can you believe that? For colored ribbons. For glory. He ended up getting crushed by the Russians and British." He raised his fingers to count off the wars. "Anyway, then there was the Crimean War, the Franco-Austrian War, the Franco-Prussian War, and the War to End All Wars. Just 21 years later, this idiotic war started. Now, the Brits, French, and Russians are fighting the Germans and Italians and Japanese. Confused?"

"Yes," Obasi said.

"Here's all you need to know." To illustrate his point, he grabbed salt and pepper shakers from several tables and moved them around on the one where they were sitting. "It's like a never-ending game of chess with different players moving the same pieces over the same countries with pretty much the same result: lots of dead people and the angry survivors plotting revenge in the next stupid war. Hitler's no different."

He sat back and downed his coffee, and waved at the waiter for a refill.

Rogers tried to stay up to date on events by listening to the BBC when it was in range and by picking up and reading English-language newspapers when he could find them. But he had had no idea how bad things were until he sat at the café watching the roundup of innocent Jews. "How could people be so stupid?" he asked again, taking a final sip of his coffee and waving Obasi to follow him.

It was getting dark, and Rogers had an appointment to keep. He checked the paper the chief inspector had given him and headed southeast across several canal bridges toward the distant twin spires of the Moses and Aaron Church in the Jodenbuur neighborhood. Once again, he was stunned: a large white sign hung at the neighborhood entrance: "Juden Viertel" on one line and "Joodsche Wijk" underneath, meaning Jewish Quarters in German and Dutch. Remnants of ten-foot-high barbed wire fences that had blocked many of the streets going into the quarter still stood, and Nazis patrolled the bridges, checking identity papers. Rogers noted the address on the paper and located the café near the Sint Antoniesluis Bridge, which went over the Oudeschans Canal and led onto Jodenbreestraat, the Jewish Broadstreet. Sitting outside, Rogers ordered more coffee for himself. For Obasi, he ordered a beer.

"Captain Rogers?" the waiter asked as he set down the drinks. Rogers jumped up.

"Yes, I'm Captain Rogers."

"Come this way, please. You have a telephone call."

Rogers gave Obasi a quizzical look and followed the waiter inside the café. He spoke for a few minutes on the phone and returned to his seat. Leaning over to Obasi, he whispered, "Drink up. It's going to be a long night."

As the sun set, Rogers led Obasi on a twenty-five minute trek northwest through Dam Square and over The Emperor's Canal, the middle of Amsterdam's three main canals and, at 102 feet, the widest. They turned right on *Keizersgracht* and started to stroll down the narrow cobblestoned street when Rogers stopped abruptly at the sight of three German soldiers leaning on stacks of bags and wooden crates lining the canal. He turned Obasi around and whispered, "I don't think they spotted us. Go back across the bridge and wait for me there. But you don't know me. Understand?" Obasi nodded and wandered off.

The soldiers tensed as Rogers stopped across from them at a building with the word *"Groenlandse"* written in large white letters on a second-story wooden double-door. That was short for *De Groenlandse Pakhuizen*, meaning Greenland Warehouses. The narrow five-story, red-brick building, with stepped gables, was one of three identical and abutting warehouses built in 1620 to store whaling products, including 50,000 liters of blubber in large cement pits in the basement. The buildings had wide double doors on each floor to facilitate the loading and unloading of goods. As soon as Rogers knocked on the main door, it creaked open, and he slipped inside.

He was greeted by an old man wearing shabby clothes and holding a candle with fingerless gloves. "Are you Mr. Maduro?" Rogers asked. The man didn't say a word. Instead, he waved for Rogers to follow him into a small room at the back of the largely empty warehouse. As he entered, a small lantern lit up, and a man in a long dark coat and fedora rose from behind a desk, extending his hand.

"You must be Captain Rogers," the man said. "I have been hoping you would come for several months now."

Rogers shook his hand, took the proffered seat in front of the desk, and asked, "You have a load for me?" He had learned not to ask too many questions of his customers. All that mattered was the price and the destination. And even though he'd never met Maduro, they had done business through shipping agents many times before. So, Rogers knew he was good for the money. Maduro, who appeared to be in his fifties, steepled his fingers in front of his worried face and studied Rogers through half-closed eyelids.

"I do," Maduro said. "I have a very precious cargo that I need transported to Gibraltar. It is more, shall we say, dangerous than my previous shipments. Is that a problem?"

"Maybe not. How much?"

Maduro reached in a drawer and pulled out a shiny metal bar, tossing it across the desk to Rogers, who caught it in the air. "That is half a kilogram of pure gold. It is all I have. My bank accounts have been seized by the Nazis."

Rogers did the math quickly. There was a little more than two pounds in a kilogram. So, this weighed around sixteen ounces, and the price of gold was $35 an ounce. So, it was worth between $500 and $600, which was a year's salary for some of his men.

"That, of course, is just a down payment," Maduro said. "Our relatives in Gibraltar will pay you one-hundred times that if you deliver the cargo alive and unharmed."

"How am I supposed to get this cargo past the Germans outside, and the inspectors at the dock?"

"There will be no problem with the customs officials. As for the Germans, they are following me," Maduro said, handing Rogers a piece of paper with a map drawn on it. "They will stay outside after you leave and go to the location on this map. There, you will find a truck with a large crate on the back. The driver will take you to the dock. But you must set sail tonight."

"So, you're not joining the cargo?"

"I wish I could. But that is not possible given my shadows. They let me come to my warehouse to finish turning it over to a Gentile—the elderly gentleman who greeted you. They think we are signing papers. But they will never let me out of their sight."

"Really?" Rogers said. "What's your hat size?"

Outside, the German soldiers jumped up when the warehouse door creaked open. A man in a white captain's hat stood in the dark doorway and shook hands with another man in a fedora and dark coat with the collar turned up. He kept his back to the Germans as he strolled away. The soldiers shouldered their rifles and marched after him down the poorly lit street. With his face still obscured by the upturned collar, the man scooted across the bridge over the canal, bumped into Obasi, who puffed on his pipe, and dropped a paper on the ground.

"Go find the truck on the map and have it driven to the ship," Rogers said, looking up from under the fedora. "I'll meet you there after I shake my entourage." Obasi bent down and scooped up the paper, glancing briefly at the approaching soldiers. Rogers hurried down the street and cut into an alley. The soldiers broke into a run, not noticing the black man in the shadows, and followed Rogers. The first solder tripped on something and fell flat on his face. As the two others helped him up, they found the dark coat and hat that their real target had been wearing. They pulled their rifles off their shoulders, cocked them, and scrambled after Rogers, whose footsteps echoed in the distance.

The evening fog had rolled in, and most of Amsterdam was a ghost town, the residents fearful of the Nazi occupiers even if they had legitimate reasons to be out just before curfew. Rogers knew the Germans would recognize him even if the streets weren't empty. So, he ran flat-out down an alley, panting and pumping his arms, trying not to fall on the slippery streets while checking over his shoulder. He slowed down only to peer around corners. Pounding footsteps echoed closer and closer no matter how fast he ran, no matter how he dodged and weaved through the shadowy alleys and over the narrow canal bridges.

To avoid two Dutch policemen strolling through the square ahead, smoking and chatting and not paying much attention to their surroundings, he flattened himself against a building wall. The footsteps behind Rogers thumped louder and closer, as did muffled voices speaking German. He was trapped. The two policemen turned off the square, leaving puffs of smoke behind them. Rogers had to move. He stuck his head around the corner far enough to glance into the square, making sure it was safe. He looked behind him, judging his chances of outrunning his pursuers as opposed to staying hidden in the dark; he chose to run.

Headlights flashed into the square as soon as he stepped out of the alley, forcing him to leap back against the wall, banging his head on a low windowsill hard enough to see stars. He hoped the driver hadn't spotted him. A flatbed truck, hauling a large wooden crate wrapped in a thick rope, crept through the square, rolling to a stop in front of Rogers' hiding place. He looked back and considered running that way, but the voices were too close. He'd have to gamble and remain motionless, trying to fade into the rough brick wall, doing the best he could to control his breath and the tell-tale puffs of condensation in the frigid night.

Obasi stuck his head out of the open passenger's door and signaled for Rogers to jump in. Rogers shook his head "no," waving for Obasi to leave the square, pointing his thumb over his shoulder while making a throat-cutting motion with the other hand. Obasi slammed the door shut, and the truck raced out of the square, tires squealing, its cargo bumping up and down.

It was now or never. Rogers sprinted zigzag across the square. Bullets pinged off the buildings near him as he skidded into another dark alley. The three Nazi soldiers from the warehouse ran into the square, shouting and pointing, trying to figure out which way he had gone. They picked the wrong street.

Not long after, Obasi's flatbed truck rumbled onto the quay and stopped at the *Peggy C*. It sprang to life; a boom wheeled over the deck and lowered its steel-wire cable and hook. Obasi jumped out and attached the hook to the thick rope lashed around the crate and swung his arm over his head in a circle to signal the crane operator to lift away.

The three Nazi soldiers from the square staggered onto the quay, out of breath and angry, clicking on their flashlights, making their way like blood-hounds to the idling truck, as they scanned the faces of sailors stumbling and singing in the dark, and others smoking on the ship decks above. Their cigarette tips flickered like red fireflies.

Cookie and Seamus hustled down the gangplank to help as the boom cranked the crate high into the air. "If this is the last of the load, where's the Old Man?" Cookie asked Obasi, scanning the back of the truck.

Obasi leaped off the flatbed, checked out the approaching soldiers, and raised his eyes up to the sky. Cookie tilted his head to the side, confused. Obasi moved his eyes upward over and over.

"No need to be making faces at me like I'm some kind of drooling idiot. The question is simple enough," Cookie said. Obasi continued the eye roll. Frustrated, Cookie imitated Obasi and took a glance up: Rogers dangled from the back of the crate, holding on to the rope for dear life.

Cookie and Obasi remained motionless as the Nazis approached, shining flashlights on their faces, under the truck, and into the cabin. One of them inspected the driver's papers; another patted down Seamus and pushed him away. Cookie sweated rivers in the cool night. Rogers sweated above him, hoping the Germans gave up soon. A man only has so much endurance.

"What seems to be the problem here?" asked Chief Inspector De Klerk, stepping out of the shadows like a ghost in full uniform. As he puffed on a pipe, blue smoke swirling around his face, the Germans swung their weapons around in surprise. Seeming to be without a care in the world, the inspector strolled over, took the papers away from the truck driver, flipped to a page, and tapped on it with the stem of his pipe.

"See, everything is in order here. I inspected the ship myself," he said in English and repeated it in German. "Special late delivery to catch the tide. Signed by Reichskommissar Seyss-Inquart himself," he said in English and German as he pointed his pipe up at the crate, indicating a large sticker on the side. One of the Germans shined his flashlight on the sticker and then on the inspector's face. After conferring among themselves, the soldiers snapped off their flashlights and returned the way they had come, dejected and still angry. The truck puttered off behind them.

"Off you go, gentlemen," the inspector said, stepping back into the shadows, watching the Germans depart, and apparently hanging around to make sure the *Peggy C* left safely.

Obasi nudged Cookie, pointing to a puddle under Seamus' shoes where he had pissed himself. They laughed and teased him good-naturedly and hurried to slip the mooring lines off the metal bollards on the dock. Once the last looped end of the thick hawsers splashed into the water, the trio jogged up the gangplank.

As the crate swung over the deck, Rogers let go and dropped down, his knees buckling when he hit the metal with a thud. Ducking his head to avoid the crate as it was lowered into Hold Number One at the ship's bow, he jogged over to help Nidal and a new crew member haul up the gangplank faster so they could avoid any more inspections and catch the ebb tide. Only after they were done did Rogers get a good look at the new sailor with a bushy beard and a bosun's whistle. "What the hell are you doing here?" Rogers yelled.

"You didn't tell us he was captain," the new sailor snapped at Nidal.

Nidal glanced from one man to the other with impatience. "You said get a crew. I did. I found two new firemen and a replacement bosun and his two mates," Nidal said to Rogers, pivoting to the new crew member. "You said you and your mates needed work and had to get out of Amsterdam before the Germans rounded up all the foreigners. I hired all three of you. Now, get to it and weigh anchor. Yalla." Without waiting for a response, Nidal headed up the ladder—what landlubbers call stairs—to the wheelhouse.

Rogers grabbed the shirt of his new bosun and yanked him in close, glaring straight into his eyes, seething and almost unable to control himself. "Do as you're told. You won't get a second chance with me this time," Rogers said, shoving him away.

The new bosun was a weathered American whose full name was William Critchfield, but who everyone always called Bosun. He spat and stuck a cigarette in his mouth, slinking away like a water rat on short bowlegs to organize the crew for departure. His squinty brown eyes and lantern jaw seemed to be in constant motion, a predator on the prowl.

Rogers yelled up to Nidal on the ladder: "Any passengers show up?"

Nidal stopped in his tracks, "We have loaded all the cargo we could arrange on such short notice, but no people."

Crestfallen, Rogers waved for Nidal to continue on his way. They couldn't wait another second to escape. He scanned the deserted dock for any activity, spotting the chief inspector with his glowing pipe stepping into the light and waving. He searched the nearby roads for headlights as he lumbered along the deck to the stern as the ship pulled away, ending at the very tip of the poop deck. His eyes stayed fixed on the chief inspector until he faded like a melancholy dream into the mist.

CHAPTER 3

Dawn had arrived some time earlier, yet the sun remained hidden behind a leaden wall of thick clouds, heavy with the promise of snow. The ocean's white-capped swells rolled the *Peggy C* as it made its way south to the English Channel, traveling barely over half speed at six knots so as not to put too much strain on the damaged engine. Chief Turani was always fretting about the engine, complaining he hadn't had enough time in port to pick up all the necessary replacement parts. Now, Turani was forced to wait in the stifling heat below deck like a worried mother hovering over a sick child.

The crew settled into their routines and split up their sea watches, normally four hours on duty and eight off. But there weren't enough men to fill all the watches on the bridge, the deck, the engine room, and the stokehold, where firemen shoveled coal to heat the two Scotch boilers that powered the triple-expansion steam engine. The stokehold was a godawful place where temperatures often topped 120 degrees and the air was always thick with coal dust.

Nidal divvied up the assignments for "port and starboard watches" of six hours on and six hours off, and each man was also given multiple jobs in rotating watches, including shoveling coal, which created a great deal of angry grumbling. The one exception to the schedule was Cookie. His sole job was to keep the men fed and hydrated. He cooked all the meals, did the cleaning, baked the bread, and dispensed the water rations—28 quarts a week per man from the padlocked hand pump in the passageway.

During the first dog watch—one of two two-hour watches between 4 p.m. and 8 p.m.—Cookie served up the biggest meal of the day: a feast of steaming corned beef pie, fried pumpkin, and potatoes, washed down with endless pots of tea and hot coffee, or what passed for coffee in wartime—a blend of coffee beans and chicory, served with a little of the rationed sugar and Nestle's Condensed Milk. At the dinner, half of the crew, except officers, sat together at a long wooden table and, for the most part, ate in exhausted silence.

Bosun presided at one end of the table, removing a green and gray tweed Irish cap from his sloped forehead, and putting it on the table. As a rule, he would eat in the officers' saloon, because he was considered a petty officer fourth in command. But he preferred to avoid Rogers as much as possible, telling everyone he needed to eat earlier than usual because the ship was so shorthanded, and he had to rest before taking over the "Dead Watch," as the Brits called it, or "Midwatch," as it was known by Americans, on the bridge at midnight. No one appeared to believe him, or care, especially Rogers, who tolerated him despite their history from years ago when Bosun's deceitful ways and constant grousing almost triggered a ship mutiny. Nonetheless, he was good at his job as foreman of the deck crew and skilled at marline-spike seamanship—everything to do with knots, splicing, and proper use of ropes—as well as overseeing the never-ending preventative maintenance of the ancient *Peggy C.*

Sitting near Bosun were the new men he brought aboard: Able Seaman Lonnie Evans, a deeply wrinkled Alabaman with a hook for a left hand, and a jug-eared young Welshman who stuttered under pressure named Hywel. He was an ordinary seaman, the lowest ranked sailor with limited skills.

Assistant Engineer Dunawa took the seat next to Lonnie, who sneered and moved across the table. "So, how'd somebody like you get to be a deucer?" Lonnie asked, using the slang for an assistant or second engineer, his southern drawl dripping with contempt.

"I started out as a nipper on British schooners in St. Vincent, and then trained at the Swansea Nautical College," Dunawa said matter-of-factly in a thick Caribbean accent, dropping the "h" in words like "that" and the "g" at the end of words.

"So, you was a British boy and then a college boy," Lonnie said, emphasizing the word boy with a laugh.

"S-s-swansea?" Hywel said. "That's in Wales, for training m-m-masters."

"Is that right?" Bosun asked. "Hows come you ain't no captain?"

"Captain Rogers was the only one who would hire a negro for something other than a steward. So, I became Chief Turani's assistant," Dunawa said as he gulped down some tea. "I will be master of my own ship someday, and you, Able Seaman Evans, can come work as my steward." The table erupted in raucous laughter; Lonnie shoved a fork full of corned beef into his mouth and glared back with his best bulldog face.

"But engineers can't become mates," Bosun said, sneering with a mouth full of bad teeth. "Not the same skills. Nothing alike, I say."

"I needed the work," Dunawa said with a shrug. "Besides, I can learn both jobs."

"No, no, no," Bosun said, brandishing a fork full of pumpkin at Dunawa as if casting an evil spell. "A deck officer is a profession. An engineer is just a trade. Everybody knows that."

"Fortunately for me, the Old Man does not see it that way. He says the experience will make me a better captain. And then you can come work for me, too."

Bosun shook his head in disapproval and changed the subject. "So, anyone know where we're headed?" During war, it was traditional for merchant sailors to sign onto a ship without knowing its destination.

"Cap'n said set a course for Gibraltar," said Helmsman Juan Cardoso, a grizzled Spaniard with a thick white beard, sitting at the other end of the table next to Seamus. Next to them were the two new firemen: Shakir and Amar Dogar, Punjab Muslim brothers wearing identical white woven kufi hats with thin black stripes and large, square sweat rags punctured with holes tied around their necks. The rags were issued monthly to members of the "black gang," as firemen and trimmers, who shoveled coal down a chute to the firemen, were called because of the ever-present coal dust on their face and hands and clothes.

"And the load?" Bosun asked.

"You saw as much as we did," Cardoso said, sopping up gravy with a handful of fresh bread. "Looked like the usual sundries: cheese, barrels of fish, coffee, and tea and whatnot."

"I know that," Bosun snapped. "I meant the last crate."

"No idea, jefe," Cardoso said. "And, if you're smart, you won't ask. The Old Man and Mr. Nidal like their secrets."

"I did some earwigging and heard 'em talking about a wee bit of Scotch and fags under the table," Seamus said. "Don't really matter none. We get paid the same for whatever."

"Unless we get caught," Bosun said. "Germans don't take kindly to contraband."

"Believe me, we sailed the *Beschermer* and know Germans don't care what we carry," Shakir said in his clipped, hurried Punjabi accent.

"How do y-y-you know, boyo?" Hywel asked.

"A U-boat stopped us near the Bay of Biscay. The First Officer took our papers to the German captain, who said he would have to sink us, though a neutral merchant, because we were carrying contraband. It was not true. We only had general cargo, barbed wire, nails, brass tubes—hardly illegal stuff. But the Germans said it was contraband because we were sailing for South Africa, an 'enemy country,' as they called it. They gave us less than thirty minutes to abandon ship," Shakir said, stopping to take a sip of tea. "Everyone ran to the lifeboats in such a hurry that many forgot their boots, some grabbed kit bags instead of food, and others even left their licenses behind."

"Good luck getting work on any ship without those licenses," Bosun huffed, shaking his head.

"W-w-what did they do with the s-s-ship," Hywel asked.

"What'd you think, you eejit?" Seamus said, slapping the Welshman on the back of the head.

"I don't k-k-know," Hywel said, pushing Seamus' hand away.

"They blew it up with a torpedo," Shakir said. "We rowed as fast as we could and barely got out of range before the tin fish hit the old rust bucket. It split in half. A ball of flames rained burning debris down on our heads. And when the bow wouldn't sink, they shot their deck gun at her until she went under. All the while, something must have fouled the whistle cord because it blew loud as a banshee until it went under. Very sad." Shakir shuddered.

"But that wasn't the worst part," Amar interjected as the two brothers took turns interrupting each other and continuing the yarn. The other sailors put their forks and cups down. "The U-boat pulled up near to us, and the captain shouted through a megaphone that he was sorry, that they were coming off a long mission and had no food or water to spare. He threw us a compass and shouted directions for shore. But the fog wouldn't lift, and even with a compass, we couldn't make much headway in the heavy swells. We pulled and pulled the oars until our hands were rubbed raw with blisters but still got nowhere."

"It was freezing cold in the lifeboats," Shakir said as his brother took a bite of food. "We were battered by rain and sleet, and the wind whipped up white horses all around us," he said of the crests on the towering waves that lashed the lifeboat and drenched the men. "Then a mighty comer flipped us over, and we had to fight to right the boat and climb back in. Two of the seventeen mates in the boat didn't make it, and we lost most of our emergency supplies. We bailed water as fast as we could with our frozen hands and our boots, barely keeping ahead of the waves crashing over the gunnels."

"For ten days," Amar added, "we drifted with only biscuits to eat, only a couple of tots of rum a day to keep us warm, and a large tin of cigarettes. We had to use blankets to catch the rain for drinking water. On the third day, one of the young lads from engineering, a wiper I think he was, wouldn't wake up to bail. He had been working in the engine room when the captain rang 'Finished with Engines.' We all knew that could mean only one thing: Come on deck and abandon ship. In his panic, the wiper hit his head and had to be carried onto the lifeboat. Slurred his words a bit, threw up some, but seemed to do fine for a while. Then he wouldn't wake up. I told the First Mate at the tiller that I thought he was dead." His voice faded off. He cleared his throat, staring off into the distance. His mates at the table sat transfixed, worry on their faces like children listening to a bedtime horror story, only one that was too real.

Cardoso, the Spanish helmsman, pulled out a square plug of tobacco, shaved off several flakes, and rubbed them between his hands, taking the shreds and tapping them into his yellow clay pipe. He lit up and puffed in silence.

"I couldn't find a pulse and his eyes didn't move," Shakir said. "But the Mate says to burn his fingers to be sure. He handed me a butt, and I pressed it against the seaman's hand until it burned a hole in his flesh. A terrible smell, I tell you." Cardoso looked around the table at the disapproving glares from his mates and tapped out his pipe on the heel of his shoe. Shakir waited for the smoke to die out and resumed his story. "The poor boy didn't react, so we took the hook out of our boat and the after-hook from one of the others, and scrounged up some Number 7 thread line to tie them to his ankle, and we dropped him overboard. Wasn't nothing else to do."

Shakir appeared too shaken to continue, so Amar took up the story. "After six days, we were running out of food. Everyone was exhausted and freezing, especially one of the first trippers, a Somali trimmer, who got all crazy. Kept trying to drink the seawater. We tried to calm him down, but he wasn't having it—just kept blabbering. When we gave up and let him be, he stood up all of a sudden and stared at the waves and kept saying, 'The water is so beautiful.' Then, as calm as you please, he jumped overboard," Amar said, putting his arm around his despondent brother, who looked around the table and worked up the strength to finish the yarn.

"By day nine, our feet, without shoes, swelled up like giant bottle gourds," Shakir said. "My stokehold boots split wide open because my feet had doubled in size. Our legs went numb no matter how we beat them or how we sat on or under the thwarts. Finally, when we were too weak to bail or pull much more, and the water in the boat was up to our waists, another merchant rescued us, praise be to God, and dropped us off in Lisbon. Forty mates survived, although some lost fingers and toes from frostbite."

Amar held up his left hand to show his missing index finger. "And to top it all, the company said our Articles of Agreement were broken by the sinking of the ship, so we were off duty and wouldn't be getting paid for those ten awful days adrift," Amar said, referring to the two-year contract some merchant sailors signed with shipping companies. That same contract always stipulated less pay for non-white crew members.

"Bastardos," Cardoso said.

Bosun looked around the table at the glum and silent men and found a darker cloud instead of a silver lining. "Gibraltar is British, and that makes it enemy territory, too. And we's heading right for the Bay of Biscay."

Seamus shrugged. "The manifest I forged for the Old Man said Barcelona is where we're heading. Gotta pass Gibraltar to get there, I suppose. Besides, it's not like we're carrying guns."

"I wouldn't put it past Mr. High and Mighty," Bosun said. "I trust him about as far as I can throw him."

"Sounds like you know him," Seamus said.

"Years ago. We worked this ship. He was third mate," Bosun said. "Wasn't called the *Peggy C* then."

"What makes you think he's dodgy?" Seamus asked.

"I has my reasons."

"Is that w-w-why he y-yelled at you?" Hywel piped in.

35

Bosun glowered at Hywel until the Welshman lowered his gaze and scraped up the last of the pumpkin. "I don't give a t-t-tinker's curse why the Old Man was so mad," said Hywel, his face turning red, muttering.

"Eat up, mates," Cookie said, toting a large steaming kettle of food out the door. "Next watch is coming soon."

Bosun followed him with his eyes. "Why's he hauling food somewhere now?" he muttered to Lonnie, pushing back his chair with a screech, and following Cookie, careful to make no noise. Stopping for cover behind one of the many tall wide-mouth cowls used for ventilation, Bosun peeked around, the faint smell of warm corned beef in the air.

Obasi, who already had opened the hatch on Hold Number One at the bow, held the kettle for Cookie so he could climb into the hold, then handed the food down to him. Bosun frowned and slipped away.

———⚬———

In the wheelhouse, a stuffy room of 15-by-21 feet, Rogers slumped in a tall captain's chair, hands clasped behind his neck, holding up his weary head. In front of him, Helmsman Cardoso kept a steady course through the Strait of Dover, the narrow entrance to the English Channel and one of the busiest sea lanes in the world before the war.

To the right of the wheel on a brass pedestal was the circular engine order telegraph used to send instructions for direction and speed to the engineers down below. Inside the glass-fronted brass frame resembling a roulette-wheel-sized clock were pie-shaped sections indicating speed and direction. When the helmsman pulled the brass handle, a bell would ring until the pointer inside stopped on the appropriate section, which the engineers would see on their engine order telegraph, and confirm that the order had been received by pulling the brass handle from side to side and stopping on the correct space.

The *Peggy C* was going half speed ahead while Rogers and Cardoso gazed at the fading light through the wheelhouse's seven almost square glass windows. The beginnings of a hard rain, mixed with blowing sleet, obscured their view, forcing Rogers to stand close to the windows for a better look with his binoculars.

"Oh, hell," he moaned.

McAllister and Nidal overheard the comment as they stepped into the wheelhouse from the starboard door to begin their watch. "Quel est …uh … What is the problem?" Nidal said, catching himself before he could finish the question in French.

"Another damn U-boat just surfaced," Rogers said. "Maybe it'll pass us by." It was unusual to see a U-boat on the surface in the Channel because it was so heavily patrolled by the British. That's why, despite the possibility of mines, Rogers had chosen this route. But, as luck would have it, the horrible weather and low cloud ceiling made the U-boat almost invisible to passing aircraft.

"Helm is being relieved. Steering two one six per gyro," Cardoso said to McAllister, "checking two-one-two per standard. Helm is in hand, rudder amidships, steering off the port pump. And we have oncoming traffic three points to port."

McAllister repeated back the instructions for the gyro and magnetic compasses, direction of the rudder, the steering mode, and which one of two pumps was driving the steering motor, and assumed control of the wheel.

Nidal took Rogers' binoculars and inspected the submarine, still a good distance away. A signal light on its conning tower flashed a message in Morse Code. "They're signaling something. What do they want?" Nidal asked, handing back the binoculars.

"Let's hope not target practice," Rogers said, only half joking.

"What?"

"Damn, damn, damn," Rogers said with growing urgency, mouthing the dits and dahs from the blinking light and translating in his head. "They want to board for inspection." Rogers rubbed his forehead, frustrated, struggling to figure a way out of this fix if he just rubbed hard enough.

"Your orders?" Nidal asked.

After a long, deep breath, Rogers said in a low voice, "Full stop, Helmsman."

"Full stop. Aye, aye, Captain," McAllister said, and pulled the two brass handles on the engine order telegraph back and forth, clanking bells down below that alerted Turani to stop. The engineer acknowledged the order by rotating the arrow around the telegraph's face and likewise halting on "full stop."

"Prepare the ship to be boarded, Mr. Nidal," Rogers said, scribbling a note that he handed to him.

"Run this to the radio room. Tell Sparks to repeat S-S-S and our location for three minutes as soon as you see the boarding party get close," he said, using the code British authorities had set up for ships under submarine attack to signal for help. "Tell him to start on the 600-meter band, but keep changing from the distress frequency to others, and to stop early if he hears a shot being fired over our bow."

"Captain, they are signaling L-R-L," Nidal said of the international code letters for "do not use your wireless."

"They won't fire directly on us because their men will be too close to the ship, but they'll warn us to stop transmitting when they figure out they don't know what frequency we're using and can't jam us," Rogers said. "That should buy us some time." He ran out the door. "I have to find Obasi."

Nidal shook his head in disbelief and headed down to the radio room on the next level, across from the captain's quarters. "On my signal, send this on different frequencies for three minutes or until they fire on us," Nidal told the radio operator, a quiet, middle-aged Brit named Charlie Jones, who everyone called Sparks, the traditional nickname for wireless radio operators on merchant ships. The name derived from the tiny electrical sparks caused by tapping the telegraph key on a metal contact to send messages in Morse Code.

"This isn't going to fool anyone for long, mate," Sparks said in a thick Cockney accent. He donned his black Bakelite headphones, which were plugged into a gray broadcast receiver with round, black-faced dials, and started tapping away.

⸺⸎⸻

Miserable sleet pelted three German sailors and an officer—all lashed with lifelines to the wire antenna above the slippery wooden-slat deck on the bow of the U-boat and struggling to aim an 8.8 cm gun at the *Peggy C*, the target several hundred yards away. Behind and above them on the conning tower—adorned with a leaping tiger emblem—the bearded U-boat commander with his white-peaked cap fixed his powerful 7 x 50 Zeiss binoculars on the distant ship, spotting a tied-up rubber dinghy from his submarine bobbing in the increasingly violent sea.

On deck, shadowy figures, obscured by the weather and approaching darkness, raised and lowered the *Peggy C*'s cargo hatches. The captain looked at his watch and at the sky, then back at the *Peggy C*. Agitated and impatient, he snapped an order to the sailors below. "Prepare to fire as soon as the boarding party departs!" he shouted, and groused to himself, "I'll be damned if we're going home almost empty-handed."

With eyes half-closed against the ferocious ocean spray, and beards and eyebrows covered in flecks of ice, the gunners loaded a thirty-three pound, brass-encased, high-explosive round into the thirteen-foot-long gun and slammed the breech shut. Without the benefit of a range finder, they calculated the elevation and took aim as best they could at the *Peggy C*'s wheelhouse.

⸺⸎⸻

Inside the *Peggy C*'s Hold Number One, a bearded German sailor, who was wearing a dark-blue doeskin forage cap with a yellow eagle and swastika on the front and the leaping tiger emblem on the side, held the long thirty-two-round magazine of his MP-40 submachine gun in one hand and the grip in the other. His finger on the trigger, he pressed the stubby barrel against Rogers' back, forcing him past wooden crates, barrels, and neatly stacked burlap sacks in the grimy, dim compartment. A German officer, also bearded and in his 20s, wearing waterproof battledress—green-gray leather coat and pants—and a visored black cap with the leaping tiger emblem, walked alongside Rogers, kicking bags, and tapping the barrels. He moved without a word.

Waving papers at the officer, Rogers tried to talk him out of the search. "Look at my logs," he said. "Everything's in order. You have no right—" The officer shoved him out of the way. Rogers persisted. "I'm American... Amerikanisch...neutral...neutral."

Obasi, carrying a crowbar, scaled down the ladder, catching up with Rogers and the officer, who pointed at one of the large crates with his Mauser M1934 pistol. With the wooden grip marked by dings and scratches, it clearly was a weapon in its own right. "Öffen das," the officer said.

Obasi deftly used the crowbar to open the large crate and pried the wooden side back so the officer could inspect the cargo inside. After holstering his pistol, the German used a small dagger to rip open one of the stacked-up burlap sacks. A torrent of coffee beans came pouring out all over the floor. He stuck the knife back in the sheath on his belt, and moved on to another larger crate. "Öffen das."

Obasi and Rogers exchanged furtive glances; the captain cursing his luck because this was the last crate loaded the night before, the one Obasi had delivered, the one Rogers rode to safety, the one they snuck onboard to avoid inspection. Holding up his hands and shaking his head, Obasi played dumb.

"Öffen das," the officer repeated louder, pulling out his Mauser and tapping on the crate, then pointing his pistol at Obasi's crowbar so there'd be no misunderstanding. After getting Rogers' nodded approval, Obasi pried open the crate, letting the open side crash onto the steel floor, scattering puffs of dust and frightened mice. The officer kept his pistol trained on Obasi, and stepped around to peer inside. There was little to see—a few sacks and small boxes stacked in the rear.

Another German sailor stuck his head through the hatch opening above and waved a bottle of Scotch and a fifty-cigarette round tin of Wild Woodbine smokes. He shouted, "*Schmuggler,*" which sounded way too much like "smugglers" for Rogers' taste. The officer shouted back. This time Rogers had no idea what he was saying. Deliberate footsteps creaked above, followed by running feet. The German sailor leaned over the hold's edge and held up ten fingers and then five fingers.

The officer narrowed his eyes at Rogers. Suspicious, he spun around, lined himself up with the forward edge of the opening above, and counted off seven steps until a stack of boxes blocked his path. He easily swatted them away. They were empty. With a flourish, he flipped his Mauser, caught the barrel in his right hand, used the handle as a hammer to tap-tap-tap on the wooden wall in front of him, then pressed his ear against it.

Stepping back, the officer crunched something under the cork sole of his black leather seaboot, something not all that unusual in the cargo holds of a ship, especially one as filthy as this one. He looked down and lifted his foot; a girl's barrette lay in shattered pieces, something that *was* unusual on any merchant ship. Obasi moved closer to the officer's back, still clutching the crowbar. The officer raised his gun at Rogers and nodded his head at the wall in front of him. "Öffen das," he said in a harsh voice.

The words were foreign, but by now their meaning was clear. Rogers had no reason to bluff, knowing that he had no choice but to comply. He ran his hands up the rugged wall, probing with his fingers until he found a loose slat, and popped it out. He tugged open a hidden door. The Germans crouched instinctively in defensive positions, guns cocked, keeping an eye on Obasi and

Rogers, but aiming at the moving door.

As the door creaked open, the hold's pale light fell on a heart-rending tableau crowded in front of cases of Scotch and cigarettes: three tearful children—boys aged six and eight, and a twelve-year-old girl—and a young woman, all huddled in a shadowy mass around a seated man in his forties with thick glasses on his doleful face and wearing a dark suit and fedora; the man held his hand over the mouth of a young boy, flush with fever, wiggling and moaning in his lap.

At first, the Germans were as surprised as the children, and seemed unsure what to do. As one, they stepped forward, swinging their weapons from the secret compartment to Rogers and Obasi, vacillating about who presented the greatest threat. Gazing into the darkness, the officer strained to identify the glittering object on the neck of the young woman, a diminutive but defiant-looking beauty in her early twenties with long black hair. His eyes widened in recognition. It was a gold necklace with an oddly shaped pendant looking like a distorted version of the Greek letter "π" or the Latin letter "M" with the first leg cut in half: it was, in fact, the highly recognizable Jewish word *chai*, meaning life. "Sind Sie Juden?" the officer said, his face turning red.

"I, uh, well, it's like this," Rogers sputtered. "You see … No, Obasi, no—"

The burly African whacked the officer on the back with the crowbar, sending him sprawling to the floor and his gun flying out of his hand. At the same moment, Rogers flung out his left arm and jostled the other German sailor's submachine gun to the side long enough for Obasi to slam his crowbar on the German's skull with a sickening crunch, knocking him out cold. Rogers knelt down by that German sailor, feeling around his neck for a pulse. Obasi stood guard above him, tapping the metal rod in his hand like a riding crop, oblivious to the German officer on the floor behind him.

The children screamed. The officer flew at Obasi, his short dagger nicking Obasi's raised right hand as he half-turned and parried the blow. Rogers spun on the floor and kicked the officer's knee, throwing him off balance, and lunged at the German's back with a furious hail of punches that whirled him around. Then came the punch, the one Rogers hadn't used since his Academy days, a resolute roundhouse to the nose. It was a blow so hard that blood spurted across the room, and the German's head snapped back as if it was going to break away from his crumbling body. The officer rolled on the floor in pain, unable to dodge the savage kicks from Rogers. Obasi wrapped his arms around Rogers and lifted him away as Rogers kicked in the air, holding the captain aloft in his steel-band arms, waiting for him to cool down.

Deafening submachine gunshots burst around them. Rogers and Obasi dove for cover amid more screams from the children. Taking advantage of the distraction, the young woman had snatched up the German officer's Mauser from the floor and stuffed it into her skirt.

In a panic, Rogers searched the hold for the shooter, spotting only an unattended submachine gun on the floor. It didn't belong to the unconscious sailor; Obasi had that weapon in his hands. As Rogers bent down to pick up the still-smoking weapon, a uniformed body fell through the hatch and smacked into the deck behind him: another German sailor out of action, the one who must have dropped the submachine gun. Nidal yelled through the hatch opening from above, "So sorry, mon Capitaine. We had a little, shall we say, disagreement on protocol. And we have another guest to bring down."

"The U-boat?" Rogers asked.

Nidal looked over his shoulder. "Maybe too dark to see anything."

⟹●⟸

From the conning tower where the U-boat's captain paced, it almost was too dark to see. The sailors manning the deck gun kept the cargo ship in their sights, a job made more difficult by the rough seas and pounding rain. A sailor stuck his head up from the hatch and shouted into the roaring wind, "British aerial patrols have been sighted in the area, Herr Oberleutnant!"

The captain scanned the dark sky for any planes. Seeing none, he scrutinized the *Peggy C.* "What the hell is taking them so long?"

⟢⟡⟣

That was the same thing Rogers was worried about. How much longer would the U-boat wait for its boarding party to return? And what would happen if they didn't? Letting the prisoners go would be a death sentence; keeping them would also be a death sentence. He studied the three of them on their knees, hands behind their heads, under guard by Obasi, Seamus, and Lonnie. The German whom Obasi had beaten lay unconscious on the floor. *Maybe I can* negotiate *something*, Rogers thought, rolling his lower lip between his thumb and forefinger, an unconscious motion he did when something was about to be decided, for better or worse.

"Now what, sahib?" Nidal asked.

"Captain," Rogers snapped. "Hell if I know what to do."

"Set them all adrift in our lifeboats, perhaps?"

Before Rogers could respond, the young woman sprang up and confronted the much bigger Nidal with surprising ferocity, shaking an index finger in his face. "We pay our way. You have the verplichting...engagement...how you say, obligation."

The man in the hat grabbed her arm, trying to calm her down. "Miriam, please," he pleaded.

"No, Uncle Levy," she said, jerking her arm out of his grip. "I am not afraid of them."

Nidal took a threatening step toward Miriam. Rogers blocked his way. "If the boarding party doesn't report back soon..." Nidal said, apparently not sure whether to complete the thought in front of everyone. He leaned into Rogers and lowered his voice, but not enough to keep Miriam from overhearing, "Perhaps we could explain this was all a misunderstanding and let them take

44

the, uh, stowaways with them."

"No!" Miriam shouted, pulling out the Mauser and brandishing it above her head. "You know what they will do to us...Mauthausen...Buchenwald."

"*Lieve* Miriam, those are just work camps," her uncle said, using the Dutch word for "dear." "We have received letters from several of our people there, and they said it was hard work, but they were fine."

"You and the other rabbis and the whole Joodsche Raad wanted to believe that."

"The Jewish Council did what we had to do to preserve the community," he said. "The Germans promised."

"They lied. Why do you still believe them after so many parents have been told their sons, perfectly healthy when they left, died from natural causes in the camps? Why do we never fight?"

"Listen to the rabbi," Nidal said. "You cannot fight the German Navy."

In desperation, Miriam pressed the gun against the kneeling officer's bleeding head. "If I kill him, you must flee," she said.

A shrill whistle from Bosun's pipe startled everyone, making them look up and giving Nidal an opening to snatch the gun away from Miriam. "The U-boat's turning about, Captain!" Bosun yelled.

Nidal turned his back to Miriam and, seeming not to care who heard, tried to reason with Rogers as he walked him to the dark side of the hold. "Captain, this is not the *S.S. Patna*. There's no honor in staying. Leave them aboard and we can abandon ship in the lifeboats and slip away in the dark. Take our chances in France. We knew this day would come."

Rogers wavered, glancing around at the children's forlorn looks—Miriam's pleading eyes, the uncle's sad face, his tense crew, the angry Germans. The angry Germans? His face lit up. Beards. All the Germans had long, bushy beards. "Or," Rogers said, "we could make a run for it."

CHAPTER 4

On the bridge on top of the conning tower, First Watch Officer Ernst Tauber, the U-boat's second-in-command, stubbed out his Jan Maat cigarette, screwed down the long firing binoculars called UZO onto a metal pedestal at the front of the bridge and, to determine the distance, trained the crosshairs on the *Peggy C*. The pedestal indicated the direction on a degree-marked ring. The captain, standing next to Tauber, decided the sea had probably become too rough to have any hope of aiming the deck gun, so he ordered the use of loaded torpedoes. "Flood torpedo tubes one and two!" Oberleutnant zur See Viktor Brauer, the U-boat's commander, shouted down the hatch, where the order was repeated back to him from below.

"We have no eels to put in tube two, sir," Tauber said, using the slang for the battery-powered torpedoes; greasy steel cigars the length of a Mercedes-Benz L3000 military truck that packed 617-pound warheads and could travel up to three miles.

The captain frowned, checking his watch. He trained his binoculars on the cargo ship's deck, relieved to see the officer and the rest of the boarding party clustered around a Jacob's ladder of rope and wood slats leading down to their dingy flopping in the heavy sea. "Prepare whatever we have!" Brauer barked in irritation.

The readings Tauber had taken with the fourteen-pound firing binoculars were only the first steps in the complex calculation of speed, distance, angle, and depth using special tools and human judgment. All the while, the predator and the prey rolled and shook in the raging sea. The UZO information plus data from a gyrocompass had to be transmitted to an electrically driven mechanical analog attack computer in the conning tower known as a Vorhaltrechner. The computer—something like a slide rule driven by gears and electric impulses rather than binary numbers in modern computers—calculated the course and speed of the U-boat and the bearing to the target.

Then the target's range, speed, and heading had to be entered—measurements that were as much judgment calls as science. Everything was fed into the Torpedo Launch Receiver, or T-Schu, in the torpedo rooms and relayed to the guidance systems of the torpedoes in the four tubes in the bow and one tube in the stern. Torpedo mechanics, called mixers, made final adjustments based on the latest shouted commands. Only then could the big-game hunter pull the trigger.

Once the direction had been determined on the UZO, Tauber called down to the hatch, "Target 1,500 meters, course 190, speed zero!" The combat helmsman repeated the command. Seated on a narrow wooden slat in the cramped conning tower, he turned the U-boat until his gauge registered 190 degrees. The rudders were controlled electronically by pushing one of two buttons on a box the size of a toaster. When they were submerged and not at battle stations, the helmsman on duty operated at a similar rudder control station on the forward wall of the control room; during docking, he manned a station on the bridge. There was an actual steering wheel in the aft chamber of the U-boat that was used in emergencies.

Now, the entire crew waited in tense anticipation for the command "torpedo los," meaning torpedo away or go. The word "fire" was never used when launching torpedoes for fear it might create confusion that something was burning inside the U-boat.

———◆———

On the targeted *Peggy C*, a German sailor fought his way down the ladder, whipped by swirling whitecaps and intense wind gusts that banged him about on the steel hull like a wind chime in a hurricane. The dingy below flipped over, rendering it useless until it could be righted somehow. Appearing exhausted, the German threw in the towel and clambered up the ladder, reaching the top of the bulwark as the ship tilted at a dangerous angle into a monstrous oncoming wave, swooshing him airborne into the other Germans.

"Shite, that was close," said the sailor—Seamus in a German uniform—rolling on the deck, coughing and spitting out saltwater. Lonnie and Bosun, also wearing captured sailors' uniforms, crowded close to the German officer. Behind them, in an oversized raincoat and large-brimmed rain hat, Miriam kept her head down to hide her face.

The groggy officer, almost too beat up to stand, shouted something angrily in German over the shrieking wind

"He said you are idiots," Miriam translated for the crew. "My U-boat can see us, so what can you do to me?"

Lonnie, a scarf wrapped around his face, pressed his submachine gun against the German's back while slipping his hook between the officer's legs, pulling hard enough to make him wince. "I think he understands now," Lonnie said with an obnoxious staccato laugh.

Careful to hide his face, Bosun picked up a circular Aldis lamp and awaited instructions. Miriam spelled out a message in German; Bosun opened and closed the shutters on the signal lamp to flash in German at the U-boat: "T-o-o. R-o-u-g-h. F-o-l-l-o-w."

Watching from the wheelhouse windows as his fake Germans signaled the U-boat, Rogers hoped the ruse would work. From what he could tell through his binoculars, the U-boat seemed to be standing down, although its bow, with the torpedo tubes, was still aimed at the *Peggy C*. Obasi, his right hand wrapped in a bandage, stood with a submachine gun next to the helmsman at the wheel, guarding the three bloodied German sailors. Dressed only in long underwear, two of the prisoners were bound and gagged and slouching on the floor, their backs against the wall under the windows. The third lay unconscious next to them, blood running down his head from where Obasi had cracked his skull.

Rogers joined Nidal in the chart room behind the wheelhouse with a large map of the English Channel spread out on a table. They hunched over it, searching for an escape. "There," Rogers said, pointing to the French coast south of Calais. "The cove just north of Ambleteuse. Didn't we drop a load there once?"

"Too shallow at low tide," Nidal objected, shaking his head.

"You don't say," Rogers said, grinning. He stuck his head through the large windowless opening into the wheelhouse and shouted at McAllister at the wheel. "Hard over left!" he said, slowly and clearly, indicating to steer 35 degrees to port toward the shore.

"Hard over left. Aye, aye, Captain."

Rogers looked at a clock over the windows: four-thirty. "Ahead, slow," Rogers said.

"Ahead, slow. Aye, aye Captain," McAllister repeated, ringing the instructions to Turani on the engine order telegraph.

"That should buy us some more time," Rogers said.

About an hour later, they entered the large cove with the submarine, off their port side, not far behind. Seamus, Lonnie, and Bosun—still in their soaked German uniforms—shoved the officer into the wheelhouse and tied him up next to his two conscious companions; the third one still lay with eyes closed nearby. Miriam followed them in, shaking the rain off her hat, and sat with her uncle in a corner.

Bosun cleared his throat to get Rogers' attention.

"Problems?" Rogers asked.

"Well, Captain, sir," he stammered, taking off his forage cap. "Me and the boys were just discussin' hows you never told us about no Jews. Especially no rabbi." He nodded his head at Miriam and Uncle Levy, resting against each other on the floor, a sneer on his face.

"What difference does it make?" Rogers asked.

"Jews is different, Captain, and you knows it—"

"Booze, cigarettes, even the Nazis want 'em," Lonnie added. "But Jews?" Bosun finished the thought. "They'll kill us for sure."

With his hazel eyes fixed on Bosun, Rogers remained silent for a moment. Lonnie's finger slid onto his submachine gun's trigger. "What if there was a reward?" Rogers asked, waiting for the news to sink before adding the bait to the hook: "One bigger than you could ever imagine."

"How much?"

Nidal, on the bridge deck outside, knocked on a window and pointed up, motioning for Rogers to come outside, which he did in a hurry. Both men tilted their heads, listening; a faint buzz grew louder. "Terrible thing to break radio silence in a war zone," Rogers said, exhilarated. "You never know what kind of company it'll attract." His gamble had paid off, and even Nidal, ever the pessimist, cracked the faintest of smiles in appreciation.

On the U boat, the German sailors abandoned their deck gun and scurried up the conning tower, disappearing down the hatch. They were pulled to the side by shipmates as soon as their boots hit the control room deck to make way for the next man sliding down the ladder. Airplane engines grew louder and closer as the submarine raced forward, submerging in a whirl of bubbles. It stopped suddenly with a shudder, trapped in the soft, sandy bottom of the shallow cove, the very top of its conning tower sticking out above the rolling surf. The periscope swiveled toward the *Peggy C.*

"Too bad the planes can't see it stuck like that," Rogers said, pausing to enjoy his little victory. "I guess now we'll have to let our prisoners go."

⟹●⟸

Inside the U-boat, all hell was breaking loose. Cans of pickled fish popped open, and their oily contents spewed all over the place. Sailors bounced off the hull and each other in the tight quarters. Brauer was furious, but remained calm, conferring with Chief Engineer Max Schmitt. "Put the electric motors slow astern and move the rudder from side to side."

The engines whined, and the boat shuddered but couldn't break loose from the oozing mud bed. Under the strain, the batteries ran over and started releasing tell-tale fumes of poisonous chlorine acid. Brauer ordered the engines stopped and instructed the crew to put on their breathing devices to wait for the enemy planes to give up because of the dark, and for the rising tide to free the submarine. He didn't dare order the conning tower hatch to be opened for fear that his position would be given away. The control room's dim red lights were used at night so no tell-tale light would shine through a raised periscope, and to help the crew's eyes acclimate to the dark before climbing out of the conning tower for a night watch. Frustrated, Brauer turned his cap backward and struggled to look through his mask into the observation periscope in the control room.

<hr />

On the *Peggy C*, it didn't take long to arrange the departure. The dingy had been righted and was relatively stable in the cove's less turbulent waters. Four men in German uniforms boarded the dingy under the *Peggy's C*'s port-side lights and in full view of the U-boat. Soon, the dinghy disappeared into the pitch-black night and fog and headed toward shore. The periscope followed them.

The wind had died down a bit, but the hard rain continued as everyone on the *Peggy C* waited, anxious and, in some cases, terrified about what was going to happen next. Rogers and Nidal hung over the darkened starboard side of the bridge deck's wing—a narrow walkway extending past both sides of the wheelhouse—unable to see more than a few yards out, unable to hear above the crash of the waves. Waiting. And waiting. Interminable waiting.

Cookie appeared on the deck below, tossed a Jacob's ladder overboard, and secured it to the bulwark as the dingy broke out of the darkness. The four men aboard hurried up the rungs. The last one turned before ascending and tossed the German officer's cap into the dingy, kicking it away. He waved at the captain and first mate—it was Seamus again.

Rogers patted Nidal on the back as they rushed into the wheelhouse, where Obasi guarded all four German sailors on the floor. Miriam approached Rogers, confusion on her face.

"Why not let them go?" she asked, indicating the prisoners.

"They'll come looking for us—"

"Instead," Nidal said, finishing the captain's sentence. "They will find the dingy, wonder what happened, and search for some time."

"Surely they will radio for other ships to catch us," the rabbi said.

"Would you want the whole German Navy to know you'd lost your boarding party?" Nidal said. "No, they'll have to come after us themselves."

"Unfortunately for them, they won't be able to, even when high tide sets them free in four hours or so," Rogers said.

"I don't understand," the rabbi said. "Why not?"

"The beards," Rogers said. From their faces, it was clear no one had any idea what he was talking about; Rogers enjoyed the suspense. "They haven't shaved for weeks," he finally explained. "They're coming home from a long mission, short on fuel, and I'll bet ammunition."

The German officer spit out his bloody gag. "Look here, old man, you can't outrun my ship. They know you were heading south." Heads snapped around at his flawless, American-accented English. "Princeton," he said in reply to their unasked question. "I'm Leutnant zur See Walter Weber, uh, ensign to you Yanks. And I'm sure I can convince my companions to forget about this unfortunate misunderstanding, with appropriate compensation, of course. Say a case or two of Scotch and some tins of Woodbines. The crew would welcome a replacement for those horrible-tasting Jan Maats."

"Nazis always lie," Miriam said. "They will sink us. They only kill Jews."

"We're not Nazis, ma'am. We are German sailors. We couldn't care less about Jews," Weber said in apparent exasperation. "What do you say, old man?"

The captain paced, tugging on his lower lip, and took stock of Weber. He had the build of a linebacker with broad shoulders and a thick neck. His curly flaxen hair was greasy, as was his scraggly beard. His gray-blue eyes were cold, and there was something about his strained smile that reminded Rogers of the worst of his Academy days, the kind of smile that presaged a dagger in the back. Rogers grabbed Weber's undershirt. "What I say, old man, is I've seen what you do to neutral ships. Now that I think of it, it might be better for us if they found your bodies, too."

The rabbi tugged Rogers away from the German. "I did not flee Nazis to become one," he said.

Weber spat out more blood, his swollen and bruised face grim. "You don't know Oberleutnant Brauer. He'll never give up."

Rogers and Nidal exchanged worried glances at Brauer's name. Seamus perked up, too. "Lock 'em up," Rogers said to Obasi. Two of the Germans carried the unconscious sailor as Obasi marched them all out and down to the secret hiding place in Hold Number One.

A relieved Miriam scooted over to Rogers, arms open as if to hug him, pulling back at the last minute and shaking his scarred hand instead. "Thank you, Captain," she said. "I must return to the children." As she opened the door, Miriam called out to the rabbi: "Both horse and driver he has hurled into the sea." She smiled and carefully closed the door behind her.

Uncle Levy chuckled at Rogers' quizzical face. "It is the 'Song of the Sea' from Exodus. A prayer of thanks for the Israelites' escape from the Egyptian chariots across the Red Sea. A prayer, by the way, sung by the Prophet Miriam," the rabbi added, amused. "Appropriate, no?"

Rogers shook his head as he walked with the rabbi into the chartroom to discuss the next move with Nidal.

"Let's take the long route," Nidal said, drawing his finger across the map north around Scotland and down the western coast of England.

"Course, sir?" McAllister asked.

"A direction they'll never expect," Rogers said. The baby-faced helmsman looked back at him, confused, not wanting to question his authority but needing clarity. Rogers took pity. "Sorry, son. Head due west for thirty minutes until we're over the horizon, and then course 230 degrees out of the English Channel. Full speed ahead."

"Course due west for thirty minutes, then 230 degrees, full speed ahead. Aye, aye, Captain." McAllister rang instructions to the engine room and spun the wheel for west.

"Bwana, your plan is too risky. Let's go to Monty or B.A.," Nidal said, referring to Montevideo and Buenos Aries. "There must be Jews there to take them in."

"We don't get paid unless we deliver them to Gibraltar."

"If we ever get to Gibraltar. This is hopeless," Nidal said and stormed out, dejected.

"It is not hopeless, you know," the rabbi said in his soothing baritone voice. "It is like the tale of the wise man condemned to death by a vain king."

"Rabbi, stories are for children," Rogers said, his attention focused on charting the course.

"The wise man persuaded the king to spare him from execution by promising to teach the king's horse to fly within a year."

"That was stupid."

"No," the rabbi said. "The wise man had three reasons, assuming the horse survived the training, of course. First, the king was old and might die in a year. Second, the wise man was also old and might not live out the year." He paused and studied Rogers' face for a long time.

"And the third reason?" Rogers asked, glancing up from his charts to break the uncomfortable silence.

"What would the Greeks say, Captain?" Rogers shook his head and frowned. "As the great poet Solomon ibn Gabirol once said: 'A wise man's question contains half the answer.'"

CHAPTER 5

The fog was burning off at the beginning of another gray day, but the sun was refusing to completely break through the clouds as the *Peggy C* plodded along at six knots, a slow speed that Turani told the captain, in no uncertain terms, was all he dared squeeze out of the engine. Rogers wasn't buying it; engineers were born pessimists.

"Come on, Chief, just a few more revolutions is all I'm asking!" Rogers yelled into the voice pipe, a brass tube used for communicating between the wheelhouse and engine room.

"The pressure is already dangerously high. Push it any harder and something's going to break!" Turani yelled back over the rumbling and clanking and constant deafening hum of the huge pistons churning up and down. After a long silence, he surrendered to the inevitable. "I'll see what I can do, Captain."

"That-a-boy," Rogers said, capping the tube with a rubber stopper and returning to his captain's chair. He could see Nidal and Seamus through the large opening to the chart room behind him. Both were working at a desk, sorting through stacks of documents, and flipping through a copy of *Lloyd's Register of Shipping*. The logbooks, registration papers, permits, and inventories were all in the name of the *Peggy C*.

"What's the name this time?" Seamus asked.

"We have to hurry, so keep the same number of letters," Nidal said.

Seamus counted seven letters on his fingers as he mouthed the ship's name. "Titanic it is, then, Mr. Nidal."

The first mate slapped the back of Seamus' head. "Something that starts with a 'P,' imbècile."

Rogers yawned and stretched, rising from his chair to leave. "You have the watch, Mr. Nidal." He put his hand on the door handle, stopped abruptly, then turned. "Teach the horse to fly. That's what the Greeks would say."

"What, Captain?" Seamus asked.

"That's the rabbi's third reason. Teach the horse...never mind. Use *Pegasus*. P-E-G-A-S-U-S."

Once the name was selected, it didn't take long for Nidal to organize the crew to carry out the change in identity. He kept a compartment full of all the needed supplies: scrapers, brushes, rollers, stencils, chipping hammers, paint of various colors, flags, and emblems; all tools of the trade for a ship that sailed through dangerous waters smuggling dangerous cargo for dangerous men.

On the forecastle deck at the end of the bow, with the ship moving ahead at dead slow, Obasi manned the donkey engine, a small steam engine used to operate the anchor windlass. That engine drove the bilge pumps that sucked out water from the lowest depths of the hull—water that had failed to drain back into the sea through bulwark holes known as scuppers. It also did a variety of other small lifting chores. On many ships, the operator was known as a "donkeyman," a job that was more like a utility player who ran the engine, worked as a fireman, and even did watches on occasion—anything that was needed. Obasi fit the description. No one ever called him donkeyman, though—ever.

He released the devil's claw chain stopper and pulled the brake on the windlass, releasing the notched-wheel cable-lifter known as a wildcat. That sent the anchor cable holding the port anchor rumbling out of the chain locker through the steel hawsepipe in the prow and plunging into the ocean with a loud splash. The anchor hit the bottom, and the chain went taut after Obasi had run out about three shackles of cable, which are twenty-seven yards each. He repeated the process for the starboard side and then waved at the helmsman.

The ship came to a dead stop.

Hywel drew the short straw. He sat in a bosun's chair—a single person seat made of a short board and rope on a hook—and signaled for Obasi, working with the donkey engine, to lower him over the port side of the ship to scrape off all but the first three letters of *Peggy C* on the prow. When Obasi didn't immediately respond, Hywel made the mistake of shouting, "Boyo, l-l-lower me over the side."

Obasi apparently was unfamiliar with Welsh slang and appeared to take great offense at being called anything that sounded like "boy." With a frown on his face, Obasi abruptly released the brake, plunging Hywel over the side, then stopping his fall with a violent jolt, drawing howls of protest. When Hywel finished scraping off the name, Obasi swung him in jerky spurts to the American flag painted on the middle of the ship, banging him like a bell's clapper ringing the steel hull. At the Welshman's plight, Obasi guffawed, his mouth wide open and head back, slapping his knees with his massive hands. Between such comic convulsions, he lowered buckets of red lead paint, an anti-corrosive primer for steel parts, and a large roller that Hywel used to cover the red-white-and-blue. Noxious fumes from the paint and the rhythmic rocking of the ship made Hywel retch green-and-yellow bile from time to time.

"Don't be s-s-so rough, boyo!" Hywel shouted as Obasi hauled him high above the deck and lowered him over the starboard side to repeat the scraping and painting process.

About an hour later, Seamus replaced the woozy Hywel in the bosun's chair, first at the prow, where he used stencils and white paint for the new letters, transforming the ship into Pegasus, the flying horse of Greek legend. Next, it was on to the blank canvas where Old Glory used to be. He sloppily painted the Spanish flag's red, yellow, and white stripes, and the black eagle of St. John. It was done well enough to fool passing ships.

Bosun lowered the American flags from the masts and raised flags of the technically neutral Spain, a country recently united under the brutal rule of Generalísimo Francisco Franco, the fascist Caudillo who depended on Italy and Germany to crush his Republican foes, but then declined to join the Axis Powers in the war—maintaining a strong relationship, nonetheless. Thus, Spanish-registered ships were relatively safe from attack by either side.

The Dogar brothers, still covered in coal dust from the stokeroom, and Lonnie used rollers on long poles to paint the red funnel black, topping it with a white diamond. Just before noon, Obasi raised the anchors, and the newly christened *Pegasus* was on her way, looking from a distance like every other tramp steamer plying the North Atlantic. The whole transformation had taken less than two hours, and there hadn't been another ship in sight, so Rogers felt they still had a significant lead on the U-boat, even if its captain had correctly guessed their route. And, because of the relatively clear weather, Rogers knew the U-boat would have to stay submerged, which meant it couldn't travel fast enough to overtake the *Peggy C* (aka *Pegasus*).

In the wheelhouse, Nidal was starting his watch when a young girl, who looked to be around twelve, held open the starboard door for Miriam, carrying a tray of porcelain cups and a pot of coffee. The girl served a cup to Helmsman Cardoso, chewing on his yellow clay pipe, and to Nidal in the captain's chair. "Gracias," the Spaniard said, grabbing the cup with one hand, never taking his other hand off the wheel or his eyes off the windows ahead. Nidal nodded. The girl took another cup into the chartroom, where Seamus scribbled away, putting the final touches on forged documents for the *Pegasus*.

"Thanks, Missy," Seamus said in his thick Irish brogue, putting down his pen to slurp from the steaming cup. "What's your name?"

"Truus," she said, picking up an artist's sketch pad from the table where Seamus was working. "Are you an artist?"

"In a manner of speaking, aye."

"Can I watch?" she asked, looking at Miriam, who nodded approval.

Seamus scooted up a chair for Truus to observe his careful penmanship and handed her a pen. She looked at him in surprise. "Use it," Seamus said, tapping on the sketchbook in her hands. "You can keep it if you want. I've got stacks of 'em."

"Oh, yes. Thank you," Truus said, not wasting a moment to begin work alongside her new Irish friend.

"Where is Captain Rogers?" Miriam asked Nidal. "I have coffee for him, too."

"In his quarters below." Nidal focused out the windows at the foaming sea and approaching fog, his frown more pronounced than usual. "He needs rest."

She ignored the hint and left by the port door. Moments later, Truus snuck out behind her.

⟹⦿⟸

Miriam found the captain's quarters with its door ajar—standard procedure for wartime because it provided a quick escape hatch in an emergency. She knocked softly but there was no reply. The door swung open. Rogers lay on a small, oak bed, his right arm over his eyes, his boots by the bed, and his soiled clothes still on. He snored lightly in a dead sleep, his head resting on a life jacket, the recommended pillow in a war zone.

Not wanting to disturb the exhausted captain, she grabbed the handle to pull the door shut when she noticed a stack of books on his nightstand—three red leather-bound books lined with cracks from age. Intrigued, she tip-toed over, set down the coffee cup, and picked up one of the hefty books: volume one of Sir Walter Scott's *Ivanhoe*. The title page said 1820, making Miriam gasp with delight. Truus peeked through the door behind her.

All around the cabin, shelves and shelves of books lined the ship lath planks painted white above a chair-rail and black below it. There were dozens of naval classics—*Moby Dick*, *The Sea Wolf*, *Captain Blood*, *The Odyssey*, *Mutiny on the Bounty*, *Lord Jim*—as well as James Fenimore Cooper's *The*

Pilot, the first American sea novel, which was published two years before the better known *Last of the Mohicans*. There were also rows of histories, biographies, philosophical works, medical and engineering textbooks—all in all, an astonishing and wide-ranging collection for a simple sailor.

Miriam drifted past the tidy cabin's two curtained portholes, small walnut dresser, and leather settee, pausing at a doorway to the captain's office, a cramped room with a tattered American flag hanging between a map of the United States, and a framed, black-and-white photo of cadets in high-collared dark uniforms titled "United States Naval Academy Freshman Class 1921." On another wall hung a framed *Times of London* newspaper clipping, yellowed with age, with the picture of a stern-faced Naval officer in dress white uniform. The headline read: "U.S. Adm. James Rogers, Naval Hero, 1860-1923."

Miriam leaned in for a closer look. A scarred hand grabbed her arm from behind and spun her around. "What the hell are you doing here?" A red-faced Rogers hissed, groggy from sleep. "No one comes into my office without my say so."

Startled, she crashed backwards into a shelf, scattering books helter-skelter over the floor. "I am so sorry, I did not...I wanted to thank you," she stammered. Truus covered her mouth and fled in terror, unseen.

Rogers plucked *Ivanhoe* from Miriam's hands.

"It is one of my favorite books," she said in futile explanation for invading the captain's privacy. "I, I am so very sorry. You see …" She appeared too embarrassed and scared to finish and darted out the door, not stopping until she rushed, out of breath, into the wheelhouse.

"How did Tuan Jake like his coffee?" Nidal asked, staring straight ahead. "They say he killed a man in America. Irritated him."

Miriam hurried into the chartroom, grabbed Truus by the hand, and dragged her away through the starboard door. Seamus, seeing that Truus had left behind a sheet torn out of her new sketchbook, stood as if to return it but stopped with a laugh at the remarkably accurate drawing of him that Truus had dashed off.

"Been hiding out on the *Peggy C* ever since, or so I hear!" Nidal shouted at the closing door, then muttered to himself, "One really shouldn't irritate such a man."

Miriam didn't stop until she reached their small assigned cabin in the petty officers' quarters under the poop deck. The cramped room featured four bunks, a settee, and a single wardrobe. Vibrations from the propeller below rocked the whole room as Arie shivered on the settee. Truus kissed his forehead and sat on a bunk while Miriam put more blankets on him. She felt his forehead and examined his throat. Looking worried, she scrubbed her face in a washbasin. The room reeked of sweaty men and tobacco smoke despite a stiff breeze rushing through the two open portholes. After checking her face in the mirror for tear tracks, Miriam closed the portholes and took Truus' hand.

They then joined the rest of the family in the crew's mess, where they sought refuge from their icy cabin and the unbearable wind and rain on deck. Here they found a comforting heat pouring in from the galley next door and the aroma of freshly baked bread, which perhaps made them feel a bit less miserable. It was as if they could close their eyes and believe they'd never fled home, still hearing the sound of their mother's clanking of pots and pans, the rooms redolent of their family's Shabbat dinners, laughter and prayers and pipe smoke—homey things children pay no special attention to until they're no more. Here the boys—Wim and his younger brother Julius—played games while the rabbi sat nearby, sipping coffee, engrossed in a tattered book.

Lonnie and Hywel, playing checkers in silence at a table, nodded a greeting to Miriam, still shaken by Rogers' anger, but doing her best not to show it. She nodded back politely and sat next to the rabbi at his own table. "Uncle Levy, Arie still feels too hot, and his throat is inflamed," she said.

"He'll be fine," the rabbi said, putting his book down on the table. "Now, what's this about the captain yelling at you?"

"What? How?" Miriam gave Truus, sitting with the boys and sketching, a reproachful look. "Did you follow me?" The young girl dropped her head and kept drawing, ignoring Miriam, who gave up waiting for an answer and turned her attention back to her uncle. "He got upset when I took him coffee and picked up one of his books."

"Books?" he said, shaking his head in wonder. "Captain Rogers was always a bit of a mystery to your father."

"Mystery?"

The rabbi hesitated, peering over the edge of his cup as he drank. Appearing to mull over what he was going to say next, he took off his thick glasses and cleaned them with his handkerchief. "Your father has done some, uh, business with the captain before."

With loud shouts, Wim and Julius rolled onto the floor, fighting over a toy soldier that Wim held out of his brother's reach, taunting him as only older brothers can. In exasperation, Miriam jumped out of her chair, separated the boys, and handed the toy to Julius. "Now, sit down and behave," she said, waiting for the boys to obey before turning back to rejoin the rabbi. In the lull, she caught the two sailors leering at her with greasy smiles as they left. "Papa did business with a smuggler?" she said, adjusting her dress as she slid into her chair.

"For favors mostly. A Jew needs favors to survive, even in Mokum."

"Amsterdam. Use English, please. And that name no longer applies. It is not a safe haven anymore."

"Your father had business all over Europe, and it depended on doing all sorts of favors—favors for customs officials, favors for bureaucrats, favors for politicians, favors for whomever would buy or trade what he was selling. It has always been thus. When our families fled to Holland from Spain and Portugal centuries ago, favors were needed to survive, and we made those favors happen by trading with our relatives all over the world. Your father was better at it than most."

"I thought he owned warehouses," she said.

"And what do you think he filled them with? At least until the Nazis came," he said and sighed. "That's why men like Captain Rogers were useful to your father."

"But why did Captain Rogers flee America? Did—"

Suddenly, machine gun bullets smashed against the outside wall in a rapid *rat-tat-tat*, ripping holes through metal and shattering window glass. A series of explosions was followed by warplanes screeching overhead, diving and blasting machine guns at one another and pulling up inches from the ship's newly painted black funnel. The children shrieked and ran into the arms of Miriam and the rabbi, who hugged them close as they huddled underneath the wooden table for protection from the deadly hail of bullets.

———⟫●⟪———

On the bridge deck, Nidal searched the foggy sky as high-pitched engines and sporadic gunfire swirled somewhere around him; flashes of explosions and tracer bullets cut through the clouds. Rogers rushed up from his cabin just as a flaming Royal Air Force Spitfire streaked over *Peggy C's* stern. They crouched for cover and held onto their hats. With a thundering splash, the crippled plane crashed into the sea off the port bow. Bullets from unseen planes ripped a trail of holes across the deck. Then, as quickly as they had come, the sounds of the dogfight faded away, replaced by the pounding of rain on the metal deck and waves clawing at the hull.

———⟫●⟪———

Miriam crawled to the shattered door window, inching up to peek out into the swirling fog. Nothing moved. She bent down to comfort Truus, clinging to her dress, shaking and whimpering. At the sound of a faint buzz, Miriam rose for another cautious glimpse outside. Dead ahead, a Spitfire trailing black smoke dropped into view, not just on a collision course with the *Peggy C,* but heading right at a petrified Miriam. It pulled up at the last second, a Nazi Messerschmitt on its tail blasting away with its MG-17 machine guns at 1,200 rounds per minute.

The two planes zoomed over Rogers and Nidal on the bridge with guns blazing, vanishing into the gray-black clouds. Nidal slapped Rogers' arm and pointed up: a man dangling from a parachute floated from the clouds and landed hard in the sea several hundred yards ahead of them off the starboard bow. Miriam rushed onto the deck, and when she was able to locate the fallen airman floating on the roiling sea, she looked at the bridge and, with her eyes, seemed to implore Rogers to help. He shook his head and mouthed the words "not safe to stop."

Shocked, Miriam tore a roped life ring from the bulwark and tossed it overboard as the ship came alongside the downed airman, a desperate, impossible toss that somehow found its mark, and the airman held tight as he was dragged along in the ship's wake. She fought to reel him in, but the weight was too much for her, and whenever she pulled him closer, the rope would rip over her hands, tearing her skin. With tears in her eyes, she mouthed "help" to the two men on the bridge.

Nidal nudged Rogers: "Now what, oh great white father?"

CHAPTER 6

The captain and first mate laid the unconscious British officer down on a bunk, blood spurting from a severe wound on his right arm and covering his blue-gray uniform. They tore off his jacket and shirt and covered his shivering body with a blanket, leaving the arm exposed. He couldn't have been over twenty-years-old, his brown hair close-cropped, his face pale, his lips blue under a pencil-thin mustache, the type favored by swashbuckling actors like Errol Flynn.

Cookie tended to him with a primitive medicine kit, anxiously pressing at the wound with a towel while flipping through a ragged copy of the *Ship Captain's Medical Guide*. "It won't stop, Cap'n."

Miriam nudged Cookie aside. "Move, please." She poured alcohol over her hands from a bottle Cookie had and probed the airman's wound with her long, thin fingers, dabbing at it to clear the blood obstructing her view. She flipped through the kit full of instruments and medical supplies Cookie had set next to the bunk and, not seeing what she needed, held up her hand, pinching her forefinger and thumb together. "Do you have, um, pincet of tangetje to remove bullet?"

"Pliers?" Cookie asked.

"Yes, or smaller, for splinter."

With a quick nod, Cookie hurried off. Rogers and Nidal struggled to keep the moaning British officer still.

"Hold this down," Miriam said to Rogers, pointing to the towel she was holding over the wound. "Press hard." She found scissors in Cookie's kit and cut off the airman's bloody T-shirt, out of which she fashioned a two-inch-wide strip that she wrapped around his arm just above the wound. Using a wrench from Cookie's kit as a windlass, Miriam twisted the tourniquet until the bleeding stopped. "Hold, like this," she said, placing Nidal's hand on the wrench.

Cookie rushed back clutching a greasy pair of pliers. Miriam examined them suspiciously, but having no alternative, poured alcohol over them, and rubbed them on her skirt to remove as much grime as she could. After Rogers lifted the towel, she slipped the pliers into the wound, moving around with delicate precision, ignoring the patient's yells and attempts to grab her hand. Rogers wrested his hand away and pinned it down, letting him howl.

With a slight tug, Miriam removed the shattered remains of a Messerschmitt's MG 131 13-mm machine gun round from the officer's arm, dropping it into Cookie's outstretched hand. She poured more alcohol over the wound and sprinkled yellow sulfa power over the gash to disinfect it. As she bandaged the arm with a roll of gauze and cotton, Nidal eased up on the tourniquet. "Please, clean and replace every few hours. Yes?" Miriam said to Cookie.

She stood on shaky legs and stumbled out of the cabin, fighting to catch her breath in the frigid night air. Gripping the bulwark's wooden cap rail to calm trembling hands covered in blood, she was apparently lost in thought in the feeble light of a waning crescent moon. Shining between scudding clouds, the moon cast oddly shaped dancing shadows on the deck and the rolling ocean as far as the eye could see.

Rogers snuck up on Miriam, pulling her out of her reverie with a gasp. "Sorry," he said in a soft voice, ostensibly begging forgiveness for disturbing her, but more so for how he had treated her in his cabin, and for his damn temper. "Thanks for bailing out Cookie. He's not much of a doctor—drunk or sober." His joke fell flat, so he tried again, this time with a cheerier voice. "How'd you know what to do?"

"I studied to be doctor," she said, staring stiffly forward into the ocean.

"You've done this before?"

"Only on dead bodies."

A cannon's distant boom and a flash of light startled Miriam, causing her to lean, unthinking, against Rogers; he hesitated, then put his arm over her shoulder, not sure what else to do. "I'm sorry I snapped at you," he said. "I, uh, I like my privacy."

She shrank away, and they both stood side-by-side for a long awkward moment, the waves lapping against the ship, the cool air electric and clean after the storm. Rogers wracked his brain for a way to end the silence, settling on returning to the scene of the crime. "So, why is *Ivanhoe* a girl's favorite book?"

Miriam glanced at him out of the corner of her eye, "Rebecca," she said.

Rogers nodded, "Of course, a Jew, a healer—"

"A woman who stood up for herself."

"She needed a knight to save her," Rogers said with a grin.

Turning to face him directly, Miriam glowered at him with her chestnut eyes. "She understood chivalry. The men did not—like you."

"What?" His grin faded away.

"You would have left him to drown."

Failing to hold his tongue, he spat out, "Look, lady, chivalry's fine in books but—"

Seamus, running up out of breath, interrupted before Rogers could finish. "Pardon, Captain, we're having a wee problem with the Germans."

———⟫●⟪———

Rogers ducked into his nearby cabin and emerged carrying a Colt M1911 pistol, a vintage World War I gun with a brushed blue finish and checkered walnut grip, and joined Seamus in a jog to the front of the ship. Descending into Hold Number One, they found Obasi and Lonnie standing guard with the confiscated submachine guns. Inside the hidden compartment, two of the German sailors, still dressed only in long underwear, were holding Bosun's arms tightly, and one pressed a jagged piece of glass against his neck.

"Stupid donkeyboy let them grab Bosun," Lonnie said, emphasizing with a sneer his substitution of "boy" for "man" in Obasi's never-used donkeyman job description. Obasi glared back.

"Shut up," Rogers said.

"Let us go and he lives," Leutnant Weber said.

Without hesitation, Rogers shot the right foot of the German holding the glass, barely missing Bosun's feet. The German dropped the shard and fell to the ground, crying out in pain and clutching his foot. Bosun spun around and punched his other captor. Obasi and Seamus joined the fray, swinging their guns at the sailors. A deft fighter, Weber tackled Lonnie as if he were still on the Princeton football team, knocking the submachine gun out of his one good hand. They dove for it across the floor.

A gunshot from Rogers' Colt knocked the submachine gun out of the German officer's reach. Everyone froze. The Germans carefully raised their hands, fear on their faces. Weber jumped to his feet and furiously charged at the captain. Again, without hesitation, Rogers aimed the pistol at the German's chest and pulled the trigger. Shocked by the blast, Weber patted his body, searching for a wound, and finding none, raised his hands. "Did I miss?" Rogers asked sarcastically, having deliberately shot past the leutnant. "Wanna try that again?"

"My men are cold and hungry," Weber said. "You cannot treat us like this, like animals."

Rogers considered the request for a moment. "All right. I'll have some food and blankets sent down. And your clothes once they've dried. Now, back in."

"And a doctor for those two," Weber said, dragging the wounded sailor next to the still unconscious sailor on the floor.

Rogers nodded and turned to leave; Bosun blocked his way. "Thanks, Captain. You saved—" Before Bosun got the words out of his mouth, Rogers slapped him so hard he fell to his knees.

"Don't ever let that happen again," Rogers said. He tossed Obasi a key and headed up the ladder. "Lock all the weapons in my dayroom cabinet. At once."

When he reached the deck, he found the rabbi uttering "tsk, tsk" with a disapproving expression on his face. "Are you animal?" the rabbi asked. "You shoot a prisoner and slap your own man?"

"I have no time to argue with Nazis," Rogers said. "And you don't know Bosun. He's poison."

"That is not God's way."

"And what would your God have me do?"

The rabbi put his hand on Rogers' shoulder. "Why do men like you want easy answers for such hard questions?"

"Because in times like these, I need a little fear to keep this ship afloat."

"The Germans would agree," the rabbi said, locking eyes with Rogers.

"Now, wait a minute …"

"Brute strength, blame, willful ignorance," the rabbi said. "Are you any different? You must learn violence is futile."

"So, running is your answer?" Rogers asked.

"My brother said I would be killed. 'Collaborator,' they called me. It was not my choice to serve on the Jewish Council. And I did not agree with many things the other members said. But I did say we had no choice but to cooperate with the Germans."

"I take it Miriam didn't agree."

"Miriam," the rabbi huffed in mild exasperation. "She thinks she is one of the Maccabees. Always wanting to fight. My brother named her for the wrong prophet. Should have called her Deborah."

"Who?"

The rabbi pressed on, ignoring the question. "For Jews, such anger has consequences. As a people, no matter where we have lived, we Jews have had to go our own way and not make noise to survive. My brother understands this. But Miriam would not listen to us."

"Your brother? Mr. Maduro?" Rogers asked. The rabbi nodded. "I thought he was coming with you. I'm sorry, but we waited as long as we could."

"The Germans suspected, correctly, that he had more assets than what they had already confiscated. They always watch him. Not me."

"I hoped he'd escape after I got his guards to chase me," Rogers said. "What will happen to him?"

"He is a very resourceful man, but I fear for him." The rabbi stuck a finger in Rogers' chest. "Now, we were talking about you, young man, not my family. Remember what it says in Proverbs: 'He who is slow to anger is better than the mighty.'"

"Sorry, but I'm not much for religion."

"Well, let me put it in layman's terms for you," the rabbi said in his soft, soothing voice while taking hold of Rogers' arm. "Have you ever heard of Aesop's eagle and the arrow?"

"Not another story." Rogers tried to pull away, but the rabbi held onto his arm.

"The eagle was soaring proudly one day when he was mortally struck by an arrow."

"So, it died and—"

"As it fell to the earth, it saw something that made it shudder." He paused for dramatic effect, trying to keep the captain's attention. "It realized that the fletchings at the end of the arrow were its own feathers." Rogers appeared not to get the point. "Think about it, Captain, before you make another enemy." The rabbi shook his head and strolled away.

Early the next morning, Wim, walking with a distinct limp, and his younger brother Julius were clacking pieces of wood in an imaginary sword fight across the bridge deck. Truus, her long hair in pigtails, chased after them, stopping to peer into the wheelhouse through one of the windows. She drew an angry glare from Nidal that sent her away shrieking. She followed the boys down the ladder to the next level, the boys laughing and whooping with delight past the half-opened door of the captain's quarters.

As she reached the door, Truus stopped to peer inside. Rogers and Obasi sat together on the settee pouring over a book, Obasi moving his fingers slowly as he mumbled some words. "But though I was terri...terri..." Obasi said with difficulty.

"Terrified," Rogers patiently said. He spotted Truus and frowned; she squealed and fled. Shaking his head, Rogers returned to Obasi's reading lessons. A few moments later, Miriam strolled up to the open door, ready to knock, but stopped and stood in silence, her smile getting bigger the more she listened.

"Fifteen men on the dead man's chest. Yo-ho-ho and a bottle of rum," Obasi read, unsure about the pronunciation but pushing ahead like any good student eager to impress his teacher. He leaned back when he finished, appearing frustrated. "What means Yo-ho-ho?"

"Nothing, really," Rogers said. "It's a cheer. Something you say when you're happy." He tapped the book. "Continue."

Miriam covered her mouth and pivoted to sneak away before she could burst out laughing. Rushing down the deck in wild abandon, the two sword fighters smacked into her, pushing her back over the eighteen-inch steel storm plate at the bottom of the door and sending her sprawling onto the floor of

Rogers' cabin. Oblivious to the collision, the boys kept up their running battle, laughing and shouting. At the thump of Miriam hitting the floor, Obasi sprang to his feet and stuffed the book under his shirt. He hurried out of the cabin without a word or even acknowledging the fallen woman as he stepped over her.

"I am so sorry," she said as she picked herself up and backed out of the room. "I was searching for the children."

"Wait," Rogers said, joining her on the deck. "So, how's your patient?"

She continued walking, appearing to ponder the question. "Which one? The one you shot, the one you hit, or the one you wanted to let drown?"

Rogers didn't take it as the insult she may have intended. "The Brit. How's he doing?"

"He will recover...Captain *Larsen*," she replied straight-faced.

"It's Rogers," he said before catching on. "Wait. Larsen? Wolf Larsen? *Sea Wolf*? You've read that, too? What kind of girl are you?"

"My father wanted a boy. In Amsterdam, boys read about the sea."

"Well, I'm no Larsen."

Miriam opened the door to the crew's mess, but Rogers didn't want to let her go. "Ahab, maybe," he said, drawing from her what he was pretty sure was the flicker of a smile. He had forgotten for a blessed second where they were and the trouble they were in.

⸻⸻➤●◄⸻⸻

Yet in a remote cove not too far behind them, the danger had not forgotten them. There, on a desolate, rocky beach, a German sailor kicked at a half-deflated rubber dinghy. Next to him, Brauer picked up a U-boat officer's hat with the leaping tiger emblem on it, then threw it down in disgust.

⸻⸻➤●◄⸻⸻

No, Rogers wasn't giving thought to their pursuers; he was too lost in conversation with Miriam as they stepped into the crew's mess.

"The *S.S. Patna* is whose ship?" Miriam asked, spotting Truus and the other children at a table where Cookie served tea and biscuits from a can for a tea party.

"There you go, m'lady, gents. Your afternoon repast is served," Cookie said with a dramatic bow before returning to the galley to the applause and cheers of the children.

"Truus," Miriam said sternly. "You must not give me a fright like that. Tell me where you go." She poured some coffee for Rogers and herself, and they made themselves comfortable at a table away from the children. "*Patna?*" she said, picking up their conversation where it had left off.

"*Lord Jim.*"

"*Tuan Jim*, of course. Why does Mr. Nidal call you those silly names?"

"I like books. He thinks they make me...soft," Rogers said. "Why does your uncle call you names?"

"He does?"

"Said you should be named Deborah, whoever that is."

Miriam chuckled. "In the *Book of Judges*, Deborah convinced a general to march into battle against hopeless odds."

"Is that supposed to be funny? At least I think Mr. Nidal is joking," Rogers said.

"But Lord Jim: Is not that an insult? He abandoned hundreds of pilgrims in a storm at sea, yes? Why would he call you Tuan Jake?"

Rogers paused before replying, his concern growing the more he thought about it. "Mr. Nidal really called me Tuan Jake?"

⸺⊸●⊶⸺

It was time for the evening watch when Rogers and Obasi entered the wheelhouse and found Nidal arguing with the British officer, whose right arm was now in a sling. Helmsman McAllister stared straight ahead, ignoring the shouting.

"We cannot drop you off in England," Nidal said.

"I must insist. As an officer in His Majesty's Royal Air Force," he said.

"Lieutenant," Rogers interrupted him.

"Basil Gaylord," he said as if his name should impress them. It didn't. "Surely you can get it through this Moor's head that my return is of utmost importance."

"There's a U-boat out there that wants its boarding party back," Rogers said.

"You will turn them over to the British authorities when we dock."

"And the refugees?" Rogers was getting agitated.

"The Jews will have to go back where they came from," Gaylord said with a haughty assurance that irritated Rogers even more.

"One of those Jews saved your life. You'd send her and her family back to die?"

"Rubbish," Gaylord said. "Truth be told, the Nazis are more civilized than you damn Yanks. Now, Helmsman, set a course for Portsmouth."

"Steady as she goes, Helmsman," Rogers said.

"Steady as she goes. Aye, aye, sir," McAllister said looking at Rogers, unintentionally moving the wheel.

"Mind your helm," Rogers said, cautioning the young sailor that he was oversteering. McAllister's head snapped forward, and he gripped the wheel tighter.

Gaylord puffed out his chest as if to intimidate Rogers, advancing on him with a menacing look, hands clenched, chin jutted out. Obasi blocked him, pressing his large Nigerian knife against Gaylord's throat. The Brit stopped in his tracks, eyes bugging out.

"Smart move," Rogers said. He nodded at Obasi. "Let him cool off for a while with the other prisoners in Hold Number One."

CHAPTER 7

"Down periscope," Brauer said, stepping down from the attack periscope in the conning tower to a control room chart table where he could examine a map with Tauber and the chief helmsman, who oversaw navigation. All three appeared haggard and bone-tired.

Tauber tapped the map. "They were heading south. They couldn't have made it far."

"They'd be foolish to go that way," Brauer said, leaning over the map and drawing a line with his finger south through the English Channel from Calais to Lorient, the largest U-boat base in France. "But even if we could catch them on the way to base, we only have one damn torpedo left, and you know as well as I do that there's a fifty-fifty chance it is defective. And how much fuel do we have left?"

"Barely enough to make it to Lorient," Tauber said.

"That settles it. We have no choice but to do a quick turnaround at base and then return to the hunt."

"Herr Oberleutnant, we've been at sea for almost two months. The men are exhausted. Shore leave is all they talk about. *Blechkoller* is already causing fights and senseless quarrels," Tauber said of the so-called "tin can disease," a type of hysteria and irrational behavior triggered by boredom and overcrowding during extended confinement in U-boats.

Brauer's crystal blue eyes, underlined by dark circles, flashed in icy anger. His slicked-back hair, sunken cheeks, and thin, parched lips made the captain resemble nothing so much as a fussy accountant, albeit a ruthless one who tallied debits in German casualties and credits in sunken ships and enemy corpses. His First Watch Officer was becoming the bane of Brauer's existence, with his judgmental eyes and rim of black hair slathered with expensive and smelly Trelacen around a balding pate resembling that of a tonsured monk. He always was raising objections, nit-picking over proper procedures, talking in superior tones about his upbringing as the scion of a wealthy family from Berlin's upper-class Schöneberg neighborhood. And he was a Roman Catholic, which Brauer, as a good Nazi, despised. "You don't play chess, do you, First Watch Officer?"

Tauber shook his head.

"Too bad. You're right. The obvious course would be south," Brauer said. "That's why we'll look for that ship coming from the north around Scotland. That gives us plenty of time." Brauer knew his gambit was risky. He didn't care. Of far more risk to him was failure or being made a fool. For some time, he had been on thin ice with the BdU, U-boat command center, because of what he had done to the commander of his last submarine.

That had been the story of his life—the outsider, the loner, the over-achieving bully who came from the son of a failed factory owner, once middle-class, who resented the sons and daughters of wealthy bourgeoisie who made fun of his shabby clothes. He was the kind of person who, no matter how hard he tried, couldn't make himself likable; whose attempts at humor were off-putting, whose smile always looked more like a sneer, and whose shyness came off as arrogance. At seventeen, he ran away to join the Merchant Marines and, with his drive and brains, rose through the ranks faster than most. When he saved enough money, he returned to study law at Hamburg University while serving in the German Naval Reserve and becoming an ardent functionary in the local Nazi Party.

Although he had some success in law after graduating, at sea is where he truly excelled, taking over command of a minesweeper patrolling the North

Sea for two years. His men respected but feared him. His superiors disliked his arrogance and fanaticism but appreciated his skill. By 1939, he was in line for promotion. Brauer was confident of a plum assignment on a destroyer or battleship. To his great disappointment, he was sent instead to submarine training school in Neustadt, and his rank remained Oberleutnant zur See, or senior lieutenant, instead of what he thought it should be: Kapitänleutnant, lieutenant-commander.

Bitter but ambitious, Brauer did well enough in school to be designated as the First Watch Officer on a U-boat to patrol the South American coast. The two-month mission was a military success but a personal disaster. The thirty-one-year-old Brauer hated his commander, Oberleutnant zur See Siegfried von Eichhain, the son of minor nobility six years his junior and popular with his crew. Von Eichhain, whose military achievements had won him the Iron Crosses Second and First Class, made sure the men were well fed and treated fairly, and he encouraged his officers to discuss politics in a way that angered Brauer no end, openly flaunting his disdain for the Nazis. He even had the gall to move a picture of Hitler from the officer's mess to a less prominent position, which he replaced with a drawing of his family's three-mast schooner.

For Brauer, the final straw came at the end of the patrol when von Eichhain evaluated Brauer as a rigid officer of average talent. Brauer had become almost inured to slights from fellow officers for being an HSO—a former merchant marine—and a reservist. But the evaluation was devastating, particularly since it meant he wouldn't get his own command, and he would have to go out on another months-long patrol under the despised captain, which Brauer endured with barely concealed contempt.

When the submarine returned, Brauer, with the support of a few of his fellow officers, condemned von Eichhain for his anti-Nazi views and for listening to foreign radio shows. It was a shocking break with the U-boat *esprit de corps*, but as a trained lawyer, Brauer knew how to build his case, and as a well-connected Nazi, he had to be taken seriously. The scandal was hushed

79

up in a hurry, with Brauer getting his own U-boat command and von Eichhain transferred to a shore job.

The new command came at a cost, however. Brauer had offended many staff officers in the BdU who admired von Eichhain, and he knew they would be looking for the slightest reason to discredit him. He was determined not to let that happen, and so he drove his sailors hard to outdo even the fabled U-Boat "tonnage king" Korvettenkapitän Otto Kretschmer. Brauer's patrols always went longer and further than scheduled, working almost to the breaking point but racking up tonnage and casualties that couldn't be ignored by his superiors. The fact that his logs were a bit vague on the tonnage and nationality of some of the ships he sank—fog, "steamer without markings," "darkened ship," or enemy planes making it too dangerous to stick around to verify the identity—was noted but not scrutinized; this was war, after all, and it was well known that most captains exaggerated their conquests.

Still, Brauer felt unappreciated by his superiors. He had completed three successful patrols and yet had only one award, the U-boat War Badge, which every commander got after two missions, and not even the Iron Cross Second Class, which the BdU handed out almost routinely. Fellow submariners joked that he, like many young officers, was afflicted with *Halsschmerzen*, an itchy neck or sore throat that could only be cured by a Knight's Cross around his neck. Now, at the end of his third patrol, Brauer had lost a boarding party to a tramp steamer.

There would be no surviving that setback. So, he ordered a full stop, and had all of his men muster in the long, tight passageway that ran down the middle of the submarine. Some had to kneel, and others hung from bunks and pipes on the side to get a view of the captain in the control room in the middle of the U-boat. Most wore gray-green denim jumpsuits left by the British at Dunkirk. Others had on a mishmash of checkered flannel shirts and wool turtleneck sweaters. U-Bootwaffe members were special that way: they wore whatever they wanted.

"Men," Brauer said over a crackling public address, enunciating in a slow and deliberate manner to make his words clearly carry the full length of the submarine. "As some of you may have heard, Leutnant Weber and his boarding party have been lost. However—" The collective rumblings of the crew took a minute to calm down before Brauer could continue. "However, there is a chance that they are alive and being held captive on an American cargo ship," he said, again waiting for the tumult to recede. "I pledge to you that we will find that ship and rescue them if alive, and if not, avenge their deaths."

Cheers erupted up and down the U-boat. "But, I need a pledge from you. The only way we can catch this ship is to return to sea immediately." Groans rippled like a slow-moving wave through the crew as the captain's words were repeated in disbelief down the passageway. "I know this is hard, but we cannot let the bureaucrats stop us for a pointless inquiry. We must do this to uphold the honor of those men, for the honor of our crew, for the honor of the Fatherland. Will you join me in that fight? Will you raise your right hands right now and swear an oath of secrecy?"

To a man, they shouted "we swear" while holding up their right hands and cheering as Brauer had hoped. His men were giving up dreams of shore leave, of traveling in luxury on a special train known as the BdU Zug reserved for submariners for weeks of rest at home, of days without stinking unbathed men crammed together in an iron coffin full of diesel fumes and fetid air, of quiet moments away from the relentless *kachung, kachung, kachung* of the roaring engines. Most of all, they would miss relief—unspoken but felt—from the gnawing terror that was the constant companion of all U-boaters at sea.

When the men dispersed, Brauer instructed the radio operator—keeper of the submarine's sea war diary—to alter the Kriegstagebócher, or KTB, as the diary was called, to say that Weber and his men were left behind in their dingy because of overwhelming aerial attacks, and were presumed lost. The radio operator re-typed the two pages and made no mention of getting stuck in the mud, or of abandoning four sailors being held prisoner on a merchant ship.

The U-boat sped south at maximum speed, often hitting seventeen knots, the prow cutting a soaring bow break. It passed a couple of lumbering cargo ships, but didn't slow down until arriving at the former French naval dockyard at Lorient on the Bay of Biscay. As they approached the stone quay, the crew, in a frenzy of excitement, hustled to clean off their uniforms, singing at the top of their lungs as U-boat songs blared from the ship's record player, "We are the U-boat men, the gray wolves on a gray sea," and "on a seaman's grave no roses bloom."

Vizeadmiral Karl Dönitz greeted Brauer and his crew as soon as they tied up at the quay, as he did for all returning U-boats. The dock was lined with flower-bearing girls from the League of German Girls—the female version of the Hitler Youth—in their military-looking jackets of fawn color suedette with dark blue skirts, white blouses, and black neckerchiefs held together with a leather slide. A military brass band played the World War I U-boat song "Den Wir Fahren Gegen Engelland" ("We Sail Against England") and other patriotic tunes. They were joined by crowds of cheering dockworkers, nurses in white capes handing out bags of fruit, girlfriends, and fellow U-Bootfahrer.

Brauer's ship flew two *erfolgswimpeln* (white victory flags) from the tall attack periscope above the conning tower, homemade pennants listing the tonnage of each merchant ship sunk during the mission; for warships sunk, red pennants were used. For tankers, white ones with red borders were flown. Four pennants, regardless of color, were the average.

"Welcome home, Oberleutnant Brauer," said Dönitz, dressed in a dark blue double-breasted overcoat, a fifteen-inch-long officer's dagger in a brass scabbard with a silver portepee—a sword knot resembling a small pompom—hanging on his left hip. Brauer suspected the white grip, with its brass pommel in the shape of an eagle clutching a wreathed swastika, was made of ivory. "Only two?" Dönitz asked in a perfunctory tone, pointing with his gloved hand at the victory flags.

Brauer braced for the expected dressing down, hoping Dönitz wouldn't deliver it as he did for Korvettenkapitän Hans-Gerog Fischer a few months earlier when he stood, arms crossed, in front of the whole U-109 crew. "Your patrol was crap," Dönitz told them as they lined up on the dock. "You'll have to do better."

With a sense of dread, Brauer held out for Dönitz his KTB, deciding to get all the bad news over with now rather than wait for the usual presentation at his debriefing. "We lost four men, I'm sorry to say, Herr Vizeadmiral."

"How?" Dönitz snapped, his cologne causing Brauer's nose to itch, unaccustomed as it was to anything that didn't stink.

"They were a boarding party—"

Dönitz held up his hand. "We will discuss that later this afternoon after you have eaten and freshened up," Dönitz said. He gave Brauer a firm handshake, handed off the sea diary to a staff officer, and turned to join the other sailors.

"Pardon me, Herr Vizeadmiral," Brauer said. "We must go back out—tomorrow."

Dönitz spun around and studied the weary captain with a sad look of admiration, shaking his head. The commander-in-chief of all U-boat forces was known to favor ambitious captains who delivered, who showed ingenuity and grit, who were hard and tireless in service to the Reich.

"I understand your anger, Oberleutnant, and I appreciate your zeal," he said, giving Brauer's shoulder a paternal pat. "We certainly could use more U-boats like yours out there right now, but that is too much to ask of your crew."

"We picked up intelligence from one of the neutral ships we stopped near Fastnet Rock about a large convoy expected in the next few days in the Western Approaches," he said, referring to the stretch of the Atlantic Ocean just west of Ireland and England. "I believe we can catch it if we hurry. And my crew, to a man, swore to me that they want to do this."

Brauer knew that would intrigue Dönitz, who was so obsessed with tonnage sunk that he compared U-boats' individual performances against each other daily, and matched them against the entire command's average. Intent on pushing the numbers higher, he often micromanaged his captains, sending them as many as seventy coded messages a day and expecting quick replies.

"A convoy, you say?" Dönitz asked, tilting his head in interest, and glancing over at one of his staff officers. "We haven't heard of any convoys in that area lately, have we?"

"Nothing from B-dienst," the officer said, referring to the German naval intelligence service that monitored and deciphered radio transmissions.

"After lunch," Dönitz said, "we'll discuss everything." He spun on his heels and shook the hand of each member of Brauer's bearded crew standing at stiff attention in formation alongside their submarine, their proud faces deathly white. He called many of the officers and Lords, as the enlisted men were known, by their first names as he handed out awards. He had a kind word or question for each of his beloved "gray wolves." Thanks to Dönitz, U-boat crews received wages almost double other military branches, and were provided the highest quality of food both onboard and onshore, including the best wine, beer, and bordellos. He also was known to write a personal letter of commendation to crews that had performed exceptionally well. All the men of the U-Bootwaffe returned the affection, calling him "Uncle Karl" and "the Grand Lion."

Brauer conferred with Obersteuermann Werner Nagel, his chief helmsman, who served as quartermaster as well as navigator but never actually steered the U-boat. Brauer wanted to make sure he understood the urgency of re-supplying their submarine quickly. Stürkorl, as he was known by the crew using the Old German term for helmsman, was in his 40s, making him the oldest person by far on the U-boat and one of the most respected. Brauer knew he could count on him to get the almost impossible job done because he always did. The same couldn't be said for Tauber, who Brauer waved over. His instructions: Re-assemble the crew from the barracks by the next afternoon for departure.

"Tell them they are not to leave the barracks except to go to the U-bootsheim and back," Brauer said of the U-boat Sailor's Home where submariners could relax and watch German movies, play card games, buy beer and snacks, and mail letters. "Our banquet and parade will have to wait until we return. But I promise they will be spectacular."

Before heading into town on wobbly sea legs, Brauer stopped in the storage barracks to retrieve his dress blue uniform from a locker in the basement. He also let base officials know of his plans. That would speed everything up once the commander-in-chief approved his departure, which he assured them would happen soon.

Brauer had an early lunch, opting for a traditional German meal, having never developed a taste for French cuisine; something about it was too effete, too foreign and rich for his working-class tastes. He wolfed down a large serving of Rouladen—thin strips of meat slathered with mustard and rolled around bacon, onions, and pickles. Served with potato dumplings, red cabbage, and gravy, lunch smelled like his grandmother's kitchen. He washed it all down with several ice-cold steins of Bavarian Hefeweizen and ended with a gooey slice of Black Forest cherry tort, coffee, and a double-shot of schnapps. Pushing himself away from the table, he felt sick.

Afterward, he luxuriated in a long hot bath at the Hotel Beauséjour, which served U-boat officers. But no matter how long he soaked, he couldn't shake that inner feeling of constant chill from long, cold months at sea.

Once done with the bath, Brauer sat down to write a letter to his wife:

My dearest Gerda,

I hope this letter finds you well. How I miss you and Hamburg. It has been too many days apart. But it won't last forever. With God's help, we will conquer our enemies and return home in peace, free of rationing and bombings and

Jews. What a glorious future we have to look forward to under our beloved Führer.

As you know, dear, I cannot discuss my missions, but I can tell you that they are going splendidly, and that I fully expect a promotion soon. Ignore those ugly rumors you wrote about in your last letter. Those were no doubt started by some who are jealous of my success, and we know who they are, don't we, my sweet? Don't worry, their time will come.

With the promotion will come more pay. Perhaps you could start looking for better housing, and yes, something with more than one bedroom. Now, don't worry your pretty head about what the doctors said. I believe God will provide. Remember Mark 11:24: "Therefore I tell you, whatever you ask for in prayer, believe that you have received it, and it will be yours." I have prayed, and we will have a family.

I am sorry for the brevity of this letter, but I must dash off to visit with Vizeadmiral Dönitz, who I am sure has something special in mind for me.

Much love,

Viktor

That finished, he tried to take a nap. After an hour of tossing and turning in his too-soft bed, and missing the constant rocking of his ship, Brauer gave up any hope of sleep and donned his clean uniform. It hung loosely on his boney frame, and he winced when, in front of a mirror, he combed his hair. His clean-shaven cheeks were sunken and pallid, his neck swallowed up by the oversized collar of his starched white shirt like a stick in a barrel. He wore his white captain's hat, despite the stench and sweat stains. It was missing the slight fold that many commanders created to make them appear more dashing. Brauer went strictly by the book, and the hat's shape was a clear signal to his crew of his rigid adherence to proper procedures.

Ignoring the falling snow, a coatless Brauer hustled over to Dönitz's command center in the Villa Kerlilon, a three-story chateau in the neo-Louis XVIII style that Brauer considered a gaudy mishmash. Gray stones and red bricks interspersed with dormer pediments and festoons in the shape of garlands were topped off with a Mansard roof. Beneath it was the recently completed fourteen-room, 10,000-square-foot reinforced concrete bunker where the signal staff worked. During air attacks, Dönitz and his staff officers could retreat down a narrow staircase in the kitchen to continue working in the bunker.

Villa Kerlilon was the middle of three eighteenth-century villas across from the base overlooking the Scorff River—the main waterway to Lorient—requisitioned by the Germans for U-boat command. The villas were built by an industrialist who made his fortune in sardines, thus the locals' nickname for the compound: "Château des Sardines."

A young lieutenant greeted Brauer at the door. "Herr Vizeadmiral Dönitz has just risen from his nap and will see you now. Follow me please, Herr Oberleutnant." He led Brauer past the grandiose, white spiral staircase in the entry hall through one of the twenty ornate rooms with high ceilings—ten of them upstairs bedrooms—to a small ten-by-thirteen-foot anteroom, richly paneled with polished parquet floors and large windows overlooking the bay. With an Alsatian resting at his feet, Dönitz sat upright at his neat desk, pouring over messages, an aide hovering over his shoulder at all times.

He waved for Brauer to take a straight-backed chair in front of him and kept reading, looking up to receive more papers from staff officers buzzing in and out of the room, snapping orders, giving rapid-fire answers to questions, and signing everything with what Brauer recognized as a Montblanc Meisterstück fountain pen. It was black with gold trim, its golden nib engraved with 4810. Brauer had always coveted the elegant pen, which was crafted in his native Hamburg, but could never bring himself to waste money on such a frivolous luxury.

Snapping the top on his fountain pen and putting it down with authority, Dönitz scrutinized Brauer as he adjusted his double-breasted blue reefer jacket. Despite his fame and rank, his uniform was modestly adorned with a standard gold eagle clutching a swastika on his right breast, and two small rows of service ribbons on his left, above an Iron Cross First Class and a bronze U-boat War Badge. A Knight's Cross of the Iron Cross dangled from a red, white, and black-striped ribbon around his skinny neck. Brauer never could get over the resemblance Dönitz had to pictures he had seen in magazines of former U.S. President Calvin Coolidge, with his severe face, square jaw, deep frown lines, and large ears, slightly jutting out.

"I see from your war diary that you had to crash-dive because of an aerial attack and that you last saw the boarding party in a dinghy. Is that correct?" Dönitz asked, his face inscrutable, holding back his famously bad temper for the moment.

"Yes, sir."

"And you returned to base with an unused torpedo?"

"Yes, sir."

Dönitz leaned back in his chair and rubbed his temples, his dark eyes staring for the longest time at Brauer, a frosty stare that made the captain's heart beat faster. Beads of sweat trickled down his forehead, and his mind raced for a response to whatever Dönitz said next. Trying not to appear nervous, Brauer glanced across the river through tall salon windows at the fifty-nine-foot high K-1 bunker, five recently completed bomb-proof concrete pens covered by twelve feet of reinforced concrete. There, submarines docked for repairs. Then he shifted his gaze to pictures on Dönitz's sparse desk.

One of them was a photograph of Dönitz's three children when they were young: Peter, Klaus, and Ursula. Brauer knew that the two sons served in the Navy and that Ursula was married to legendary Korvettenkapitän Günter Hessler, who earlier in the year, as commander of U-107, sank fourteen ships in a target-rich area off the coast of Africa, the highest single-mission tonnage of Allied merchant ships of the war. To his credit, Dönitz had not felt it proper to recommend a Knight's Cross for his son-in-law, so Grossadmiral Eric Raeder, commander of the Kriegsmarine, did it for him. Such humility endeared Dönitz even more to the U-Bootfahrer.

At last, the Vizeadmiral broke the uncomfortable silence. "Come with me," he said, bolting from his chair and moving briskly into the adjoining room, his tall frame ramrod straight. The dog, called "Wolf," trotted along at his heels.

They passed through a large Situation Room where Dönitz's surprisingly small staff of officers worked on huge maps and charts, which covered every available space on all the walls. They were known as "the staff without paunches," a result of their ten-hour work days and Dönitz's never-ending demands for more data. Brauer thought he caught disapproving stares from some of the older officers, who quickly eluded his gaze, pretending to be busy. The second room had graphs on the walls showing tonnage sunk, U-boat losses, results of every attack on a convoy, and, most important to Dönitz, the average sinking tonnage for every U-boat per-sea-day and a fever chart for the entire command.

"We call this room the Museum," Dönitz said, running his hand over his thinning hair, then smoothing it down.

At a glance, Brauer could see that his submarine's performance was above average, thank goodness, but the line on the chart for all U-boats was down dramatically. Only twelve enemy ships had been sunk midway through the month, only five in the North Atlantic, and none off the coast of Ireland, a stunning decline in successful attacks for the exalted U-Bootwaffe. Another chart showed it had been averaging forty-six ships sunk a month since the war began. Even worse was a chart showing what was known as the "exchange rate," the ratio between ships sunk and U-boats lost. In October, forty-five ships were sunk compared to two U-boats, a ratio of 23-1; so far in November, that ratio had dropped to 6-1. Brauer knew anything less than a 10-1 ratio was disastrous.

"As you can see," Dönitz said, pointing at the various charts as a half-dozen assistants worked on the figures at their desks, "the numbers are not good."

"I don't understand," Brauer said, incredulous but careful with his words so as not to imply any fault in Dönitz's strategy. The vice-admiral was known to prefer "yes men," and did not deal well with critical or pessimistic views.

"The Naval High Command has decided to concentrate submarines in the Mediterranean and in the waters east and west of the Strait of Gibraltar—to aid our Italian friends and Rommel's Afrika Korps, and to cut off oil from the Middle East heading to Britain, which, by the way, makes no sense because the tankers have been taking the long way around the Horn of Africa for some time."

Dönitz led Brauer by the arm into the second Situation Room, its walls plastered with diagrams showing local times in the various operations areas, charts for tides and currents and weather conditions, plus how long each U-boat had been at sea and its expected return date. In the center of the room stood a large globe, three feet in diameter, that allowed for more accurate calculation of distances based on the earth's curvature. It was a data treasure trove that made it possible for Dönitz to change strategy daily and to move his U-boats around like chips on a watery chessboard, gambling where to find the jackpot of another convoy.

Brauer, half-listening to Dönitz's pedantic explanation of all the information he used for making decisions, waited in anguish for the impending interrogation about the missing boarding party and the unfired torpedo, both of which were usually unforgivable. Dönitz gestured toward a large map of the North Atlantic, divided into numbered six-by-six-mile squares with smaller squares inside for position locators. Pins and flags marked the position of each U-boat and known enemy positions. Red pins marked the last known position of U-boats that had not been heard from for several days and were presumed lost. Brauer had to look twice and still couldn't believe his eyes: only ten pins marked U-boats in the vast body of water stretching for millions of square miles.

"My God!" Brauer said in shock.

"Exactly. Most upsetting. Concentration of forces at the decisive point is one of the most important principles of war. And, as I have always said, that point is the North Atlantic. The way to defeat Britain is *guerre de course*. Destroy all her merchant ships and starve her to death, then focus on the warships," Dönitz said of his strategy for U-boats. In a quiet voice with a tinge of anger, he added. "Now, we can't even get any support for locating the convoys. We are operating practically blind."

Dönitz waved at a section of ocean between Iceland and Greenland where a few U-boats were lined up. "Recently, even wolfpacks have been struggling to find convoys. It's as if the British have knowledge of our concentrated dispositions and are able to avoid them. It isn't luck, and it is impossible that they have broken our code. So, we suspect it must be some combination of radio traffic, high-flying aircraft, or some kind of new location device," he said with a wave of his hand. "Whatever the reason, it is maddening. Individual U-boats like yours are the only ones having any success."

The distress was visible on Dönitz's wan face. He had been a U-boat commander himself during World War I and had begun refining *Rudeltaktik*— the German's pack attack strategy called wolfpacks—while stewing in a British prisoner of war camp for nearly a year. Rudeltaktik had been conceived during

World War I, but never successfully implemented.

Dönitz's strategy was to position a half dozen or so U-boats in a patrol line, called a stripe, across an area west of Britain where Allied convoys were likely to sail into their net. Once a U-boat found a target, it would shadow the ship or convoy at a distance just beyond the horizon, following the merchants' towering black smoke plumes. The U-boat continually transmitted a beacon signal, allowing Dönitz to coordinate a convergence of the far-flung wolves for the slaughter.

Many captains, like "Tonnage King" Kretschmer, preferred to attack on the surface at night in the darkest hours before the moon rose. Because of their speed and low silhouette, the U-boats would slip unnoticed inside the multiple columns of ships in the convoy and wreak havoc, firing torpedoes and deck guns at point-blank range, and then speed away into the darkness before the escorting warships could catch them.

A stunning affirmation of Dönitz's strategy came in October 1940 from a wolfpack that included Kretschmer and two other top aces: Korvettenkapitän Günther Prien and Korvettenkapitän Joachim Schepke, who was so notorious for exaggerating his successes that fellow officers referred derisively to "Schepke tonnage." There was no exaggeration in this patrol, though. Over four days, the wolfpack annihilated an unprecedented thirty-two merchant ships—twenty in a single night dubbed "Night of the Long Knives" by the U-Bootfahrer—without the loss of a single U-boat.

Now, what Germans called "the Happy Time" was over, and Dönitz barely had enough wolves to howl, much less attack, in the Battle of the Atlantic. In 1935, when, at the age of forty-four, he was appointed to build up the U-boat force, only twelve U-boats were in service. By the time the war started, Germany had fifty-six U-boats, but few were the modern type fit for the Atlantic. Now, only around forty were at sea to cover the forty-one-million square miles of the Atlantic Ocean as well as the North Sea and the Barents Sea. The force's effectiveness was further reduced by the Rule of Thirds: At all times, one-third of his U-boats would be docked, another third would be heading out, and the final third sailing home.

Another complication was the United States Navy. Although America was officially neutral, President Franklin Roosevelt had expanded the Pan-American Security Zone two-thirds of the way across the Atlantic in April, which meant that American warships could help escort convoys of armed merchant ships loaded with vital supplies for Britain as far as Iceland. It was only a matter of time before such provocations resulted in U-boats sinking an American destroyer, and indeed that had already happened: with the *USS Reuben James*, killing 100, and severely damaging the destroyer *USS Kearny*, killing 11, near Iceland. It had been less than a month since those incidents, and Brauer knew Dönitz and the whole U-Bootwaffe were chomping at the bit for more action.

"Let me help, for the glory of the Fatherland and the Führer," Brauer said, seizing the opening with passion, knowing that although Dönitz was not a member of the Nazi Party, he was an ardent supporter of Hitler. And he knew that they both shared the German leader's virulent anti-Semitic views about the spreading poison of Jewry. Brauer hoped that would be a bond that would help the former lawyer win his case. "Give me ten days and a full load of torpedoes and we will, by God, find that convoy and utterly destroy every single ship, sir."

Dönitz, bursting with pride, signaled to one of his aides. "Make sure he has everything he needs. Top priority." He took Brauer's hand and held it. "But before you go...about that unused torpedo..."

Brauer, dreading this moment, had rehearsed his response over and over until it sounded impromptu, "Too many of our torpedoes misfired, so I didn't think it prudent to risk stopping and using up what little fuel we had left." Dönitz continued to hold Brauer's hand.

"'I can hardly be expected to fight with a dummy rifle,'" said Donitz. "That was how Korvettenkapitän Prien put it to me before we lost him in

March," the admiral said with a trace of nostalgia in his voice and a far-away look in his eyes.

Prien! An exasperated Brauer thought: *Why do they always bring up the late, great commander, the Bull of Scapa Flow? Yes, before he vanished somewhere south of Iceland, he sank the HMS Royal Oak in a daring raid on the British home fleet's main harbor, and was the first U-boat captain to win a Knight's Cross on the strength of sinking a total of 31 ships.* But Brauer believed he could have accomplished as much by now had he been sent to the same target-rich areas Prien was assigned, instead of always laying mines, or escorting blockade runners, or being on weather patrol—an odious assignment to alert the Luftwaffe multiple times a day of incoming storms so it could better plan its bombing missions over Britain.

But Prien had always been one of Dönitz's favorites, so much so that when Prien was on patrol and his wife gave birth to a daughter, the vice-admiral radioed him, "Little submariner without periscope has arrived. Congratulations." Brauer was upset when he heard about it. He had never gotten so much as a birthday greeting from the *Großer Löwe.*

"We've had far too many similar reports about premature explosions of torpedoes with magnetic pistols," Dönitz said of the type of torpedo that was supposed to be triggered by the magnetic field of its target. He told an aide standing nearby, "Make sure at least half of his torpedoes are set for contact pistols, and have his ship ready to sail first thing Saturday."

"Vizeadmiral, we cannot wait two days. We must leave tomorrow," Brauer said, struggling to plead without sounding too demanding.

"Turning everything around in less than twenty-four hours is unheard of. Besides, tomorrow is Friday," Dönitz said. "It's bad luck."

"Foolish superstition, sir. The enemy will not wait, and neither should we," Brauer said. "It is God's will, not false beliefs, that determines our fates." He paused, then decided to be bold. "And Lüth did a one-day turnaround last year at Wilhelmshaven, didn't he?" he said of Kapitänleutnant Wolfgang

Lüth, another top ace, an ardent Nazi, a Knights Cross winner, a prude who forbade profanity and famously searched his crew's belongings for objectionable material, which he would throw overboard. He was the type of hard-assed commander Dönitz considered a possible successor. He also was lucky, having gone unpunished though his U-43 sank while docked at Lorient because of the watch crew's negligence in his absence.

Dönitz bowed his head, deep in thought, making Brauer fret that he had gone too far. Lifting his head, Dönitz smiled at Brauer. "Friday it is. But just shadow the convoy when you find it. Send a contact report and beacon signals so I can organize a wolfpack with what few U-boots we have left."

Stunned by his good fortune, Brauer thanked Dönitz profusely.

"Good-bye and good hunting, Viktor," Dönitz said, letting Brauer escape with no accounting for the lost men. Had Dönitz forgotten? Or, Brauer suspected, did he not care to know more because men die in war? Dönitz's frequent admonition to his captain, "Be hard," echoed in his mind as he rushed outside.

As he returned to his ship, Brauer stopped at a pharmacy to pick up several round bottles of Pervitin, an alertness drug popular with the German military because it allowed soldiers and pilots to stay awake for days during the heat of battle. Early in the war, millions of the white pills were distributed, providing a jolt of energy and a sense of euphoria, making servicemen who popped them like candy more confident, even fearless. Tank crews and pilots got their doses from "tank chocolate" bars called *Panzerschokolade*; Hitler, who couldn't stomach pills, preferred getting his lift from multiple daily injections of a similar drug called Eukodal, an opiate related to heroin better known as oxycodone. German doctors were just starting to discover Pervitin's serious side effects, including hallucinations, aggressive behavior, excessive sweating, and addiction. All were common problems with an earlier version of methamphetamine.

Working with the efficiency of a pit crew at the German Grand Prix, the re-supply and repair teams took just under twenty-four hours to load food, fuel, and fourteen 1.5-ton torpedoes into Brauer's U-474, an artificially high identification number Dönitz used to fool the enemy into believing the Germans had far more submarines than they actually did. The Type VIIC U-boat was the cramped fifteen-feet-wide home for forty-five sailors, jam-packed with a maze of exposed pipes, switches, meters, gauges, valves, and hand-wheels of every size in six equal-sized compartments bow to stern.

In the bow was the "cave," the forward torpedo room with four large torpedo tubes and removable deck plates for storing more torpedoes and mines underneath. Two more torpedoes were stored atop a false wooden floor, called the "threshing floor." Chains for holding and hoisting the torpedoes hung down like steel stalactites. The curved bulkheads were lined with twelve collapsible leatherette-covered bunks with standard-issue blue-and-white check sheets, some with a metal guard rail to keep the men from falling out.

Four hammocks hung overhead. The men had to "hot-bunk" with two sailors sharing each one; four of them had to sleep on the floor until some of the torpedoes were fired. The torpedoes had to be pulled out and serviced every few days. The U-boat was so jammed with men, torpedoes, food, and equipment that it was difficult to move around, and almost impossible to stand erect.

The next compartment was for the officers and petty officers to sleep and eat, as well as for the radio room and the listening or sound room, where an operator using GHG hydrophones could detect the propellers of a single ship from eleven nautical miles away and a convoy from fifty-five nautical miles distant. It could also provide the approximate bearing and range. The operators, trained on recordings of actual underwater sounds at various distances, could also hear sinking depth charges.

Then came the control room, another row of bunks next to the ship's galley, the diesel engine rooms, the electric motors room, and finally the aft torpedo room, which also contained eight folding bunks and the auxiliary steering wheel.

Because of the short turnaround time and the brief mission, only half of the usual four tons of food had to be loaded. It was crammed wherever there was an inch of space throughout the ship, though placed with precision to avoid throwing off the boat's trim. Dried meats and bags of potatoes hung from the ceiling. Crates of onions and vegetables were squeezed under the crew's bunks while *Kommissbrot*, hard-crusted black bread in mesh-net bags, hung in the forward torpedo room between the torpedo tubes and bunks. Fresh meat and produce, which typically lasted only a couple of weeks, were stored in the small refrigerator, and canned goods were stacked in the two heads, often leaving only one head available until the food was consumed.

Although the engine room contained a small distillery for making fresh water from seawater, the output was mainly used to refill the 124 batteries under the deck. As a result, there was only enough fresh water for cooking and half a bucketful a day per man for drinking. That left almost nothing for washing hands or bathing or brushing teeth or shaving or laundry, no matter how many weeks the voyage lasted. Saltwater sponge baths were possible but unpopular because they left the skin dry and itchy, and the special saltwater soap provided the men left an uncomfortable scummy film. Every day after their generous meals were prepared in a tiny galley (only five feet by two-and-a-quarter feet) on three hot-plates and two small electric ovens, consumption had to be measured so the remaining food could be re-arranged to maintain the ship's balance.

Early the following day, Brauer returned to his ship after a fitful night's sleep, retired to his tiny quarters amidships across from the radio room, and closed the heavy green curtain behind him. He knelt and prayed, his eyes focused on a small crucifix on the wall above the washbasin with a fold-down cover that served as a small desk, a ritual he practiced twice a day and before and after every mission. It gave him the strength to carry out his duties, secure in the knowledge that he was doing God's work in vanquishing his country's enemies, that the National Socialists were doing God's will.

Inspired, Brauer rose and took command of his ship as he and his men, weary and sullen but eager for revenge, passed through "Toten Allee"—Death Row as the Bay of Biscay was known because of the swarming British aircraft, mines, and anti-submarine vessels. Then off they went on their desperate hunt for a desperate ship on the run—the *Peggy C*.

CHAPTER 8

His watch over, Rogers headed down to the officers' saloon and stopped at the door, looking at the rabbi through the shot-out circular window. Wim, Julius, and Truus were sitting at a long table. Miriam, with a kerchief over her head, waved her hands over two lit candles three times and covered her eyes. When she finished, the rabbi raised his hand over a glass of wine and muttered something that Rogers, staring at the warm family scene, couldn't make out. As the rabbi passed around a loaf of bread, Miriam caught sight of Rogers and beckoned him in. Truus ignored the bread and focused on her sketching. "Truus, eat," the rabbi said, forcing her to put down her pen and pick up a fork.

"Sorry, just wanted a cup of coffee," Rogers said.

"Please, join us to celebrate Shabbat," the rabbi said. "Surprisingly good wine. Won't you have some?"

"I never touch alcohol," Rogers said, taking one of the two vacant chairs at the table, but the only one with a place setting.

Truus and Julius whispered and snickered. Julius pointed at Rogers. "He sat on Elijah." Everyone laughed except Rogers, who jumped out of the seat in embarrassed confusion, looking down behind him to see what he had sat on.

"Julius is confused," Miriam said with a smile, patting the captain on the arm. "The seat was for Arie, but he is not well. We only set a place for the Prophet Elijah on Passover."

"And circumcisions," the rabbi said with a chortle, raising his wine glass in a toast. The children giggled. Rogers sat again, this time with great care.

"Wim, tell the good captain the story of Elijah," the rabbi said.

"Is there no end to the stories, Rabbi?" Rogers said.

"Jews have a saying, Captain: 'Why were we humans created? Because God loves stories,'" the rabbi said. "Now, Wim...."

Rogers endured the story and many others, willingly, basking in the warmth of family life, not talking about the war or danger for once, but engaging in rambling conversations with delightful children who could hold their own with the pedantic and easily amused rabbi. Rogers tried not to stare at Miriam when she tilted her head. Her wide eyes were framed by thick eyebrows and sparkling in amusement. Her husky voice flowed from exquisitely plump lips. She was lovely and whip-smart and intoxicating.

"So, who's related to whom?" Rogers asked.

"Truus and I are sisters," Miriam said, reaching over to stroke her head with affection.

"And the young scamps are my boys," the rabbi said.

"Where are their mothers?" Rogers asked without thinking.

The rabbi and Miriam exchanged worried glances. Miriam leaned over to whisper in Rogers' ear so the children couldn't hear. "They were in Rotterdam when the war started. We thought they were safe because the city had surrendered. But the German planes bombed it anyway. We have not heard from them since."

Rogers mouthed the word "sorry" to Miriam and turned to the children with a mischievous look on his face. "Miriam reminded me that I've never told you about the time I almost caught a mermaid. Would you like to hear that story?" The children cheered and clapped and leaned forward in eager anticipation.

All too soon for Rogers' taste, they were walking along the deck, Rogers and Miriam hanging back as the rabbi and children gleefully sang the popular folksong "Hava Nagila" and headed into their cabin. "It means 'let us rejoice,'" Miriam explained to the puzzled captain.

The two stood outside the cabin where they could hear the muffled voices of the children imploring the rabbi for story time. Rogers was unaware of how much he was enjoying himself. Miriam stood next to him at the rail and breathed in the cool, salty air. Both of them stared out at the mist and fog in contented silence. As the boat rocked, Miriam grabbed hold of the wooden rail, brushing against Rogers' scarred hand. "What are these from?" she asked, examining both sides of his right hand. Rogers made no effort to pull away.

"Burns," he said. "Life on a ship."

"You were saving someone, yes?"

Rogers, mesmerized by the attention and her gentle touch, smiled, half-embarrassed.

"So, you can smile," she said, lifting his hand and delicately kissing the scars. "Did it hurt terribly?" Rogers shrugged, unable to come up with words. "You are a very strange, very wonderful man, Captain Jake Rogers. I have never met anyone like you. You are not afraid." She slid closer to him, tilted her face up, and waited.

Rogers, feeling like a dope and unsure what to do next, began to stammer. "Well, I...I wouldn't say—" The ship shook with a force that almost knocked them off their feet as lights flickered.

Below them in the engine room, Turani and Assistant Engineer Dunawa stumbled around with flashlights, flicking switches and turning valves, steam spewing out from ruptured pipes and the pistons screeching to a halt.

Rogers sprinted down the ladder in the dark. "What's wrong, Chief?!" he shouted.

"We're snapping parts and having problems with the bearings in the screw shaft!" he shouted back. "I told you we weren't ready to leave Amsterdam."

"How bad?"

"Don't know. We have to come to a full stop to cool off the bearings and assess the damage."

"Let me know as soon as you figure it out," Rogers said and ran out onto the now dark deck and up the ladder toward the wheelhouse, bumping into Miriam, who was rushing down with a flashlight in her hand.

"You must come," she said in a frantic voice.

"I can't." He pushed past her and jumped two steps at a time to reach Nidal on the bridge. "We have almost no power," Rogers said. "Keep her steady and get lights on the deck." Silent flashes rippled through the fog, followed by distant booms and clacking spurts of anti-aircraft fire. "Lights! Now!" he shouted, speeding down the ladder where Miriam waited, looking for an explanation. "The ships have to see we're neutral."

Miriam took Rogers' hand and led him to the settee in the family's cabin. There, Arie groaned in his sleep as she pointed her flashlight down the child's inflamed throat. "Diphtheria," she said. "It is closing his throat. He could die without serum."

"There's nothing I can do—"

"Diphtheria is infectious. We are all in danger. We must get anti-toxin serum from hospital," she pleaded.

"Impossible," he said, turning to leave, but Miriam wouldn't release his hand.

"You are smuggler. Surely, you know someone onshore who—"

"I deal in cigarettes and booze and stuff you don't want to know about," Rogers said, shaken by Miriam's tearful plea. "I'm sorry, but it's too dangerous."

On the bridge deck, Nidal peered into the dense fog, the sounds of gun-fire, cannons, and the engines of passing ships swirling all about him. Out of nowhere, a massive destroyer's bow smacked against the *Peggy C*'s port side, hurling Nidal headfirst into the rail. Then it glided away into the dark like a whale oblivious to the minnow it had just crushed.

The collision threw Rogers and Miriam together on the floor; they clung to one another as the ship lurched with a heart-stopping screech of metal on metal. All the children, except Arie, scrambled out of their bunks, wailing and crowding around Miriam. The rabbi prayed in his bunk.

"I have to go check on the ship," Rogers said, letting go of Miriam so he could stand.

"Arie?" She grabbed Rogers' hand again, imploring him with her eyes, a soulful gaze he had trouble breaking as he bolted for the wheelhouse.

Rogers found the bleeding Nidal sprawled out on the bridge deck and helped him to his feet. Together, they staggered into the wheelhouse. Nearby, a British destroyer slid past, kicking up a tremendous wake, oblivious to the presence of the *Peggy C*. Helmsman Cardoso, still focused ahead at the wheel, puffed on his pipe. The three men gazed outside in horror, catching glimpses of the war raging all around them in the dark and fog: thundering explosions and shooting flames, cannon volleys that rattled the glass in the windows, the frantic blaring of ships' alarm sirens, parachute flares, and flashes of star shells that lit up the clouds like long-lasting sheets of lightning. As the war ships barreled out of the mist so close that their wakes battered the *Peggy C*, they felt helpless.

At dawn, an exhausted Rogers stood on the bridge deck, still unable to see through the never-ending fog, pierced only by shimmers of light from a flickering fire and the echoes of distant moans and desperate cries. Whiffs of smoke, mingled with the stench of burning oil, drove him back into the wheelhouse, gagging and covering his nose and mouth with his hand. In the chartroom, Rogers joined Nidal, his head bandaged, and Chief Turani to study a map of France. He moved his finger south along the coastline until he reached the port city of Le Havre, stopping to tap on the harbor.

"Pierre Jacquard," Rogers said.

"Pierrot le fou?" Nidal asked in disbelief.

"Crazy Pete is just the man we need," Rogers said, and turning to Turani asked, "Can we get enough power to get there, Chief?"

Turani nodded. "Just barely."

"They say he works for the Nazis now," Nidal said.

"Collaborator, resister, it's all the same to him. He only works for the highest bidder," Rogers said. "Besides, he's all we've got."

"It could be suicide," Nidal said.

"Without parts, we're dead for sure," Turani said. Nidal shrugged in resignation.

That night, hours after the sun had set, Rogers, Obasi, Seamus, and Bosun hauled provisions to a motorboat hanging on its davits over the port side. They included flashlights, ropes, and boxes of Scotch, all for the short journey across Le Havre's harbor. It was filled with tramp steamers like the *Peggy C*, providing the perfect hiding place from any nearby U-boats.

"I must go with you," said Miriam, who had slipped up on them unnoticed.

"No," Rogers said, continuing to load the motorboat.

"You do not know what to ask for."

"Write it down."

"I must talk to doctor about doses."

"No," Rogers said.

"How good is your French?"

"Why not take Mr. Nidal along, Captain?" Seamus said. "Don't he speak French?"

"He's injured, and we can't both be off the ship." Rogers looked Miriam over from head to toe, kneading his lower lip.

Not long after, the four sailors left along with Miriam, wearing pants and a dark, ill-fitting jacket, her hair tucked under a knit watch cap. She rubbed her hands for warmth in the motorboat as it crept along to the quay, where, undetected, they tied up and unloaded cases of contraband Scotch.

Rogers signaled Obasi to guard the motorboat in the shadows of the tranquil harbor. The African frowned, lit a pipe, and squatted down to wait.

The others left on a twenty-minute hike to find the notorious gangster known as "Crazy Pete"—a nickname no one dared call him to his face. They found him sitting behind a desk in the dingy backroom of a smoke-filled bar where groups of sullen men hunched over watered-down drinks in silence.

"Bonsoir, Capitaine, it has been too long," Pierre said, a cigarette hanging from the corner of his mouth. As he shook Rogers' hand, he cocked his head to one side to avoid the steady stream of smoke and picked up a wine bottle from the side of his desk. "Drink for you and tes amis?"

Rogers shook his head and pulled a bottle of Glenfiddich Scotch Whiskey from inside his jacket and set it down on the desk gently as if it were a delicate Waterford crystal. "How about a drink for you?"

Pierre's eyes enlarged in amazement before his poker face returned. Leaning forward, he picked up the round, green bottle and examined the white label with "Pure Malt" printed in red letters—what many considered liquid gold at seventy-proof. He put his hand on his cap and looked at Rogers. "May I?" Rogers nodded. Pierre snuffed out his cigarette and opened the bottle, put it under his nose, and took a long breath before letting out a sigh. He pulled a glass out of his desk drawer and poured himself two-fingers' worth, sniffing and taking a long sip, swishing it around his mouth before swallowing as if it were a fine wine. "This is very hard to find. You have more?"

"Yes," Rogers said.

"And what is it you want in exchange?" asked Pierre, whose chiseled face made him look more like a movie star than a ruthless criminal known for smuggling and robbing banks and killing anyone who crossed him. That made him valuable both to the Nazi occupiers and to the resistance. Rogers handed him a list. Pierre studied it for a moment. "Parts are no problem. This serum, not, how you say, so facile."

"How much is *not so facile* going to cost me?" Rogers asked

"Medicine attracts too much attention. Not worth it," Pierre said, wadding up the paper and tossing it into the trash.

"Les enfants mourront sans le médicament," Miriam said, anguish in her voice.

"Shut up, sailor," Rogers said, stepping in front of her so Pierre couldn't see her well enough to tell she was a woman.

"What children? How will they die?" Pierre asked, standing and leaning forward, looking with curiosity at the small, unruly sailor behind Rogers. "It hurts me in my heart to hear that. I have many children of my own."

Rogers stepped forward, "So, what will it take?"

"How many *caisses de whiskey* are we offering?" Pierre held his hands out, palms up, the knowing smile of a winner on his face. After a quick negotiation, Pierre made several phone calls. "You are in luck, mon ami." He waved over one of his gruff-looking men who had been hovering in the doorway. "Francois will lead you to the hospital. I will go first and meet you there."

"Merci," Rogers said, badly pronouncing it more like "mercy."

Pierre held up a finger. "One, how you say, problem. You must also pay the doctor."

"Wait a minute, Pierre."

"It cannot be helped. As I said, not so facile."

Rogers snatched the bottle of Scotch off the desk and turned as if to leave but ran into a stern glare from Miriam, which made it impossible to carry out his bluff. He turned back to Pierre and put the bottle down gently. "Deal."

A little while later, Rogers, his crew, and Francois waited in the shadows across the street from the rustic Flaubert Hospital in the center of historic Le Havre, hiding from a passing Nazi patrol led by a sniffing German Shepherd. As soon as the danger passed, Pierre stuck his head out of the hospital's back entrance and waved. Rogers and his crew scurried to the door and slipped inside to find Pierre and a young doctor in scrubs and a long white coat. The guide stayed hidden outside.

"Five minutes only," Pierre whispered to Rogers and ducked back outside.

In French, Miriam spoke rapidly to the doctor, who led her and Rogers into the morgue, where he counted out vials of serum, dropping them into a burlap sack, answering Miriam's questions, and often stopping to listen for any approaching footsteps. When the doctor was finished but still holding the bag, Rogers handed him a wad of dollar bills and reached for the medicine. The doctor examined the bills in disgust and yanked back the sack, saying something in French with a sneer. Rogers looked at Miriam for a translation.

"He said his price just went up," she said.

"Captain," Bosun said in a stage whisper as he stuck his head into the morgue. "The patrol is coming back. We have to go."

Rogers aimed his Colt at the doctor, who sniffed in haughty Gallic indifference and turned his back. "My offer just went down," Rogers said, slapping the doctor's head hard with his gun. "How about that?" The bleeding and unconscious doctor couldn't reply. "I'll take that as a yes." Rogers stuffed the pistol into his belt, snatched up the dollar bills from the doctor's limp hand, and tossed a couple of bills onto the floor out of a sense of fairness; honor among thieves and all that.

Miriam grabbed the burlap sack, and they all raced for the exit, stopping abruptly at the door, where they could see through the round window that the German Shepherd had stopped to pee in the yard, blocking their way. The dog finished his business and trotted away, followed soon by the German patrol.

It took nearly thirty minutes to make it back to the harbor. The curfew forced them to stop often and let patrols or suspicious vehicles pass them by before moving on to the next dark street. In an alley across from the quay where the motorboat was tied up, Pierre waited with two armed men guarding a large box next to several cases of Scotch.

"Your parts," Pierre said when he spotted Rogers. "Where to now?"

"Gibralt—," Bosun blurted out before Rogers cut him off.

"Amsterdam," Rogers said.

"Good luck, my friend," Pierre said, shaking Rogers' hand as his men picked up the Scotch and hustled away.

Laughter erupted in front of Rogers' crew, coming from across the street, right between them and the motorboat. Three German soldiers sat on the ground, lighting cigarettes, and sharing a bottle of wine between chortles and bits of boisterous German songs. Rogers held up his hand and directed everyone back into an alley to wait for the soldiers to leave or pass out.

Miriam whispered in Rogers' ear. "Why wait? Kill them and we leave."

"What kind of cutthroat do you think I am?" Rogers whispered back. "Two hours until dawn. We wait."

"You have killed before, yes? That is what the crew says. What stops you now?"

With a sad shake of his head, Rogers plopped down cross-legged, placing the Colt on the ground beside him.

"But I could distract them, and you could take them prisoner or knock them out," Miriam said. "Arie is very sick. He needs the medicine now. Please."

"I said we wait."

The chattering Germans showed no sign of leaving. They opened another bottle of wine and retrieved some bread and cheese from a backpack. Seamus and Bosun sat with their backs to a brick wall; Rogers appeared lost in thought. Miriam, fidgeting in growing agitation, stared at the Germans. Impulsively, she snatched Rogers' gun and stuffed it in her belt, pulling out her shirt to cover it. She ripped off her cap and shook loose her long hair. "Enough wait-ing. Arie will die," she said. Rogers was too surprised to stop her from dashing across the street and strolling in front of the soldiers.

"Hast du eine Zigarette?" she said in as seductive a voice as she could muster.

The drunken soldiers staggered to their feet. One of them tapped out a cigarette from a brown packet of French-brand Gauloises Troupes and offered it to Miriam. Paying no attention to anything else around them, the three German soldiers appeared enchanted with the mysterious woman in

108

pants and fought over who would light the cigarette dangling from her lips. Rogers, Seamus, and Bosun snuck up from behind and used bricks from the alley to whack the Germans on their heads, knocking two of them to their knees. The third German soldier tried to stumble away, but Miriam drew Rogers' gun and waved it in his besotted face.

"Halt oder ich schieße," she said, threatening to shoot.

He lunged toward her and wrestled her for the gun. Rogers tackled him from behind. They rolled in the dirt, grunting and trading blows. Seamus and Bosun joined the fray, trying to separate the two, who were throwing wild punches. Miriam pointed the gun at the rolling mass of bodies, not sure what to do.

"Halt!" shouted an armed German soldier who had come out of nowhere. "Hände hoch," he said, holding one hand above his head, indicating they should do likewise. "Hands, hands."

The German soldier kept his rifle trained on the *Peggy C* crew and Miriam as they stood and slowly raised their hands. Miriam let her pistol slip to the ground. When the German glanced down in anger at his colleagues on the ground, a dull thud sent his helmet flying off his head. He stood motionless for a second, staring ahead with glazed eyes, then crumbled to the ground. Obasi held up a large stick behind him and, with a wide grin on his face, said, "Yo, ho, ho."

"Tie them up and gag them. There's some rope in the boat," Rogers told his crew, picking up the burlap sack with the medicine. "And grab the crate with the parts."

Unnoticed by the others, Bosun stole a Luger from one of the fallen Germans, hiding it under his shirt. Miriam retrieved the Colt and held it in her shaky hand, clearly embarrassed and frustrated. Rogers snatched it away. "You talk a good game," he said, grabbing her arm and dragging her to the motorboat, holding the gun in front of her face. "If you're going to point the damn thing at someone, you'd better be ready to pull the trigger."

"I could not...I am sorry," she said, tears in her voice, an unexpected emotion that made Rogers unsure how to react. He put his arms around her as they walked.

"That's OK," he whispered. "You tried to do the right thing."

Once they were back on the *Peggy C*, Miriam rushed to her cabin. She took a vial from the burlap sack, measured a spoonful of serum, and poured it down Arie's inflamed throat. Then she laid his feverish head down and sat on the side of the settee. As she hummed a lullaby in Ladino—an Old Spanish dialect spoken by Sephardic Jews—she tucked the blanket under his chin. Rogers watched through the cracked open door, his stony face softening. Miriam caught his eye and, ever so slightly, a coy smile slowly emerged.

CHAPTER 9

Brauer popped a Pervitin into his mouth as he, Tauber, and four lookouts—all with swollen red eyes from the frozen ocean spray—scanned the foggy horizon from the bridge atop the conning tower. Heavy rain mixed with hail pounded their oilskin foul weather gear, nicknamed "derGrosse Seehund" or "The Big Seal." Gale-force winds tore at their floppy sou'wester rain hats with the distinctive long flap that covered their necks.

Tauber, the habitual Jan Maat cigarette hanging from his mouth, chopped his arm at the horizon. "Shadow off the port beam," he announced. Brauer pressed the binoculars to his eyes and spotted a distant ship, a fully rigged three-mast schooner blindly tacking in turbulent waters and on a near collision course with the U-boat.

"What a magnificent sight, eh, Herr Oberleutnant?" Tauber said, tugging at his wide leather safety belt to ensure it was secure as another towering wave swamped the bridge. The white, wooden ship's three masts soared majestically and had twelve fore- and aft-rigged sails plus two square sails on the foremast. It flew a Swedish flag. Tauber moved his binoculars in another direction.

"What are you doing, First Watch Officer?" Brauer asked.

"Looking for a target, sir."

"We have a cargo ship right in front of us. Loaded with contraband, no doubt."

"Should I order a boarding party?"

"Not necessary."

"Sir, the Prize Regulations say we should warn her first—"

"Might be a U-Bootfalle setting a trap," Brauer said, referring to British armed Q-ships disguised as merchant vessels that ambushed and sank at least fifteen U-boats during World War I, an idea credited to then-First Lord of the Admiralty Winston Churchill that was revived by now Prime Minister Churchill. "The British also have been arming their merchant ships. One even attacked my first submarine while we were trying to rescue their very own sailors. The hypocrites: They have set the rules, and now they'll have to live by them. As far as I'm concerned, it is unrestricted submarine warfare."

Brauer lowered his binoculars and mulled his next move. He knew the British Admiralty had taken command of all British merchant ships in 1939 and had been arming thousands of them with low-angle four-inch guns and three-inch anti-aircraft guns. The weapons on the Defensively Equipped Merchant Ships, known as DEMS, were manned by the Royal Navy with assistance from trained crew members. What worried Brauer was he didn't know how many of the merchants had been armed.

"I'm not taking any chances," Brauer said. "But I'm not going to waste a torpedo on it, either. Get the gun crew up here."

"But sir, it's hardly worth—"

"They need the practice," Brauer said, the veins in his neck popping out.

The order of "clear for guns" was shouted along. Three sailors—gunner, layer, and loader—and Second Watch Officer Wolfgang Mueller, all wearing life jackets, rushed up through the hatch. They scampered down metal rungs on both sides of the conning tower onto the upper deck's slippery wooden slats and waited, holding tight to a metal rail, carefully timing their next move. When the bow rose on a cresting wave, pulling the deck momentarily above the waterline, they dashed to their 8.8 cm gun and buckled on safety lifelines just before walls of water crashed over their heads, blinding and choking them.

Inside the ship, crew members unloaded ammunition from the magazines beneath the decking next to the captain's cabin and unpacked the shells from their individual metal containers. Others formed a line and carefully relayed the thirty-three pound brass shells hand-to-hand from the control room up through the conning tower hatch and down from the bridge through a small chute at the front to the deck. There it was held in readiness for the loaders.

"It is unarmed, sir," Tauber said.

"Hold until she's closer," Brauer said, ignoring Tauber and making a mental note to write him up for incompetence, insubordination and, worst of all for a submariner, weakness. Brauer knew this type of motorized schooner well from his early days of naval training on the much larger *Gorch Fock* in the Baltic Sea. She appeared to be 120-140 feet in length, which meant she could hold more than 125 tons in cargo. It wasn't much of a target, but he was itching for a kill to erase the stain of the last few disastrous days.

Gunnery Officer Peter Radke used a megaphone in the howling wind to relay commands from Brauer down to Mueller and the gun crew.

"Target 500 meters, course 260, speed seven," Tauber said, taking readings from the firing binoculars mounted over a gyrocompass repeater that showed true north, which unlike regular compasses was unaffected by the magnetic pull of the metal ship.

Men rushed around the schooner's deck, waving their arms and shouting.

"Open fire!" Brauer shouted.

Before Radke could repeat the command, a mammoth wave swept over the conning tower, knocking all the watch crew members off their feet and drenching the men in the control room below the hatch. As Brauer helped Radke up, one of the other lookouts held his bloody mouth and screamed, "My teeth! My teeth are gone!"

The captain examined the wounded sailor's mouth before helping him down the hatch. "Get the pharmacist mate! This man needs attention!" he shouted into the ship. There were no doctors on U-boats. Medical emergencies were handled by a lightly trained pharmacist mate, typically one of the radio operators because their work required oil-free and relatively clean hands, or sometimes by the captains, who took a medical course as part of their training.

Brauer struggled to his feet and was about to repeat his order to fire when he noticed only two gunners on the deck with Mueller; the fourth one had washed overboard and was hanging suspended over the starboard saddle tank, one of two external ballast tanks that looked like elongated saddlebags.

"Open fire!" Brauer screamed at the gun crew as they scrambled to reel in their fallen comrade by his lifeline. The schooner was dangerously close, crashing up and down over the soaring waves, picking up speed. Brauer grabbed the megaphone from Radke. "Leave him and open fire, now!"

Mueller and the other sailors—maybe they didn't hear Brauer's orders—finished hauling the sailor on deck, then unscrewed the watertight tampions from both ends of the 8.8 cm's barrel. The gunner pulled the firing lanyard and blasted off a high-explosive round. It was impossible to miss at that range. The shells ripped into the schooner's bow, sending orange flames and debris high into the air. They fired again, hitting amidships with devastating effect, the hull splitting into the air like a bucking bronco, with fragments of metal raining down on the sea. Some of the men on the schooner used knives to hack at the tangled ropes on suspended lifeboats. Flames engulfed the three masts above them, fiery embers floating all around. Others plunged into the oily waters, only to be swallowed up by the freezing cold waves or burned alive in pools of flaming fuel.

The ship was crippled but would not sink. Brauer ordered round after round fired. It was no longer target practice; it was God's will, as in Deuteronomy: "And when the Lord thy God shall deliver them before thee, thou shalt smite them, and utterly destroy them." Screaming men clustered on the schooner's stern, struggling to hold on as the ship sank, its propeller pointing nearly straight up. The attack went on for almost an hour until the gun overheated and jammed. The hapless ship swooshed below the surface, leaving a trail of flotsam and billowing clouds of black smoke.

"Should we prepare to offer assistance if we can find any survivors?" Tauber asked, searching the water with his binoculars.

"As I have told you before, Vizeadmiral Dönitz's Standing Order Number 154 is clear. We are not to pick up survivors or provide any assistance. It specifically says, and I quote, 'We must be hard in this war. The enemy began the war in order to destroy us, so nothing else matters.'"

"Hasn't that been rescinded?"

"How naïve you are," Brauer said, giving Tauber a sideways look. "Dönitz has said unequivocally that our sole mission is the annihilation of enemy ships and crews. So, as far as I'm concerned, the order stands."

"Alarm! Alarm! Alarm! Aircraft 140 degrees!" one of the lookouts shouted, pointing off the stern into the sky at two British planes coming in low across the cresting waves: they were boxy Short Sunderland flying boat bombers, four-engine U-boat hunters called Tractors by the Germans. They were drawn to the flaming battle scene like a moth to a campfire, one with a sky-high mushroom of flames visible for miles.

"Clear the bridge! Make ready to dive!" Brauer screamed as the lookouts skidded down the hatch's ladder, their feet, clear of the rungs and into the control room. The dive alarm klaxon shrilled, lights flashed, and the crew repeated "alarm, alarm" from one end of the U-boat to the other. Up above, the gunners slipped and stumbled their way across the heaving deck, scrambling up the conning tower rungs and into the submarine. In the panic, one of the men tripped and fell through the hatch headfirst onto the unforgiving steel deck and had to be dragged out of the way, unconscious and bleeding.

One of the planes strafed the conning tower as the last lookout tried to jump into the ship, bullets punching holes across his body. He fell dead on top of the hatch, pinning it open, and making diving impossible. Brauer scurried up the ladder and tried to shove the body from the opening, but it wouldn't budge. Blood poured into Brauer's eyes as the second Sunderland made another pass and blasted the dead sailor, shattering bones and tearing off bits of body parts.

⟹⊱◈⊰⟸

Anticipating the need to dive, the chief engineer shut off the diesels, closed the air induction and exhaust valves, and declutched the engine before the captain could close the hatch. Otherwise, all the air in the boat would be sucked out in a matter of seconds. "Green board!" he shouted, indicating that the battery of red and green lights known as the *Weihnachtsbaum*—the Christmas tree—were all green, and all the openings in the pressure hull had been closed.

The trailing Sunderland dropped a bomb that bounced off the water, short of the U-boat, and skipped back into the air blowing away its own tail, and sending the low-flying plane spiraling wildly into the ocean. With a howl of exertion, Brauer used his last bit of strength to thrust savagely with his shoulders against the body, managing to roll it far enough to clear the hatch. The remaining Sunderland had circled around and was closing in for the kill.

Brauer slammed the hatch shut, dogging the handle fast to secure it tightly, and yelled, "Hatch is closed!" as his grip slipped, and he fell to the control room deck, landing on his back with a painful yelp.

Struggling to his knees, Brauer realized he had no time to do anything but order "flood negative," a maneuver that flooded the Negative Tank, forcing the submarine into a stomach-churning plunge. It left a swirling bullseye of bubbles and ripples on the gray water above.

With sweat rolling down his face, Chief Engineer Schmitt took the U-boat down to 140 meters and kept it as trim as he could by turning a steel forest of red and green valves, levers, cranks, and wheels. His eyes were trained on gauges like a sweaty musician tuning several cranky instruments at once—with a gun to his head. There were controls for ballast tanks, for trim tanks, for compressors, for the horizontal and vertical diving planes, for the negative tank controlling emergency dives, and they all had to be turned precisely in the correct sequence to avoid disaster.

As the submarine descended, Brauer brooded over which lookout had allowed the plane to sneak up on them. He would get to the bottom of that soon enough. All unnecessary equipment was shut off, and they held their collective breaths.

The first explosion jolted the submarine so hard its steel frame shrieked and quivered like a wounded animal. The Sunderland's bomb had come close but did not cause serious damage. The crew hung on to anything they could and waited in silent terror. After thirty minutes and no more explosions, Brauer ordered the submarine to fourteen meters—periscope depth. Tauber manned the observation periscope in the control room and scanned the cloudy sky for any sight of aircraft.

"All clear, sir," he said, lowering the periscope.

With his back aching, Brauer gingerly crawled up into the conning tower above the control room—and below the conning tower hatch—and ordered the attack periscope raised. Once the oiled hiss of the rising shaft stopped, he turned his visor to the back of his head and sat on a metal bicycle-type seat, pressing his face against the shell-shaped rubber eyepiece buffer, which had a fixed height, unlike the observation periscope, which moved up and down. Placing his feet on two pedals that guided the rotation, Brauer gripped handles on either side, controlling the height of the periscope's extension and its field of view. Moving patiently in a circle, he had trouble making out anything in the fog.

The danger rang out before it came into focus: the tell-tale *ping-ping* of the enemy's primitive sonar system known as ASDIC. Brauer crushed the right pedal down, spinning around until he saw a looming silhouette—a British destroyer filled the lens. It was right on top of them.

"Alarm! Make your depth 40 meters!" Brauer shouted down the hatch. "Down periscope. Battle stations." The commands were echoed throughout the submarine.

All movement inside the floating sardine can ceased. No conversations were allowed. Everyone had to reduce activity to conserve oxygen. The only sounds were the soft hum of the two 375-horsepower AEG electric motors and the maddening hiss of the ventilator pumping in oxygen-rich air and sucking out the stale air through a CO2 filter. The men waited, taking off their shoes and tossing mattresses and blankets onto the passageway deck to muffle their steps. Some wrapped towels around their feet to deaden the sound of footsteps even more.

Ping-ping, ping-ping, ping-ping echoed all around the submarine like footsteps approaching a coffin, and the swishing of propellers churned ominously overhead. *Ping-PING!* The sound of the second, louder ping sent a chill down Brauer's spine; it meant the signal had ricocheted off the hull, putting his U-boat in the crosshairs of the enemy above. He practically jumped down from the conning tower into the control room and rushed over to the listening room where the hydrophone operator could pick up sounds underwater through the eleven small receivers embedded on each side of the bow.

Brauer took the operator's hydrophones, pressing the cups on his ears. *Bubbles, faint but growing louder.* He ripped off the hydrophones and signaled for the crew to brace themselves. Only one thing creates bubble sounds like that—sinking depth charges (*Wasserbomben*). "Prepare for Wabos!" Brauer shouted.

The first horrifying click of a depth-charge trigger was followed by violent explosions one after the other, rattling the boat, making it buck and seesaw, and knocking any standing crew member off his feet. Lights flickered. Shattered glass dials and depth gauges shot debris careening through the air. Burst pipes spewed water into some of the compartments, and paint chips fell from the ceiling.

"Exhaust valves making water!" someone shouted from the engine room.

Out of control, the ship plunged deeper until the sweaty chief engineer could swivel enough valves to bring the potentially fatal free-fall to an unstable halt at 140 meters. At that point, the ship's bow was pointing up at almost a 45-degree angle. The steel hull creaked and moaned ominously under the tremendous pressure. Sailors not needed at their battle stations rushed on padded feet through the narrow passageway to the forward torpedo room, careful not to trip over the overturned toilet pails sliding around the narrow aisle between the diesel engines, spreading gag-inducing human waste everywhere. The buckets were used when the lines at the heads were too long, or the ship was too deep and under too much water pressure for the toilets to be flushed. The weight of the sailors brought the bow down level with the stern.

Brauer stood erect in the control room, in the middle of the submarine, precisely where his men could watch him in the dim glow of the blue emergency lights. Calm, almost nonchalant, he held onto a pipe above him, his head cocked to one side, listening for the next inexorable attack. Brauer knew he was on a kind of stage; the crew took their cues from him. If he projected confidence of survival, they too would be confident, or at least less terrified, believing that the captain had everything under control.

The destroyer's propellers gyrated above, coming and going like a relentless Grim Reaper thrashing ever closer for the deadly harvest. The hydrophone operator signaled to Brauer that he heard incoming depth charges. The captain waved for his men to hunker down. The ones who could see him passed along the signals to their shipmates farther away. Shock waves from the exploding depth charges hammered the submarine like a kettledrum; more pipes ruptured, spewing more water. Gauges burst, and light bulbs shot out of their sockets, leaving the men in complete darkness. The ship shuddered and plunged and pitched. Cries of pain rang out in the dark tomb.

Brauer was operating blind. The pipes gushed, the ventilator hissed, and the damaged steel hull creaked even louder from the increasing water pressure. And, like a blind man, Brauer was surprisingly overwhelmed by heightened sensitivity to the smell of Kolibri, the sickeningly sweet-smelling cologne and deodorant sailors used in a vain attempt to cover body odor and to scrub off the saltwater encrusted on their faces. The cologne was part of an odious brew of diesel fumes, moldy food, and a faint hint of dangerous chlorine gas coming from damaged and wet batteries.

The next round of low-pitched detonations jarred the submarine but with less intensity. Technicians working frantically with flashlights were able to get the emergency lights on. The engineering crew, eyes red and infected from the fumes they had to endure, patched a leak in a large pipe with a rubber sheet and a piece of wood to counter the water pressure.

"Should we leak some oil to make them think we're sunk?" Tauber asked Brauer in a low voice.

The captain mulled that idea over for a moment and brightened up when a better one occurred to him. He led Tauber to the listening room and asked the operator if he could tell when the depth charges hit the water. He said he thought he could. "Good. Signal First Watch Officer Tauber when you hear them," he said and instructed Tauber, "Start your stopwatch on his signal and stop when the blasts go off. Do you understand?"

"Yes, sir." He held up his watch, ready to push the starter button. After a moment, the operator raised his hand, indicating he heard the splash and bubbles. Tauber clicked on the stopwatch as Brauer looked over his shoulder. At the twenty-eight-second mark, the depth charges exploded, shaking the boat but not causing significant damage. Tauber restarted the watch. It took thirty seconds this time. After a third wave of depth charges exploded at the twenty-six-second mark, Brauer looked at a gauge and sighed in relief. Tauber and the operator gave him a questioning look.

"The Brits' Mark VII Wabos sink at five meters per second," Brauer said. "They are detonating at no more than thirty seconds, meaning 150 meters is the deepest the British have set them to explode. We are at 190 meters. So, we'll wait them out." He stretched and yawned. "Have the men get in their bunks and stay still to preserve oxygen. It's going to be a long night. And shut off the gyrocompass. I want total quiet." The humming of the spinning disc inside the compass died away.

Brauer stepped over to Schmidt, "L.I., do the best you can to keep our depth at 190 meters with as little noise as possible," he said, using the informal title for the Leitender Ingenieur or chief engineer.

"Aye, aye, Herr Oberleutnant," Schmidt said, knowing that what the captain was requesting was easier said than done. He hovered over the two planesmen seated side-by-side on an L-shaped leatherette-topped bench in front of what looked like two steering wheels on the starboard side of the control room. A helmsman sat at the shorter end of the L, ready to steer using two electric buttons. The planesmen controlled the vertical position of the U-boat with two electric buttons for up and down, or manually with the wheels, if necessary, while Schmidt kept a close eye on the manometer to monitor the depth and the inclinometer for trim and an array of other gauges and dials.

It was as much an art as a skill because even subtle changes in the water's temperature or salinity could throw off the U-boat's buoyancy. To keep the U-boat trim and at the proper depth, the planesmen had to carefully, and in precise order, turn gears and flywheels to adjust the air-to-water ratio in the ballast tanks in the bow and stern, and constantly adjust the angle of the diving planes to counter the currents and swells of the ocean. They were used to performing these tasks well; doing so quietly, and during such a prolonged attack, was another matter.

The rest of the crew did as they were told, although most of them couldn't sleep, shivering uncontrollably in their bunks in the forward and aft torpedo rooms. Because Brauer ordered the electric heaters turned off to save the batteries, the cold was unrelenting. Condensation covered the pipes, and every breath created a visible cloud. Some of the sailors wore double layers of long underwear under their leather coats, which never seemed to dry out. None of their clothes were ever completely dry, not even after hanging them in the engine room near the blazing hot diesels, which didn't run while submerged, so there was even less heat than usual in the submarine.

While they waited, Smutje, as cooks were called on German ships, prepared oatmeal porridge that duty stewards served the men from a "long boat," a deep, bucket-shaped container. There was no mess for the Lords, so they always ate at their stations or bunks on small, collapsible wooden tables lined with racks called Fiddles that kept the food from falling off. The officers ate in a separate midsection wardroom between the listening room and the galley on a folding table in the aisle while sitting on the lower bunks. The walls around them were lined with small lockers for storage of personal items and covered with a veneer of varnished wood, a homey touch amid all the steel.

Brauer could see the surprise among the crew when he walked through their quarters, whispering small talk and handing out chocolates. He tried to smile once or twice but, on his cadaverous face, it came off looking more like a grimace. Dripping in sweat despite the cold, he told one frightened-looking young sailor, "It's small potatoes," and he kept repeating it in reassuring tones to others, meaning what they were enduring was nothing compared to the bigger challenges facing their beloved *Vaterland*. Of course, that saying wasn't original to him. He had overheard another officer, perhaps from U-505, talk about it over dinner one night and thought it was a nice patriotic bromide he could use to give the appearance of nonchalance in an emergency, even if it wasn't at all what he felt.

Brauer also took time to check that sailors who did fall asleep were securely wearing their stale air filters—potash cartridges in a large metal box attached to their chests with a rubber hose leading to their mouths; their noses were clamped shut. The devices were vital because carbon dioxide could reach dangerous levels after hours underwater. Still, the captain knew his men hated the contraption because the potassium compound inside the canister heated up after a while like an electric burner. They knew that waiting for long stretches underwater was not what U-boats were designed to do.

They knew, too, that the word "submarine" was something of a misnomer. As Vizeadmiral Dönitz often explained, U-boats weren't underwater vessels at all but "diving vessels." They stayed on the surface most of the time for maximum speed, maneuverability, and range of visibility. On the surface, U-boats could race along at more than seventeen knots and get a better view of targets than through a periscope, particularly at night when there wasn't enough light to pick out the blacked-out merchant ships. Underwater, the U-boat's range was only sixty-to-eighty nautical miles, and its top speed was around seven knots, which was too slow to keep up with all but the most ancient of merchant ships.

That meant it had to wait in a stationary position like a mine for an unlucky target to approach, or as Dönitz described it, "like a beast of prey which did not hunt for its food but crouched instead in the undergrowth and waited for its quarry to run into its jaws." The other disadvantage of being underwater was that the electric batteries that charged everything, including air filtration, had a limited lifespan of a day or two depending on how much activity there was aboard. The air, unfortunately, was likely to run out before that.

After twelve hours underwater, during which Brauer lay down in his quarters but couldn't sleep, the drum roll of depth charges became less frequent, the propellers churned like eggbeaters farther away, and the pings stopped. Brauer ordered the chief engineer to start the pumps and raise the submarine to periscope depth. On the way up, the ship stalled. "Too much water, Herr Oberleutnant. We'll have to bail it out to go any higher," Schmitt said, wiping his grease- and soot-covered face with his hands.

It took another hour for the crew, using buckets, to shovel enough water into a tank and then air-pressure pump the liquid into the ocean for the ship to resume its ascent and stop at periscope depth. Brauer sat at the attack periscope in the conning tower and scanned an ocean glistening in the early morning sunlight. No ships or planes in sight. He ordered the ship to surface.

When the conning tower cleared the waterline, Brauer didn't wait to vent the pressure that had built up inside the boat. He unclipped and flipped open the conning tower hatch with a loud, metallic clang, grabbing his hat as it flew off his head. He was half sucked out of the hatch from the sudden change in air pressure, which made all the sailors inside grab their ears in pain. With relief, they sucked in the cold, fresh air rushing inside. Despite being drowsy and headachy from carbon dioxide poisoning, they let out wild cheers.

"Watch crew to the bridge!" Brauer shouted down the hatch as he climbed onto the bridge, still streaming out seawater. The four members of the crew hustled up the ladder and assumed their positions at three, six, nine, and twelve o'clock to cover the sky and vast ocean from all directions, double-checking that their steel safety lines were clasped securely to handles on the tower's casing.

Brauer had put the fear of God in his whole crew when he told them about U-106's bizarre but avoidable accident the previous month. Its four lookouts had not strapped in, apparently fearing it would take too long to unhook themselves if a plane attacked on what was a clear day, but it was a day with forty-mile-an-hour winds whipping up huge swells. That was a deadly combination for a U-boat moving too slowly with the current to surmount a monstrous wave. Another such wave crashed over the conning tower from behind, sweeping all four members of the unsuspecting watch crew overboard. Their bodies were never found.

Inside the U-boat, Funkmaat Franz Vockel, a radio petty officer, sat in his cramped room at a Telefunken Type E 436S receiver and pressed his right hand to his earphone—the left ear was always left uncovered so orders could be heard. He scribbled furiously on a notepad, taking down a message that couldn't be received earlier when they were deeper than periscope depth.

When the short transmission finished, he flipped open a codebook and scrolled through to find that day's Naval key for his Enigma machine, a wooden box containing what looked like a black typewriter with two keyboards and a scrambler unit of three rotors at the top. The device resembled a combination lock for a bike—with the 26 letters of the alphabet on each rotor. Vockel changed out one of the rotors and adjusted each one to start on a letter designated in the codebook.

As he typed individual letters on the lower keyboard, the rotors turned, and an electric charge went through the scrambler, which generated a random letter that would light up on the top keyboard—called a lamp board. With three rotors, there were 17,576 possible combinations, which made the Germans believe their code could never be broken. A second operator wrote down the illuminated letters. At the end of the message, Vockel opened the *Kurzsignalbuch*, a codebook of short messages with tables in water-soluble red ink on pink blotting paper that, like the Naval key book, could be dissolved quickly by dropping it into the bilges or the ocean. For additional security, each military branch had a unique version of the encryption machine, and multiple versions within the branch; the U-boat version was called Enigma Triton.

Vockel decoded the message, ripped off the note, dashed up into the conning tower, and popped his head up through the hatch. "Herr Oberleutnant, there's radio traffic about a robbery of medicine and ship parts in Le Havre," Vockel said, holding out the notepaper.

Brauer glared at him with an irritated expression of "why should I care?"

"By American sailors."

With a smirk on his face, Brauer shouted, "Check!" down the hatch to Tauber standing below Vockel. He was rooted silently on the bridge, taking deep breaths, his eyes glancing all around, waiting for the shuddering roar of the diesel engines to kick in. It occurred to him that in his anger and haste for revenge, he'd made a near-fatal mistake; he'd endangered his ship and crew for a mere schooner, he'd remained on the surface far too long for far too many rounds, and he'd ignited a fiery beacon for the enemy—actions he would have a hard time justifying to the BdU, particularly with Tauber onboard. He prayed for forgiveness and mulled over what he'd do to the incompetent lookout.

Something caught his eye as he swallowed a Pervitin and wiped the sweat off his brow. He focused his binoculars on the only thing in sight amid floating bits of shattered wood and torn canvas in an iridescent oil slick: a fully equipped lifeboat that was completely empty.

CHAPTER 10

Rogers struggled into his quarters dead tired, hoping to get a few hours of sleep before his next early morning watch, and was surprised to find Miriam walking around the cabin, holding something in her hands and perusing his bookshelves. "Is something wrong with Arie?" he asked.

"No. Uncle Levy is taking care of him," she said, spinning around in surprise. "I hope you do not mind me coming. I do like to read."

Rogers stood in the doorway, uncertain how to react. "Help yourself."

Miriam walked over to him, shut the door, and held out the framed picture of U.S. Navy midshipmen she had found hanging on Rogers' office wall. "This is you, yes?" she asked, pointing to one of the cadets in the picture. "But your name is not Rogers."

"You should go."

"Why did you leave Annapolis?"

"What?"

"Is that where you killed someone?"

"You really should leave," he said, opening the door, his voice tight.

Miriam pushed it closed again and edged up next to Rogers. "You fought over money? A girl? Your honor? You tried to do the right thing, yes?"

Clearing his throat uncomfortably, Rogers backed away. "There was nothing noble about what I did, if that's what you mean."

"Then you ran away?"

"Wasn't my choice."

Miriam set down the picture and clasped Rogers' face in her hands, which Rogers enjoyed for a moment before thinking better of it, and turned and opened the door. "Please, it's not a good idea for you to be in here."

Ignoring his plea, Miriam floated around the room, checking out the books again until she found a copy of *Anna Karenina*. She plucked it off the shelf. "So sad about Anna and Count Vronsky. Forbidden love." She tossed the book on the bed.

"Yeah, sure...but," Rogers said in confusion.

Miriam took another book from the shelves: *Sea Wolf.* "And what about Maud? Was not she first true love of Humphrey?" She tossed that book on the bed, too.

"I, uh, I don't remember," he said, paying close attention.

She plucked *The Sun Also Rises* off the shelves and held it in Rogers' face as she eased the door shut behind her. "Jake. There is the wounded Jake in here. Not like you, yes?"

"No, no, he's not. But—" he said, starting to catch on to the game.

Miriam shoved him onto the bed and crawled on him, kissing him hard on the lips and pulling on the buttons of his shirt.

⸻⸻⸻

A hammer slammed down on a hand being held down on a table. The Le Havre gangster Pierre, bruised and bloody, whimpered and squirmed, unable to pull away from the two U-boat sailors in their leather battledress pinning down his arm. "You were doing so well, Pierre," Brauer said. "Now, don't tell me Amsterdam again."

"Jake...said Am—," Pierre said. "Wait, don't—."

Brauer pressed a German Navy Bordmesser rig knife against Pierre's left little finger, drawing a trickle of blood. "They told me that no crime happens in Le Havre without your knowledge. You are disappointing me." He pushed down harder on the pocketknife's three-inch blade; BUND was emblazoned on its black handle.

"One of the others, he says...Gibraltar," Pierre muttered.

"Good, good," Brauer said. "So, Captain Jake Rogers of The *Peggy C* is making way to Gibraltar. Correct?"

Pierre shook his head "yes" emphatically.

"With the stolen parts you sold him?"

The trembling Pierre nodded "yes" again, the implications of what he admitted slowly dawning on him. His eyes widened in terror. Brauer, in a cold fury, nodded at one of the soldiers, who slammed Pierre's forehead with the butt of his submachine gun.

A ray of soft moonlight from the porthole cast a spotlight on Miriam's enchanting face, which looked like a cameo on a pendant outlined in shadows; her skin was smooth as ivory yet flush with a rosy glow around her cheeks. Her gentle breathing tickled Rogers' neck, but he couldn't bring himself to take his numb arm out from behind her head for fear of waking her and ending a perfect dream, one he had never had before or could ever have hoped for. Vagabond sailors like him knew only fleeting and impersonal affairs. He drank it all in—the warmth of her legs wrapped around his, her long dark hair draped across his chest, her perfume enveloping him like the fragrant lilacs on the farm his mother had once taken him to as a kid. As he lingered half-awake in her arms, danger, responsibility, war, and all regrets faded away. Miriam's eyes slowly opened. She smiled, kissed him on the lips, and snuggled even closer before drifting back to sleep. A knock on the door broke the spell.

"Captain, our watch starts in ten minutes," Cardoso said.

"Thanks, Helmsman. I'll be right there."

Despite his best effort, Rogers woke Miriam when he carefully extracted his trapped arm.

"Where are you going?" she asked in a sleepy voice.

"My watch. Sorry," he said, pulling on his pants.

"What time is it?"

"A little before four a.m."

Miriam shot out of the bed to dress. "I must go to our cabin before anyone wakes." Rogers blushed and looked away. Miriam laughed, standing defiantly naked in the dim light, her ribs sticking out like a washboard from malnutrition. "You do not need to be shy." With a giggle, she danced over to him on her skinny legs and tiny feet, hugged his neck, and kissed him. Rogers hugged her back, not wanting the moment to end, and reluctantly letting her loose to finish dressing.

"What now?" she asked as she gathered up her clothes from the floor.

"At the end of my watch in a few hours, I'll fix you breakfast," he said.

"Why not Cookie?"

"We're shorthanded, so he only does twelve hours a day. We're on our own for breakfast."

"I can cook."

"Oh, you haven't lived until you've tasted my fried pumpkin," he said with a chuckle and turned to leave.

"You did not answer my question."

With a sigh, Rogers sat down on the bed and pulled her close. He kissed her forehead and her cheeks and her neck and her lips. "I, uh, I don't know what happens next. If we survive this—"

"*When* not if."

"*When* we survive this, we can decide what happens. I have my men and the *Peggy C* to think about, and life on a tramp is no life for a woman." She gave him an exasperated look. "Even a tough broad like you." He tickled her; she stifled a squeal.

"Tramp?" she said with exaggerated horror. "I am no beggar."

Rogers laughed. "Tramp steamer. Ships like ours, going from port to port looking for loads. Like tramps. Like beggars. Get it?"

Loud knocking startled them. "Sorry to bother you, Captain, but Mr. Nidal wants you to know that he would like to be relieved. Cardoso is already on the helm," said McAllister, the young helmsman.

"Tell him I'll be there straight away."

"Aye, aye. Captain." McAllister's footsteps rang out on the metal deck as if he was deliberately making it clear he was nowhere near the captain's door.

In the moonlight, Rogers fixed on Miriam's chestnut eyes, so full of fire and determination yet suffused with a haunting sadness. He didn't move. "Go," she whispered. "You are right. We do not have to decide anything now. Only..." She paused as if at a loss for words. "Only when we can be alone again." After one last long embrace and kiss, Rogers pulled away.

Later in the afternoon, Rogers and a radiant Miriam strolled together into the wheelhouse unannounced, catching Nidal reading *Robinson Crusoe*, which he quickly hid behind his back. At the wheel, McAllister nodded his hellos and went back to watching the ocean through the windows.

"Helmsman, compass card," Rogers said, quizzing McAllister as part of his training.

"Has thirty-two cardinal points, each eleven and one-quarter degrees, sir," McAllister said.

"Correct."

"We're back up to full speed, Captain," Nidal said. "Should make Gibraltar by dawn."

"That's cause for celebration," Rogers said. "Tell Cookie to break open a barrel of salt beef for dinner."

"Aye, aye, Captain," Nidal said.

"And the Montrose Saint-Estephe 1925," Rogers added.

"I like *Robinson Crusoe* very much," Miriam said to Nidal. "How do you like it?"

"He just looks at the pictures," Rogers said.

Miriam, erupting in laughter, covered her mouth, trying desperately to stop the giggles before fleeing back outside. Rogers trailed after her. Nidal watched them with disappointment written all over his face.

That night, Rogers sat at a long table in the officers' saloon alongside Miriam and the rabbi and across from their officer "guests:" Weber and Gaylord, freed from their confinement in Hold Number One. Nidal and Turani had begged off, pleading other duties. A white linen table cloth was set out with Limoges china, sterling silver flatware, and Waterford crystal glass goblets; incongruous elegance for a tramp, but Rogers enjoyed it for special occasions, and sometimes with potential customers he was trying to impress. He also had set up a gramophone, softly playing American jazz records.

The children chatted at a nearby table. Obasi lounged in a corner holding Rogers' Colt in his lap, a pipe clenched in his teeth. Cookie set down a plate of butter and warm bread, which smelled like it had just come out of the oven, and he returned to the galley to whip up more magic.

"To what do we owe this honor, Captain?" Weber asked in his flawless American English, wearing his dried uniform covered with flecks of blood from his beating. His face was black and blue around his broken nose, and his right eye was swollen shut.

"A celebration among officers," Rogers said. "And don't worry Leutnant Weber, your men will share in the feast."

"What in bloody hell is there to celebrate?" Gaylord said in his haughtiest upper-crust English accent. He was wearing one of Rogers' work shirts, his right arm in a makeshift sling.

"Your freedom," Rogers said. "Tomorrow. Gibraltar. And you can take the Germans with you as my gift to the cause."

Showing no reaction, Weber shifted his attention to Miriam. "So, Doctor, it looks like you did a fine job on my new cellmate."

"I do not have medical degree. The Nazis kicked all Jews out of university," she said, picking at the salt beef.

"Unfortunate," Weber said, sniffing and swirling the wine before taking a sip, his face lighting up with surprise and pleasure. "The National Socialists can be such brutes. But their time will pass, and we can sort things out after the war." His cold blue-gray eyes zeroed in on the children across the room; Wim ducked under the table, terror on his face.

Gaylord downed his wine and filled his glass, though he was getting tipsy. "Here, here. All the bloody political parties are the same. Nazis, Tories, Labor, Democrats, Republicans. Scoundrels all. Not like us, eh, Leutnant? Military men have a code of honor."

"Was it honor when the Nazis destroyed my country?" Miriam said in a sharp tone.

Gaylord muttered to himself, "You Jews bring these things on yourselves."

The rabbi threw down his fork, almost breaking a plate. "No one deserves what has been done to us by Nazis like Leutnant Weber."

"I am not a Nazi," Weber said, turning to help the disabled Gaylord cut his meat. "We just do our duty. Don't you agree, Captain?"

"You know what? You remind me of the old guys cheering one of the last Confederate Civil War veterans at a Baltimore ceremony when I was a kid," Rogers said, leaning forward to make his point. "They praised him for his honorable service to the cause and for doing his duty to defend his country. Now, I don't know whether that guy owned slaves or even supported slavery. Didn't make any difference. You know why?"

"No," Weber said suspiciously, as if waiting for the other shoe to drop.

"Because if his side had won, millions of people would still be slaves, and the United States of America would be the shattered states of America."

"But Captain, don't forget, Britain and France declared war on us," Weber said.

"What?" Gaylord said, blurting out the words with a spray of wine. "Now, look here. You chaps had just invaded Poland, our ally. Hitler knew perfectly well we had promised to defend the Poles if they were attacked."

"We were attacked first," Weber said.

"Pssst," Gaylord hissed.

"Think what you will, but we are fighting for a just cause, for a united Europe, one free from Soviet communism," Weber replied in a calm yet chilling voice. "I admit that Hitler can be crude, but he raised my country from the ruins. He ended our starvation, gave people jobs, and took back what was rightfully Germany's. He saved my country."

"Have you not read *Mein Kampf,* Leutnant?" the rabbi asked. "Is fighting the Jewish peril how you save your country?"

"Nothing more than 'fantasies behind bars.' That's how Hitler describes that book," Weber said. "I repeat, we are fighting to save our country from foreign aggressors, not for a particular leader or party."

"You can tell yourself that, but whether or not you're a member of the Nazi Party, you are what you voluntarily fight for," Rogers said. "And you can't be an acolyte and claim you don't understand the religion. No, you and your kind make evil leaders like Hitler possible by pretending you're only fighting for ribbons and medals."

Cookie popped his head in and waved at the children, who followed him through the door, jumping up and down and jabbering in excitement, all except Wim, who remained in hiding under the table.

"Ribbons and medals?" Gaylord spat out. "I fight for my country because, as Lord Nelson put it, 'England expects that every man will do his duty.' Have you no sense of duty or honor?"

"I get paid for what I do. Duty and honor have nothing to do with it," Rogers said, sipping a glass of water between bites of boiled potatoes and peas.

"'*Dulce et decorum est pro patria mori*,'" Gaylord quoted.

"That old lie? I prefer Wilfred Owen's to Horace. There is nothing sweet or fitting about dying for any country," Rogers said. "You're just dead."

———————

With his captain's white hat turned backward, Brauer looked through the attack periscope, tracking a cargo ship with two masts and a tall funnel as it floated in and out of the swirling mist. He pulled his head back, irritated, and wiped off the lens with a silk handkerchief wrapped around his right index finger, then pressed his face against the rubber-covered sight. "Target's speed eight knots, range two-thousand meters, Number One," he said to the ship's bosun—referred to as Number One—who was sitting behind him at the fire-control center entering data in the attack computer. Nearby, a combat helmsman was at his electronic steering station in the cramped conning tower. "Down periscope. Surface!" Brauer yelled down the hatch.

"We're too close to Gibraltar," Tauber replied from the control room below.

"We need the visibility to get a clean shot."

"It is an unnecessary risk, Herr Oberleutnant."

"Do not question my orders," Brauer hissed. "Ever."

———————

The children marched back into the saloon with a beaming Cookie in tow carrying dessert plates. Truus giggled joyfully as she set one in front of Miriam.

"Blintzes?" the rabbi said. "How in the world?"

"We taught him," Truus gushed as the children served the others and returned to their table, coaxing Wim to sit up with them and enjoy the rare dessert, which he did but avoided looking at the adults, Weber in particular.

As everyone drank coffee and scraped up the last of their blitzes, Gaylord guzzled more wine, slopping some on his borrowed shirt, lit an unfiltered Woodbine, and took a long, deep draw. "Now, Captain, you mean to tell me you don't have some sense of loyalty to America?"

"The *Peggy C*'s my country," Rogers said, helping himself to the last forkful of his blintz.

"Oh, come now," Gaylord said, puffing out his chest to recite more poetry: "'Breathes there the man with soul so dead—'"

Rogers finished the stanza: "'Who never unto himself has said, this is my own, my native land.' They're just words."

"Just words?" Gaylord slurred, his voice rising indignantly and smoothing down his pencil mustache with the back of his index finger. "Serving my country is more than words. It is my honor. A man without honor, Captain, as the poem says, will return 'to the vile dust, from whence he sprung / Unwept, unhonour'd, and unsung.' That is a fate worse than death, I'd say."

"Patriotic blather to con suckers like you two to fight over God knows what every generation or so," Rogers said, pointing his fork at the guests.

"Nonsense?" said Gaylord. His face contorted and turning red, he sat up in his seat as if ready to hurl himself across the table to settle the argument.

His German cellmate held him down. "Gentlemen, please."

"He's no gentleman," Gaylord spat out. "Even if he can quote Horace and Sir Walter Scott. Why, the man's nothing more than a...a pirate."

"I'm no pirate," Rogers said.

"Rogers?" Weber said, amused as if an idea had just struck him. "Captain Jake Rogers?"

"Oh, jolly good," Gaylord said, slumping back in his chair and guzzling another full pour of wine before slamming the glass down on the table. "Jolly Rogers."

Gaylord and Weber, heads tilted back, howled in laughter, patting each other on the back. "So, Captain, how did such an erudite gentleman such as yourself come to be a pirate, I mean, sailor?" Weber asked between guffaws.

Rogers and Miriam exchanged glances. "Bedtime for the children," she said, pushing away from the table. "Thank you for a lovely dinner, Captain."

⟫●⟪

Brauer squinted at the darkness from the conning tower bridge, focusing on a ship slipping in and out of the fog. Behind the ship, a waxing crescent moon cut through the haze and shined a flittering spotlight on the silhouette: a three-islander. The captain clicked on his flashlight and searched through the pages of *Merchant Fleets of the World*, a Kriegsmarine handbook that showed the sizes, characteristics, and silhouettes of all known cargo ships. The ship in the distance matched the *Peggy C*'s book silhouette, although because of the position of the dim moon, Brauer couldn't make out the name on the bow or the color of the poorly lit flag on the hull. "It is them," he said to Tauber, standing beside him, struggling to attach the fourteen-inch-long firing binoculars to its pedestal with his yellow, cigarette-stained fingers. "Open all bow caps, now," Brauer said into the hatch.

"Open all bow caps," the combat helmsman in the conning tower below repeated.

"Herr Oberleutnant, our men may be on that ship," Tauber said urgently. "Shouldn't we send a boarding party first?"

"As you pointed out, we are too close to Gibraltar and, I might add, we are sitting ducks even in this moon," Brauer said in a soft, controlled voice dripping with menace. "We do not have time for niceties."

Chastened, Tauber returned to his binoculars. "Target's range two-thousand-three hundred—," he said, popping up his head as the ghostly mist swallowed the target, making a clear shot impossible.

"Well?" Brauer asked, waiting for further commands from Tauber, who,

137

as First Watch Officer, was responsible for firing torpedoes during surface attacks.

"Spread shots from tubes one and two," Tauber said into the hatch. "Depth three meters."

"Tubes one and two ready, sir," the combat helmsman inside the submarine said.

———————◦———————

Weber propped up Gaylord, singing drunken shanties at the top of his voice as Obasi led them away at gunpoint. Miriam and Rogers said goodnight to the rabbi and the children and hung back on the deck, standing shoulder to shoulder, leaning over the rail.

"So, your African bodyguard does leave you alone?" she asked.

"Obasi? He's not my bodyguard."

"Then why does he hover over you like mother chicken?"

"I pulled him out of a jam once."

"How do you pull someone out of jam?"

"Not jam, *a* jam," Rogers said with a laugh. "It was a fight. Three against one. I pulled Obasi out of that jam. Now I can never make him believe we're even."

"Even?"

"All square," he said. "You know, all paid up. Get it?"

Miriam shook her head, confused, and snuggled against his shoulder with a face that was the very picture of domestic bliss. Something Rogers spotted out of the corner of his eye made him stiffen. He cocked his head and squinted into the dark, listening intently. "What's that?"

———————◦———————

"Permission to fire, sir?" Tauber asked. Brauer nodded. "Tube one and two...Torpedoes los!" Tauber shouted, pulling the firing lever on the side of the UZO pedestal.

"Tube one and two...torpedoes los!" the combat helmsman inside the conning tower repeated.

Following the double-whoosh of the torpedo launch, the U-boat's bow lurched up as Tauber studied a stop watch for more than a minute, estimating how long it would take for the torpedoes, traveling at thirty knots, to reach their mark. Unlike pointing and shooting a rifle, everything about firing a torpedo was complicated. Once targeting information had been fed from the UZO or periscopes through the attack computer to a torpedo, the internal guidance system and depth-keeping device had to maintain the diving rudders on target as the torpedo was driven forward by two counter-rotating, two-bladed propellers. If the pistol or trigger was of the magnetic type, the torpedo had to run just under the target. If it was a contact pistol, it had to travel at the correct depth and angle to hit the hull and trigger the warhead.

It also had to keep plowing forward.

In this case, nothing worked. Disgusted that there was no explosion, Tauber shook his head at the captain. The elusive target slipped back into the shadows, and the Germans waited in tense silence for another opening. It was a gamble fraught with danger. An exposed U-boat could become the prey instead of the hunter. In the moon's glaring spotlight, it could be spotted on the surface, where air patrols and enemy submarines and surface vessels of all types could slip up on it through the maddening fog.

"Oh my God, look!" Tauber yelled, wagging his finger frantically at a faint phosphorescent trail in the ocean streaming out of the mist and heading directly for the U-boat. The watch crew, looking in other directions, tensed but maintained discipline and did not take their eyes off their assigned quadrant.

"Circle runner!" Brauer yelled, focusing his binoculars on the approaching bubbles and holding his breath. He looked at Tauber, and they both started to pray. One of their torpedoes apparently had a damaged steering or guidance system—perhaps caused by the depth charges after the schooner sinking— and now was coming home to roost. There was no time to take evasive action or to warn the unsuspecting crew below. All they could do was wait for the inevitable. The bubbly wake plowed closer and closer, like a sea monster just under the surface charging a helpless victim. It hit the hull with a loud, metallic *CLANK*. Nothing happened.

"Contact torpedo?" a much-relieved Tauber asked, crossing himself to the disgust of Brauer.

"Must have been," Brauer said. "A magnetic one would have exploded for sure. I can only assume the contact angle was too small to trigger the pistol."

"Lucky for us."

"It wasn't luck, First Watch Officer."

In the faint moonlight, a sudden clearing revealed the elusive merchant ship closing in fast, a lamb leading itself to the slaughter unawares. Brauer had no time to do new calculations. "Tube three...Torpedo los!" he shouted without waiting for Tauber, who pulled the firing lever.

"Tube three...torpedo los!" came the repeated command inside. The lone torpedo whooshed and plowed through the choppy water. The Germans waited, motionless, holding their collective breath.

◄►

Aboard the *Peggy C*, a gust of wind parted the wall of fog long enough for Rogers to make out, just beyond a tramp steamer, a dreaded sight on the horizon: the low-slung shape and circular top of a U-boat. "Oh hell." He sprinted up the ladder to the wheelhouse, leaving Miriam to scour the sea. "Mr. Nidal, right full rudder!" Rogers shouted. The *Peggy C* rocked from the concussion of the blast. Miriam ducked in fear as Rogers jerked around and caught a glimpse of the towering flames on the distant exploding merchant.

"All ahead full, Mr. Nidal," he shouted at the wheelhouse. "Let's get the hell out of here...And kill all the lights."

—⟫●⟪—

At the same time, the German officers on the conning tower bridge trained their binoculars on the rising hulk of a ship, split in the middle like a twig, orange flames and black smoke filling the air. Men ablaze jumped off the decks, their howls of pain and terror echoing in the cold distance. To identify the ship for the KTB, Gunnery Officer Radke trained a small, portable Aldis lamp on the hull: "The City of Dingle" were the words on the bow. A large Irish flag in green, white, and orange was amidships next to towering letters: "EIRE."

"Damn," Brauer said.

In the distance behind the U-boat, a dull explosion created a small geyser. Tauber swung around with his binoculars. "Battery must have run out," he said of the rouge torpedo that had exploded when it sank to the ocean floor. He turned and was surprised to see he was talking to himself; the captain was nowhere to be found. Tauber gave Radke a questioning look.

"What's the Old Man so upset about?" Radke asked. "Never heard him use a curse word before."

"It's not them," Tauber said.

"A kill's a kill, eh?" Radke said with a shrug.

"They're Irish." Radke appeared confused. "Vizeadmiral Dönitz has given strict orders against attacking neutral Irish ships so as to keep the Republic of Ireland out of the war," Tauber said. "There'll be hell to pay at the BdU."

No one was exempt from the Grand Lion's wrath when mistakes like sinking the wrong ship were made, not even one of his top aces like Kapitänleutnant Fritz-Julius Lemp. He had created a worldwide outcry on his first patrol two days after the invasion of Poland—and only hours after France and England had declared war—when he mistook the British passenger liner *S.S. Athenia* for an armed merchant cruiser. He said he was confused because it was blacked-out and traveling at a high speed in a zigzag pattern, something neutral ships did not do. He fired two torpedoes without warning and sank it, killing 112 civilians, including 28 U.S. citizens. He offered no help to survivors. After realizing his mistake, Lemp made his men swear an oath of secrecy—twice.

The first sinking of a British ship during the war was condemned as a war crime. Germany, fearing America would be drawn into the war, denied any responsibility. A furious Dönitz also covered for Lemp, ordering him to remove the incident from his KTB, and told the BdU staff to alter his own war diary. In punishment, he made Lemp spend his leave confined to quarters to study the silhouettes of foreign ships. On the same day Lemp sank the *Athenia,* British Prime Minister Neville Chamberlain made a momentous decision: He ended Churchill's decade-long exile from government and named him the new First Lord of the Admiralty, the same job he held during World War I. The Admiralty greeted the announcement with a gleeful fleet-wide message: "Winston's back."

Lemp eventually got out of Dönitz's dog-house and had the distinction of commanding the first U-boat to dock at the newly captured French base at Lorient in July 1940. He went on to sink 20 ships and was one of the first U-boat captains to win a Knights Cross. But the star-crossed commander could never shake his bad luck. His U-110 disappeared on May 9, 1941, and all hands were presumed lost.

CHAPTER 11

In the cool of the night, Miriam slid out of her bunk and dressed in the dark as quietly as she could amid the children's soft breathing and the rabbi's snores. Wrapping a shawl around her shoulders and holding her shoes in her hands, she tip-toed away, silently closing the door behind her. The rabbi rose up in his bunk and shook his head. He laid back down, eyes wide open, praying.

Miriam hurried along the freezing cold steel deck from the stern to the captain's quarters amidships and, making sure no one was watching, slipped inside. Rogers was waiting, reading in the low light above the settee. He threw down the book and jumped up as Miriam ran into his arms and covered him in kisses.

"You're freezing," he said as they hugged and gasped for air.

"You will keep me warm," she said.

When she grabbed his belt buckle, Rogers pulled her hand away. "We have to talk."

"Yes," she said, reaching for him with a hunger and affection that Rogers had never seen from any other woman. "Later." She pushed him towards the bed, refusing to take no for an answer.

"Wait, please," Rogers pleaded. "I can't lead you on. There's no future in this. All I know is life as a sailor. No matter my feelings for you, the sea will always call me back." Miriam hesitated with a sly smile and listened silently as he continued to protest. "Don't you see? I'm not good enough for you. I mean, maybe I really am nothing but a pirate."

"Yes, yes," Miriam said with a giggle. "Because of you, my family has a future. My future and yours is now, even if it is only one more beautiful night." She shoved him onto the bed. "Tonight, you are my pirate."

———————◦○◦———————

At dawn, Rogers stood at the wheel beside Helmsman Cardoso, expertly steering the *Peggy C* into the narrow Strait of Gibraltar. Pinpoints of light from countless naval ships and merchant steamers flickered in the evaporating fog; above it peeked out the tip of the 1,400-foot Rock of Gibraltar, a limestone promontory known by the Romans as one of the two pillars of Hercules, the other being the 2,700-foot Jebel Musa across the strait in Morocco.

Since the early eighteenth century, Gibraltar, the tiny British colony of less than three-square-miles on Spain's southern tip, had been a strategic chokepoint for Great Britain to control access to the Mediterranean. It had a major air base there, and its deep, well-defended harbor was home to the British naval formation Force H comprising aircraft carriers, battleships, and cruisers. Even the Rock itself was a weapon of sorts. It provided natural protection from frequent air attacks. More than thirty miles of tunnels bored through the limestone provided room for up to 30,000 soldiers, a power plant, water supply, and even a hospital.

The *Peggy C* docked near several Red Dusters—British merchant ships flying a red flag with the Cross of St. George in the upper left canton—apparently waiting for the formation of a new convoy. Once the mooring lines were secured, Rogers took his logbooks for the newly named *Pegasus* down the gangplank and handed them to a waiting British Naval officer, Lieutenant Spalding, who greeted him warmly. The *Peggy C* sprang to life as the crew hustled to offload the crates and bags they had picked up in Amsterdam. It didn't take long.

"Where to from here, Jake?" Spalding asked, handing back the documents he had skimmed before stamping.

"Not sure," Rogers said. "Depends on what I'm able to pick up. But, first, I need a truck to deliver a load into town."

Spalding arched an eyebrow. "I thought we'd unloaded everything."

Rogers gave him a "don't ask" look.

"Oh, I see," the lieutenant said in a conspiratorial tone. "That will require a small surcharge, I'm afraid."

"I don't have any more Scotch left," Rogers said.

"Well, I do have a load for Malta."

"Malta? Are you crazy?"

"How badly do you want to deliver your load?" Spalding said, examining Rogers like a professional gambler looking for his tell.

"Bad enough," Rogers said, maintaining his poker face. "But sailing through Bomb Alley?"

"It's not so bad now," Spalding said. "The Germans have diverted most of their aircraft to the Russian front."

"So, what kind of load?" Rogers couldn't help but feel he was being set up for a no-win situation, kind of like drawing for an inside straight. No matter how tempting the pot, the odds were never in your favor.

"Aviation fuel," Spalding said.

"Jesus, liquid dynamite? No thanks. There are better ways to commit suicide," Rogers said, his stomach turning.

"Not to worry. Lots of steamers have made the journey with no problem at all," Spalding said with a greasy smile that left no doubt he was sugarcoating things. Rogers' shoulders sagged; he was unconvinced. "Let me sweeten the pot, as they say. Take as many of the fuel drums as you can hold, and I'll not only get you paid a premium, I'll also throw in a pass to get you through the Suez."

"You can do that?" Rogers had drawn that inside straight and was about to cash in for an escape from the pursuing submarine—if he could survive carrying a load of highly explosive fuel through waters likely swarming with U-boats.

"It'll be waiting for you in Valletta," Spalding said with the confidence of a man who knew he held all the cards. "Or … you could take your load and your, uh, new ship back into the Atlantic."

Rogers knew he had no choice, and he knew from news reports that Malta was vitally important to the Allies because it was the only base between the major British strongholds in Gibraltar and Alexandria, Egypt. The tiny island between Sicily and Libya had been under siege since June 1940, attacked daily by Italian and German warplanes. Some said it was bombed more than just about anywhere else in the war, including London during the eight-month-long Blitz the year before. Since it was traditional not to tell crews where the ship was heading until after departure, Rogers was confident his crew wouldn't abandon ship in Gibraltar, where there was little work and few bars. Even if some did leave, Rogers had learned there was no shortage of desperate men looking for work in every port.

"I'm willing, but my crew may not be, considering the dangerous cargo," Rogers said.

"Not to worry, Captain," Spalding said. "The barrels will be labeled as something other than fuel, and I'll make sure your manifest says you're coming from Lisbon and heading for Istanbul. I'll get you loaded straight away so you can sail tonight." Rogers nodded. "Now, how many tons can you hold?"

Tonnage is a complicated question for cargo ships because it can mean weight or volume of space. It comes from the old English word "tun," meaning cask or barrel, and it typically designated a wine barrel, which, in the quaint British terminology of olden times, is made up of two "butts," with two "hogsheads" per butt. Parliament standardized a tun as holding 252 gallons and weighing 2,240 pounds. That became known as a "long ton." Duties on imported wine were based on the number of tuns a ship could carry—a measure of volume of space, not weight. The number of tuns was derived by dividing the cubic-feet capacity of enclosed space—minus non-revenue generating areas like living quarters—by one hundred. That calculation yielded the "net register tonnage," which is what Spalding was really asking for. U-boats measured their sinking success in "gross register tons," a ship's total enclosed space. It took 100,000 tons to win the coveted Knights Cross.

For the *Peggy C,* none of these calculations included all the hidden spaces used for contraband, an omission Lieutenant Spalding politely ignored as he quickly organized the loading of aviation fuel desperately needed by the Royal Air Force. Within the hour, trucks rumbled up the dock loaded with barrels with freshly stenciled labels of "cooking oil" and "sardines." They actually contained a key to winning the Battle of Britain the year before: British Air Ministry-100. The BAM 100-octane aviation fuel, developed by Standard Oil of New Jersey, gave the modified Merlin engines of British Spitfires and Hurricanes thirty percent more horsepower for taking off and climbing. They also could fly 25-34 miles-per-hour faster than they did before the Blitz, an improvement in performance that startled and befuddled German pilots.

Shortly after the Battle of Britain ended, the RAF's Air Chief Marshal Arthur Tedder said publicly that three things led to victory: the bravery and skill of the pilots, the engines Rolls Royce made, and "the availability of suitable fuel." The Germans quickly figured out what he meant when they discovered the fuel—dyed a distinctive green so it wouldn't be confused with other fuels—in a downed Spitfire. But they couldn't adapt their warplanes' engines to the higher-octane fuel and were stuck with using the less efficient 87-octane gasoline, primarily derived from coal gasification.

⟫●⟪

After dark, the promised covered military truck rumbled up next to the *Peggy C.* A powerful searchlight on the peak of the Rock scanned the dock in slow circles. Uniformed dock police patrolled the area in pairs. Rogers, careful to time everything to avoid detection, hustled the rabbi, Miriam, and the children into the back of the truck, pulling down a cloth to cover the opening. He hopped into the passenger's seat with a small bag in his hands and gave the driver directions. They drove past the John Macintosh Square, the center of city life dominated by an imposing three-story city hall, built in the early 1800s by the Portuguese immigrant Aaron Cardozo as his home. It turned out to be the largest private mansion in Gibraltar.

Cardozo was the first Jew allowed to own property in Gibraltar, but only after the direct intervention of a close friend whose fleet he supplied: Admiral Horatio Nelson, the British hero of the Battle of Trafalgar. The truck drove on cobblestoned streets past tall palm trees and old stucco buildings with towering arched doorways, ironwork balconies, and Spanish stained glass before turning onto a winding alley barely wide enough for the truck. It rumbled to a stop in a secluded square.

As the truck idled, the rabbi climbed out of the back and knocked on an apartment building's massive wooden door. The others waited behind the truck in the dark shadows with Rogers, who scanned the silent street with growing concern.

"I don't like this," he whispered to Miriam.

"No, it is alright," she said. "We have family here. The British have protected Jews in Gibraltar for centuries. There are even four synagogues. I peeked out and saw that we passed the Nefusot Yehuda Synagogue on our way here. It is known as the Flemish Synagogue. My ancestors and other Sephardic Jews in Holland helped build it. So, we are quite safe."

"Still, where are all the people? Are you sure we're in the right place?"

"Of course. Uncle Levy has been here before." She paused and pressed her warm body against him. "We will miss you," she said.

"I will miss you and...Oh, I have something for you." Rogers opened the passenger's door, removed a cloth-wrapped package from the bag, and handed it to Miriam. She glanced inside with a delighted gasp: the three red leather-bound volumes of *Ivanhoe*.

"I cannot take these," she said, handing them back.

"Please. It'd make me happy," Rogers said, pushing them away gently.

"I … I have nothing for you," she said, touching her throat. As she felt for her necklace and unclasped it, she set down the books on the truck bed and held up the jewelry so Rogers could see the dangling gold symbol. "I know this is not your faith. But will you keep it in memory of me? The symbol means chai—life—and it is one thing I value very much," she said, stepping closer and adding in hushed tones, "like you."

Rogers bent over and removed his hat so she could put it around his neck. "I will always remember you," he said, replacing his cap and holding her face, leaning in for a final kiss.

The loud slam of a door made everyone jump and turn their heads to the building where the rabbi stood in stunned silence, shaking his head in disbelief like a mourner at an unexpected funeral. With head hung low, he plodded to the truck.

"Gone" was all he could manage to say.

"Who?" Miriam asked.

"The British have evacuated almost all the civilians," the rabbi said. "We heard rumors of some leaving. But not all. We cannot stay."

Rogers' face turned stony. "Miriam, you and the children get in the back. We have to get out of here," he said in a stern voice. "Rabbi, a word?" After making sure Miriam couldn't hear, Rogers grabbed the rabbi by the collar and shoved him against the truck. "Where's the money?"

"With my relatives?" the rabbi mumbled. His body trembled.

"And where are they?" Rogers whispered through clenched teeth.

"London, Madeira, Jamaica maybe. No one knows for sure."

"Of course," Rogers said in disgust. "You know we can't go back that way. So, you'll just have to stay and find another way to pay."

"That is not possible."

Rogers tightened his grip and leaned into the rabbi's face. "Let *me* tell *you* a story, Rabbi. It's about what happens when sharks attack a sick whale. The water gets so red with blood and guts that they can't see a thing, so they end up tearing each other apart. But they don't care. They want what they want, and they don't care who gets hurt."

"And the sharks are your crew?"

"Oh, no, Rabbi," Rogers said. "That's nothing compared to what my crew will do when I tell them there's no reward and that all we have to split among fifteen men is a half a damn kilo of gold."

"We cannot stay. We don't know what the British will do with us. They may even send us back home...to die."

Stepping back in frustration, Rogers kneaded his lower lip between his thumb and forefinger. "Where in the hell are you safe?"

They returned to the *Peggy C* in glum quiet. Miriam led the children to their cabin and tucked them into bed, kissing each one good night.

"Why do we have to leave?" Truus asked between sniffles. "How will Papa know where to find us?"

"I am sure the captain will tell him when he sees him again," Miriam said, pulling the covers up to the little girl's chin. "Would you like me to tell him for you?"

Truus nodded and closed her eyes, drifting off to dreamland in the middle of a crisis, as only children can. Miriam sat beside her, holding back her sobs, making sure all the children were calm before slipping away.

In the captain's quarters, the rabbi paced in front of Rogers. Seated on the settee, the captain fixated through the open door of his office on the picture of the grim-faced admiral on the wall.

"What are you going to do?" the rabbi asked. When Rogers didn't reply, he turned to see what was holding the captain's attention and stepped into the office to get a closer look at the admiral's framed obituary. He took it off the wall and sat next to Rogers, holding the frame in his lap. "Your father?" the rabbi asked.

"Grandfather. My mother's father," Rogers said.

"This man was important to you?"

"I only met him once. But, yes, he was important to me," Rogers said and paused, taking the picture from the rabbi, hanging it back on the office wall, and leveling it with care. He strolled around his quarters, deep in thought.

"We haven't much time, Captain. Have you decided what you're going to do with us?" the rabbi asked, a tinge of urgency creeping into his voice.

"Something the admiral once said to me keeps running through my mind," Rogers said. "He said, 'Remember, family is everything.' Ironic, since he had disowned my mother when she ran off to marry my father, a lowly sailor in his eyes. I rarely saw my father and almost never saw him sober. 'Family is everything,' the admiral said. That was the night he bailed me out of jail."

"Jail?" the rabbi gasped, leaning forward and cupping his chin in his hands, his mouth hanging open in amazement.

"He had a friend give me an apprentice job on a steamer heading for Europe. And that was the night he said I could never come home again."

"Why? What did you do?"

"Cost him everything," Rogers said. "No promotion. Ostracized after they quietly arranged his forced retirement. All because of a grandson he'd never met, a grandson who didn't even know he existed. Maybe it was his way of apologizing for how he had treated me and my mother. 'Family is everything.'"

Nidal knocked on the door and stuck his head inside. "The men are assembled, Captain."

"What have you decided?" the rabbi said, his chin quivering.

Rogers stopped pacing, let out a deep sigh, and fixed him with a hard stare. "Whatever I say to the men, you must agree. Understand?"

"Yes, but—"

"Just stick to the story with everyone, and that means everyone," Rogers said, muttering under his breath, "Maybe Moses was on to something."

They headed to the crew's mess, where the other fourteen crew members were gathered in the tight quarters, looking upset and muttering in low, menacing tones to one another. The room fell silent when Rogers entered and joined Nidal at the front of the group of sweaty, smelly, grimy men. The rabbi stayed outside and watched through the cracked open door as the voices got louder and angrier. He recoiled in surprise when Miriam sidled up next to him and held a finger to his lips, pointing at the brewing trouble.

"Listen, listen, listen, damn it!" Rogers yelled, waving his hands for silence. "I'm telling you we've got no choice. The reward's in Palestine."

Miriam turned to her uncle in wonder, her eyes widening, and mouthed the word "Palestine?"

"Pay us what you've got now," Bosun said, clenching and unclenching his stubby fists.

"Got nothing worthwhile to give you," Rogers said.

"Where's the money for the load we just delivered?" Seamus asked, his thumbs stuck in his suspenders, attached securely to his belt.

"Spent on medicine, bribes, coal, supplies," the captain said. "We'll get something once we deliver our load to Malta and get the Suez pass. You can take your share of what we get in Valletta and stay there if you want. But the big money's in Palestine. There you can stay in Haifa or work the *Peggy C* through the Suez to Bombay and spend your money away from this damn war."

Lonnie stepped closer to confront Rogers. Obasi jumped in between them and blocked Lonnie's way, holding his knife in his right hand. "Make your move, Sambo," Lonnie growled.

Rogers eased Obasi away. "Calm down, everybody."

"So, give us what you and the Jews got. They always got money," Lonnie said to murmurs of agreement from the rest of the crew. "We ain't goin' no further without it."

Rogers advanced on Lonnie, going nose-to-nose with him. Menace was visible on both men's faces—kindling waiting for a spark. Neither man would back off; every member of the assembled crew held their breath. Lonnie lowered his cruel eyes, reaching his hook out to tug at the chain necklace around Rogers' neck.

"You're just sweet on the girl," he said with a sneer. The crew snickered.

Rogers shoved Lonnie away. When ominous grumblings replaced the crew's chuckles, Rogers scrutinized each man, sizing them up, calculating who would move first, who was on his side, and who was wavering. And who might have a weapon. Almost as one, the men edged closer to the captain and Nidal. Rogers, arms akimbo, stood his ground. And then he did what every smart gambler does in a bind: the unexpected. He bellowed with laughter. The crew looked at one another in astonishment.

"All I want is the money," Rogers said with a sly smile. "When have I ever really been sweet on any girl for long? As soon as I get what I want, I sail on to the next port. Eh, Cookie?"

"That's a fact, Captain," a relieved Cookie chimed in.

"She's just, uh, entertainment," Rogers said. The room echoed with laughter.

Looking on from outside, a horrified Miriam pressed her hand to her mouth and fled, tears welling in her eyes. The rabbi chased after her.

Bosun didn't join in the laughter, his arms crossed tightly across his chest. "It's too dangerous."

"It is, and I can't guarantee we'll make it," Rogers said. "But if we do, each one of you will be rich."

"How can we trust you? You haven't told us what the reward is—"

"Fifty thousand."

Collectively, the crew gasped.

"That's right. Fifty thousand dollars. That's what their family in Haifa has promised if we deliver them there. And equal shares for all—from Master to the lowest ratings. That's more than you'd make in two years or three."

Rogers let that sink in. Most of the crew made less than $100 a month, and if they could divide $50,000 by fifteen, they would realize it was $3,334 each, enough to buy a small house in cash or several cars, or for the average sailor, thousands of pints of beer at the best London pub. It was an unbelievable amount of money for a tramp sailor, the kind of man who Rogers knew would blow all that cash on booze and women and gambling, and would be back at sea within a year moaning about how unfair life was, how they'd been cheated—and how much they hated being sailors.

"Now, are you with me?" Rogers asked.

Most of the sailors nodded in agreement—with the notable exception of Bosun and Lonnie—and filtered back to their jobs preparing the ship to sail.

Nidal hung back. "They will turn on you at the first sign of danger, Captain."

"And you?" Rogers asked.

"As you always say, 'Mine is not to reason why,'" Nidal said. "The prisoners?"

Rogers paused, then shook his head. "We could turn them over to the British here. But then again, they could cause us a lot of trouble if they squealed about our refugees, which they would no doubt do to get even. And then there's Gaylord. He'd be even worse. Nah, we'll have to let them all go after Suez. But let Gaylord stay out of his cage as long as he behaves."

———◦———

On the way to the wheelhouse, Rogers picked up a tin of gingerbread cookies in the galley and strolled to the cabin Miriam and her family shared. He found Miriam, holding the railing and staring expressionless into the clear star-lit night, a shawl draped around her shoulders.

"Don't scream. I'm right behind you," he said, pulling a cookie from the tin and offering it to her with a smile. To his surprise, she shook her head without turning to face him. "Thought the kids could use some cheering up."

"They are sleeping."

"Why the long face? Didn't your uncle tell you? We're heading to Palestine, where you'll be safe. I thought you'd be happy."

"The British still control Palestine and do not want to upset the Arabs. They search every ship for Jews because of Aliyah Bet."

"Ali what?"

"Aliyah Bet. Illegal immigration," she said. "We hear they send Jews away or to internment camps."

Rogers, struggling to hide his surprise that Palestine of all places wasn't safe for Jews, put his hand on Miriam's shoulder. She moved away. "You will get into Palestine," he said with firm reassurance. "You might have noticed that I'm pretty good at smuggling people in and out of places."

"Yes, so you can get your money."

"You'll be safe," Rogers said in a less confident voice, trying to figure out what had happened. What had he done wrong?

"I am learning that Jews are never truly safe anywhere," Miriam said.

"Sure, I can understand that—"

"No. No, you cannot understand until you see them take everything," she said, her lips trembling, a torrent of words pouring out of her mouth as if a dam of repressed horror had burst wide open. "At first, it was little things. Sorry, no Jews in parks. You must register and carry papers with "J" for Jew. You must carry B2 identity cards used for bastards. You cannot be in schools or have government jobs. Thugs from the Dutch National Socialist Movement forced shops to put up signs saying, 'Jews Not Welcome.' Every month something new. Every month, we were told not to fight back, it would not get worse. Yet it did. You cannot understand the dread, walking around every day afraid, every day getting hungrier, more humiliated, hopeless."

"So, that's what I saw in the streets," Rogers said, stunned by the realization that he had been so blind. "I had no idea. Why didn't your family just leave?"

"And go where?" Miriam said with a snort. "No country will take Jews. Holland has no mountains or forests for hiding. And, sadly, even the Jewish Council helped them by telling all Jews that we would be safe if we voluntarily registered."

"But your uncle said—"

"He was a fool. They all were fools who would not fight back—until February. A fascist was wounded in a fight with Jews and died. Dutch and Germans surrounded the Jodenbuurt with barbed wire fences. They took many hundreds of Jews as hostages and deported them. Some were my friends. They have not been heard from again."

Miriam's voice grew hoarse, and when the sea wind blew her hair away from her tear-stained face, Rogers reached out to comfort her. She pulled away and gazed unblinking into the darkness.

"That struck the match for many non-Jews, and me," she said, wrapping her shawl tightly around her neck. "Most of Amsterdam went on strike on the twenty-fifth of February to support Jews. We could not believe it. First, all the trams stopped. Then government offices and shops closed. Students and teachers left classes. The shipyard workers put down their tools. I joined many thousands of my countrymen, Jews and gentiles, in marches and protests— against my father's and uncle's wishes. Even Wim snuck out with me. The Germans did not know what to do. It was—it was ... glorious. And then ...."

Miriam's voice drifted off. Rogers waited, transfixed, afraid to break the silence, sickened at what he'd heard, horrified by what he might hear next.

"And then," Miriam said, gasping for breath and grabbing the railing. "And then, the next day, Wim and I were marching hand-in-hand with thousands of others and ran into a group of the WA, the armed force of the NSB Dutch fascists. One of them was a boy I had grown up with named Luuk. A sweet gentile who would carry my books to school. We even kissed once. There he was, in his black uniform carrying a rifle and shouting curses against Jews just like the others. His face was very red, and there was spit coming out of his mouth. When he saw me, he stopped and stared. I could not move. Stupidly, I think I smiled. His friends saw who he was looking at and shoved him toward me and Wim, shaking their fists at us. The crowd pressed too hard behind us, and we could not run away.

"His new friends shouted dirty words, and they came over, pushing Luuk in front of them, goading him, telling him that Jews like me were the enemy and that a real National Socialist would never tolerate being smiled at by such scum.

"When they got close, Wim let go of my hand and jumped in front of me and put up his fists to protect me. They laughed and spat on him. Luuk had known Wim since he was baby. That did not stop him from smashing the butt of his rifle into his face. The others joined in and stomped on him, breaking his leg. The WA and Luuk threw me to the ground and kicked and punched me. Marchers tried to rescue us, and fighting broke out everywhere until we heard shots. The Germans were shooting into the crowd and throwing hand grenades at us. I saw one boy on a bicycle shot in the head. His brain splattered on a building. The last thing I remember was Luuk's face, smiling and laughing with his friends, Wim's blood and my blood on his hands."

"I'm so sorry. I didn't   "

"It was that day that my father decided we must flee Holland, no matter how, no matter the cost. Uncle Levy tried to talk him out of it. My father told his brother that he and all the other members of the Jewish Council would eventually be killed by the Dutch as collaborators or by the Germans when they no longer found them useful. That same day, much of the resistance ended. The Jewish Council pleaded for no more protests so the Germans would not deport any more Jews."

Miriam turned her cold, blank face to Rogers: "Men are such cowards.

'The sound of the trumpet wakes Judah no longer—'"

"Why are you quoting Rebecca to me?" Rogers asked, confused about the reference to the Jewish heroine in *Ivanhoe*.

"'Her despised children are now but the unresisting victims of hostile and military oppression.'" The rabbi opened the door, stopped by the demeanor of the glum-looking pair. "That is what she said," Miriam said. "You can look it up yourself. I will return your books. I do not want them anymore."

She brushed past the rabbi. With a forlorn glance at Rogers, he shut the cabin door.

CHAPTER 12

With a fair wind across her stern and a slight nip in the air, the *Peggy C* chugged east through a placid Alboran Sea, the 750-mile stretch of the Mediterranean leading to Sardinia. The water was a deep blue, and the skies a glorious turquoise. Miriam and her uncle, wrapped in blankets, sat in folding chairs on the forward well-deck below and between the bridge and the forecastle deck, reading while Truus sat cross-legged, drawing in her sketchbook. The three boys lounged nearby, listlessly playing games, their usual jabbering and hijinks reduced to grunts and murmurs. Pacing back and forth nearby, the newly freed Gaylord puffed on a cigarette, paying no attention to the others.

"I still do not understand how the captain thinks he will get us into Palestine," Miriam said. "And who does he think will pay the reward?"

"Rest assured, my dear brother always thinks of these things and makes plans for them. Even when we were children, he was always planning, always thinking three moves ahead like a Grand Master in chess, a game he played very well, by the way." The rabbi took Miriam's hand. "One Hanukah, our father gave us a large globe, and your father was always putting pins in the countries he said he would visit for business someday. He would go to the library after school and research them, and then he would find someone who had relatives there or who knew someone to whom he could write. He couldn't have been more than ten years old, and he was already plotting his future," he said, his deep brown eyes barely visible under his tufts of bushy eyebrows.

"I know about that globe. He gave it to me," Miriam mumbled. "Why are you telling me this?"

"Because he eventually traveled to all those countries, made contacts with those he had written, and greatly expanded the family business. One of the men he met in his travels was a professor in Manchester, England, named Chaim Weizmann."

"The Zionist?" Miriam asked, lifting her chin from her chest and turning to her uncle. "He met the president of the World Zionist Organization?"

"Yes. They became friends, and because of him, your father began donating money to the Palestine Land Development Company that bought property in Palestine and trained Jews to be farmers so that after two-thousand years of diaspora, we Jews would have a home."

"Father never spoke of leaving Holland."

"He didn't want to. But as I said, he was always planning ahead," the rabbi said. "He watched with horror the rise of Hitler and Franco and Mussolini and Stalin and the NSB in our own country. That convinced him we had to be prepared to flee someday, just as our ancestors have always had to flee. And when you and Wim were attacked, he decided that time had come. He said Gibraltar was the only safe place for us. But I'm sure he must have had a backup plan for Palestine because of all his connections there. Now it is up to Captain Rogers."

"But Jake had never even heard of Aliyah Bet. He has no idea the danger we face."

The rabbi raised an eyebrow at Miriam's use of Rogers' first name. "The captain assures me that he can get us past the British authorities. He has gotten us this far. We must have faith."

"I have no faith in him...or any man."

"*Liefje, liefje, liefje,*" he said using the affectionate Dutch word for dear. "I know what he said hurt you, but I do not believe he meant it." A single tear rolled down Miriam's cheek from the corner of her eye.

Miriam had good reason to be skeptical. Modern-day Palestine was a volatile territory carved out of the old Ottoman Empire at the end of World War I when the French, British, Russians, and Italians double-crossed their Arab allies, who they had promised an independent homeland in exchange for revolting against the Turks. Instead, the victors divided the conquered Middle East territory into "spheres of influence" based on a secret treaty, later validated by a Mandate from the League of Nations, for Britain to administer Palestine.

To add salt to the wounds, the British government's "Balfour Declaration" of 1917 promised support for a Jewish national homeland in Palestine, roughly the area of the ancient kingdoms of Israel and Judah east of the Jordan River. The Hebrew folksong "Hava Nagila" was written in celebration of the declaration. When the majority Arabs revolted, the British government formed the "Peel Commission" to study the problem. It recommended partitioning Palestine to create an independent Jewish state. Almost no one was happy.

As the Arab revolt worsened and Jewish immigrants flooded in to escape growing anti-Semitism in Europe, Britain double-crossed another ally. In the White Paper of 1939, Britain rejected the idea of partition and instead said there should be a Jewish homeland in an independent Palestine, one ruled jointly by Jews and Arabs, who vastly outnumber the Jews. And to placate the Arabs' fears of being overwhelmed and out-voted by Jewish immigrants—and to keep them as allies against the Germans—the plan severely limited the number of Jews who could enter Palestine. It also curtailed their ability to buy land. This made almost no one happy, again. As a result, the Royal Navy had a fleet of ships patrolling the waters off Palestine to stop and search suspicious vessels for Jews. Ever since, they've maintained a dangerous gauntlet the *Peggy C* would have to run.

At the sound of an approaching hummed sea shanty, "Blow the Man Down," everyone looked back. When Cookie stepped out of the galley, they returned to what they were doing before. Cookie carried two long poles slung over his shoulder. Two buckets in his right hand clanked together like cowbells as he shuffled past the melancholy family. Turning to take in the scene, he seemed to think about it for a moment before calling out, "Alrighty, boys, no lollygagging on this ship. Captain's rules. Time for some peggies."

The boys gave him puzzled stares and looked at Miriam; she shrugged. "The boys and I do not understand," she said. "Could you repeat in English?"

"I am speaking the King's English," he said with a chortle and tried again, enunciating each word with care. "I said, no moping about. It is time to do some chores—what we British sailors call peggies because peg-legged sailors could only do light work. Understand?"

When the boys hesitated, Cookie held up the two poles and buckets. "Fishing. For dinner." Electrified, Julius and Wim leaped to their feet and cheered. Arie ran over to Miriam and buried his head in her lap, clinging to her for protection.

"Go," Miriam said, waving on the older boys while stroking Arie's hair. "But do what Mr. Cookie tells you to do, and no playing around the sides."

"Bulwarks, ma'am," Cookie said.

"Yes, bulwarks," she replied with a smile. "And put on life jackets."

They groaned when Cookie tossed bulky jackets to them. "You heard her! On with your Mae Wests."

"Why are the jackets called that?" Wim asked.

Cookie shook his head and laughed. "Never you mind. Now, mates, we only have about an hour at dead slow before the Chief finishes his maintenance. So, it's off to the poop deck we go," Cookie said, spinning around and marching toward the stern. As the boys walked alongside, they whispered and giggled. "What's so funny, boys?"

"Julius thinks you said a bad word," Wim said.

"What?"

Wim leaned in and whispered, "Poop."

Cookie guffawed. "Poop doesn't mean poop like that. It's the raised deck at the stern."

"Why is it called poop if it is stern?" Julius asked, his body shaking with laughter. "And what means stern?"

"It doesn't mean that kind of poop. It is from the French word *la poupe*, and that means stern, and stern means back of the ship. Understand?" Cookie handed Julius an empty bucket and Wim one bucket full of shiny, squirming objects. The boys studied the slender, six-inch-long fish in wonder. Wim struggled with both hands to hold the bucket, a curious look on his face.

"Sardines. Make the best bait. Netted this morning," Cookie said as he waddled on his bad hip to the stern. The boys scrambled up the ladder to the poop deck and ran to hang over the metal taffrail, watching the spumy wake churned up by the *Peggy C.* "Now, look here, boys," Cookie said once he made it to the railing. "If you're going to be mates on my ship, you need to talk like a sailor."

He set down his poles and waved for the boys to stand beside him, turning them to the front of the ship. "Here we stand aft at the stern on the poop deck." When the boys giggled, Cookie cuffed them on the back of their heads with gentle taps. "Pay attention. The front of the ship is fore, and the very front is called the bow or prow or stem. The upper deck there is the foc's'le deck. The right side facing forward is starboard, the left is called port. Going forward is called *ahead*; backward is called *astern*. Understand?"

"Yes," the boys said in unison.

"*Aye* is what sailors say."

"Aye, Skipper," they shouted with glee and saluted.

"I'm not the skipper, boys. The skipper is a captain. But never call Captain Rogers that or he'll throw you overboard," Cookie said.

"Why?" Wim asked.

"You can call him Master or Captain, or, if you are the First Mate, you can call him Father. But, never, never Skipper. That's an insult for a steamship captain. This isn't a fishing boat with a skipper. Understand?"

"Aye, aye, Mr. Cookie," Wim said.

"No, laddie," Cookie said, shaking his head and suppressing a laugh. "You say 'aye, aye' when you've been given a direct order. It means 'I understand, and I will comply.' Can you remember the difference?"

"Aye!" Wim and Julius shouted.

"We're going to make sailors out of you yet," Cookie said, handing each boy a pole and instructing them how to hook a sardine on the end of the twenty-foot line. Cookie tossed each line out behind the barely moving ship and lodged one end of the long poles in a closed chock on the deck, creating a secure clamp for the poles on the rail. "Now, each one of you hold a pole and wait for it to bow. Then we'll pull in your catch."

It didn't take long. Julius' pole bent down with a jerk, and the boys whooped and hollered for help. Cookie tugged in the line and pulled a foot-long fish over the rail, letting it flop on the deck to the delight of the boys. He held up the wiggling fish, reddish with black spots, huge eyes, and a dorsal fin of long spikes. "Lovely blackspot seabream, mates. Good eating fish," he said, pulling out the hook and dropping the catch into the empty bucket, covering it with some water from the other bucket. "Now, Wim, it's up to you."

As Cookie recast Wim's line, a pod of three gray bottlenose dolphins, in unison, soared out of the water close behind the *Peggy C*. They followed along as if dancing with the ship, their long snouts open and sucking in air, sliding gracefully back under the surface, only to repeat the acrobatic display in ones and twos, flying high over the surface with white bellies exposed. Sometimes they flipped; other times, they twirled or stayed in perfect lockstep with the ship's forward motion with only their dorsal fins visible, a magnificent ballet that left the boys frozen in awe.

———⟶⊰●⊱⟵———

On the deck below them, Hywel sanded the round metal stanchions lining the bulwarks while Lonnie used a sharp-edged chipping hammer to scrape off rust from the deck. Bosun slopped on gallons of gooey red lead paint, choking on the noxious fumes. He stood to light a cigarette. "Hywel, when you're finished there, the 'tween deck hatch coaming has been bent. Look after it." In the distance off the starboard side, a cargo ship billowing clouds of thick, black smoke gained on the *Peggy C.* "Hywel, belay that. Go alert the captain that we've got company."

"Aye, aye, Bosun," Hywel said, dropping his sander and jogging around the superstructure.

⸺⸻⸗●⸲⸻

On the bow, Rogers, large binoculars hanging from a strap around his neck, leaned against the bridge's rail and waved at Miriam and the rabbi, but Miriam refused to acknowledge him. Gaylord briefly nodded and continued his agitated pacing. McAllister took readings on a sextant under Rogers' watchful eye.

"Now, look through the telescope and line up with the lower limb of the sun," Rogers said. "You want to see it balance on the horizon like a golf ball on a fairway. Does that make sense?"

"I'm from Scotland, Captain," McAllister said, grinning.

"Right. Now swing it in an arc to refine your measurements. Record the time and the degrees."

"All done, sir."

"Good. Head into the chartroom and plot our latitude using the Nautical Almanac, and what formula?"

"Latitude equals zenith plus declination."

Rogers nodded. "And head down to the taffrail and stream the log." The ship's "log" was a brass gauge about the size of an alarm clock mounted on the poop deck's rail, called the taffrail, that measured speed. Resembling a large brass dart, it was connected by a stiff braided line to a rotor with four vanes. The gauge measured the rotor's revolutions as it was towed behind the ship over a set period of time to record the distance traveled, and thus the speed in knots, short for nautical miles per hour. "Come back with your estimate for how long it will take us to get to Valletta traveling at 10 knots."

"Aye, aye, Captain," McAllister said, handing back the sextant on his way into the wheelhouse.

Rogers had already done the calculations and knew their latitude was thirty-six degrees and thirty minutes north, and the distance was around 800 nautical miles, which meant nearly four days to Malta. But he wanted to see if the young Scot could arrive at the correct answer. Rogers knew he desperately wanted to be master of his own ship someday, and he had to admit that McAllister showed lots of potential.

After they dropped their load in Valletta, it would be another four days to Haifa, around 2,000 nautical miles in all from Gibraltar. An easy run, particularly compared to the awfulness of the North Atlantic, and most likely out of reach of Brauer's U-boat. The German captain would be crazy to attempt the dangerous passage through the Strait of Gibraltar, which was swarming with British warships.

"B-B-Beggin' your p-pardon, Captain," said Hywel. The Welshman touched his forehead as if saluting. "B-b-bosun wanted me to inform you that a s-s-ship's approaching one p-points abaft the s-s-starboard b-beam, sir."

Rogers wrinkled his brow and moved as far as he could to starboard on the bridge wing and trained his binoculars on an approaching cargo ship, a three-islander similar to the *Peggy C* flying the red Turkish flag with a crescent moon and star. Heavy smoke was pouring out of its tall funnel, and it was flying a white flag with a large red "X." "They're flagging for assistance. Get everyone out of sight."

"Aye, aye, Captain. P-P-Putting out a lot of s-s-smoke. Must have engine p-p-problems," Hywel said.

"So, why is it closing on us?" Rogers asked, shooing Hywel away to corral everyone inside.

As the ship approached within a few hundred yards, a man on the bridge in a merchant marine uniform and a captain's visored cap waved pleasantly at Rogers; several crew members idled on the deck, and a woman with a scarf over her head walked a stroller back and forth, a not uncommon site on merchant ships, which sometimes took on passengers or, more rarely, had female crew members. Rogers lifted his binoculars to inspect the ship when it drew almost parallel with the *Peggy C.*

Out of the blue, the crew sprang into a frenzy of action. The woman tore off her scarf, revealing a man's face. The others stripped off a fake bulkhead covering a 75 mm gun. Panels slid open below the deck, exposing six 5.9-inch guns. A German War Ensign—a red flag with a swastika in a white circle—was raised above the wheelhouse. More crew members dragged back tarps to uncover four 20 mm guns.

Rogers spun around to make a run for safety, but machine gun bullets ripped across the *Peggy C*, spraying wood chips, shattering windows, and tearing through Rogers' right leg and arm, knocking him into a screaming heap as he clutched the chai necklace with his left hand. From the wheelhouse, Nidal and McAllister frantically crawled on hands and knees and dragged Rogers away, leaving a trail of blood on the bridge.

Inside the wheelhouse, Nidal couldn't find enough rags or apply enough pressure in the right places to staunch the spurting holes in Rogers. Obasi broke through the port door and crumbled at Rogers' side, tears pouring down as he moaned and tore off his shirt to press it against the wounds.

"Get me the medicine kit, yalla, yalla," Nidal snapped at McAllister. The Scotsman ran to the galley, and back up with the bag, tore through it for gauze and bandages. Nidal splashed alcohol over the wounds, wiping them with towels and pressing on gauze. Blood continued to ooze out.

Rogers lifted his head and said in a shaky voice, "Raise the stop signal flag. Only, take your time...to stop. Sneak Miriam and...and Weber up here."

Nidal motioned to Obasi and McAllister, "You heard him, sailors. Move." McAllister gave three long blasts on the ship's whistle and ran outside to hoist a blue flag with a white "X," the international signals that the ship was stopping,

When she rushed into the wheelhouse with Obasi, Miriam took charge, cleaning Rogers' wounds and helping Nidal with a tourniquet and bandages. Obasi rocked on his knees next to them, head in hand, his shoulders shaking in sobs, a helpless giant clutching his bloody shirt.

"What happened?" Miriam asked, wiping her brow with the back of her hand.

"Hitler's pirates," Nidal said. "We thought they were just a rumor."

"Pirates?"

"The Nazis convert cargo ships like ours into warships with hidden guns," he said, standing to look through the shattered window. The pirates were launching a motorboat. "They'll be boarding soon."

Bosun and McAllister escorted Weber into the wheelhouse and held him by his arms in front of Nidal. "Helmsman, go tell Sparks to send the R-R-R distress signal," Nidal said, referring to the British code for a merchant ship under attack by a surface ship.

"No, no!" Rogers whispered hoarsely. "Don't do that. The prize, Mr. Nidal—it's our only chance...Prize." Nidal kneeled and put his ear near Rogers' mouth.

"What prize?" Miriam asked.

Raising his hand for silence, Nidal strained to make out what Rogers was trying to say. When the captain's head fell back, Nidal snarled at the German. "Leutnant Weber, you will come with me. If you do not do exactly as I say, we will kill your men most horribly, and then you." He pointed at Miriam. "She will make sure you say correct things."

"Why should I?" the German said, stiffening up. "The pirates will slaughter you all."

"Perhaps," Nidal said, standing to face Weber. "I do not fear death. Alhamdulillah. The question is, how much do you love life?"

"I see your point, old man," Weber said with false bravado.

Nidal grabbed his arm and headed for the ladder, stopping in mid-step to wipe his bloody hands over the dried blood splatters on the lcutnant's jacket. "We don't want any questions about before," Nidal said and pointed him to the steps.

Weber marched down and across the main deck, stopping at the rail above the Jacob's ladder. Miriam, carrying a stack of books, stood next to Nidal, blood staining both their clothes and hands. The man in the merchant officer's uniform from the neutral Yugoslavian steamer, who appeared to be in his late 40s, climbed up the ladder from the motorboat and hopped aboard, stopping with a stunned expression on his face at the sight of a German officer. "Who are you?" the officer said in German, which Miriam translated for Nidal in a whisper.

"I might ask you the same thing," Weber replied in German, watching two armed men dressed as civilian sailors scamper over the rail from the motorboat.

"Heil Hitler. Kapitänleutnant Hermann Dietz," he said, giving the Nazi salute.

"I'm Leutnant zur See Walter Weber, U-474," Weber said, half-heartedly returning the salute. "We captured this ship, and now we're taking our prize to Tripoli." Weber nodded up to the bridge at Bosun, dressed as a German sailor and clutching a submachine gun. McAllister, in civilian clothes, leaned on the rail next to him. Seamus, also dressed as a German sailor, peered out from a shattered window, watching Miriam for any sign of trouble. Sitting tied up on the floor in front of him, and out of sight were the three gagged German sailors in their underwear.

"Not much of a prize," Dietz said in flawless American English.

"Even less so full of bullet holes," Nidal said. "You nearly killed my captain."

"We need food, and we need to move fast," Dietz said. "Been getting too much resistance since we dropped our eggs outside of Valletta."

"We can spare some food, can't we, Mr. Nidal?" Weber said. Nidal nodded.

"And your registry and cargo manifest. Our current identities are drawing too much attention," Dietz said.

Taken aback, Weber opened his mouth as if about to say something, but Nidal's glare shut him down. "We, of course, brought them for your inspection," Nidal said. He took the books labeled *Pegasus* from Miriam and gave them to Dietz.

As Dietz riffled through the pages with an expert's eye, his expression darkened, and he clenched his jaw. He flung the books at Nidal in a fit of rage and aimed his pistol at him. The two guards raised their submachine guns. "Do you think I'm an idiot?" Dietz said, smacking Nidal's head with his gun and knocking him to his knees. "Your real books. Now." Dietz raised his fiery eyes from the prostrate Nidal and reached up to grab Miriam. "I told you, no time for warnings." He nodded to the guards. "Toss the girl overboard."

Miriam screamed and tried to wrestle loose, but Dietz was too strong and handed her off to the two guards. They dragged her by both arms to the rail, looking back to double-check their orders while dodging Miriam's kicks and fighting to keep her under control. Nidal signaled to Lonnie, Seamus, and Bosun to raise their weapons. He stood, tapped Weber, and pointed to his armed men on the bridge, careful not to draw Dietz's attention away from Miriam. Weber hesitated, appearing to be calculating his odds, and made up his mind only after the two guards had Miriam halfway over the bulwark, shrieking and flailing.

"Kapitänleutnant. I'm in command of this ship!" Weber shouted. "We're not killing anyone."

The guards lifted Miriam back onto the deck, awaiting instructions from

Dietz, who waved his hand for the men to release their prisoner. Miriam jerked out of their clutches and sought refuge behind Nidal.

"Last chance," Dietz said.

"Now, Mr. Nidal, are there other papers?" Weber asked.

Rubbing his bruised face, Nidal nodded and signaled to McAllister on the bridge, pointing at the books scattered on the deck and indicating he should bring him the real logbook and manifest. McAllister ducked into the wheelhouse and hurried down the ladder to the deck with the new documents for Dietz, who inspected the registration papers for The *Peggy C* as well as log books and a color drawing of the ship with its markings. The papers said the ship was transporting barrels of cooking oil and sardines from Portugal—nothing worth confiscating. "How long ago did you change names, and where?

"A week or so," Nidal said. "English Channel."

"So, the *Peggy C* has not been a common sight around here, eh?" said Dietz. "Might be just what we need to get the hell out of the Mediterranean All my papers are as phony looking as those for the *Pegasus*."

After McAllister left to get the supplies, Dietz lit a cigar, cupping the lighter's flame against the cool breeze, and scrutinized Weber's black-and-blue face. Miriam translated for Nidal. "So, you're one of Brauer's boys, huh? My old shipmates in the U-Bootwaffe tell me he can be a real piece of work."

"You were a U-Bootfahrer?" Weber asked, surprise registering on his face.

"During the last great war," Dietz said, taking long, deep draws of the cigar and blowing the smoke at Weber. "Too old for that now. The OKM stuck me with that nearly worthless steamer. Surprisingly, though, it gets the job done," he said, referring to the German Naval High Command.

The Nazis called disguised surface raiders like Dietz's ship Auxiliary Cruisers. They were the bane of merchant ships on the Seven Seas, collectively sinking millions of tons of cargo with mines—most carried more than 200 of them—and their hidden arsenal. They also took dozens of ships as prizes to be repurposed by Germany. The captains of what some called "high seas Houdinis" were supposed to follow the Prize Regulations—a 1935 agreement between England and Germany—and fire warning shots across the bow, forcing the ship to stop for inspection, and then allowing time for the crew to abandon ship before stripping the vessels of food, water, and fuel. And, only after all that, they would blow the ship to smithereens with everything from anti-aircraft guns to torpedoes to detonation charges. Some even carried two flimsy Heinkel He114B seaplanes hidden in their holds, often with British markings, to scout potential targets. One was disassembled in crates; the other could be lifted by a crane from the hold and lowered into the ocean in no time.

As the crew of the *Peggy C* discovered, Dietz didn't believe in firing a warning shot before attacking. His first barage, like headshots into a herd of cattle, were usually aimed at the bridge, creating havoc and casualties and putting a quick end to any resistance. Both of his seaplanes had already crashed, so he had to get close to his targets to be sure what he was attacking. To avoid detection, the raiders changed identity often, using fake funnels, paint, and neutral flags to match the description of ships listed in the Kriegsmarine handbook *Merchant Fleets of the World*.

Hywel, Obasi, and the two Dogar brothers, the firemen covered in coal dust, hauled crates of food onto the deck and helped lower them into the German motorboat. Once his boat was as full of supplies as it could hold, Dietz stubbed out his cigar, gave Weber another Nazi salute, and sped off with his two guards and their bounty.

When the Germans were out of earshot, Miriam confronted Weber. "Do not expect me to thank you," she said defiantly.

⋯⟫●⟪⋯

Lieutenant Spalding focused his binoculars on a three-island steamer off the coast of the British naval base in Gibraltar with a funnel painted red topped by a black stripe bordered by thin white lines. Its name was barely visible in the hazy morning: *Peggy C.* "Now, I wonder who Jake sold the name to?"

"The paperwork was in order," said a young aide standing next to him.

"Did you get the captain's name?"

"Robert Johnson, sir. He sounded American. Should we stop it for an inspection?"

"Let it go, but get headquarters on the phone," Spalding said. "We may have a problem."

"Smugglers?"

"Not sure. But bears watching."

A few hours later, a periscope poked up from the rough Atlantic west of Gibraltar, and focused on the fake *Peggy C.* The water bubbled and churned, and a conning tower with a leaping tiger emblem emerged. As soon as the U-boat surfaced, the hatch opened, and gunners poured out to man the deck gun; four lookouts assumed their positions at each quadrant on the bridge. Brauer climbed up to the bridge with Tauber and Gunnery Officer Radke at his side. "Check and mate, First Watch Officer," the captain said in satisfaction. "Open fire. And try not to kill our men."

"Captain, it is clearly marked as a neutral American ship. We should board first and rescue our men if they are still aboard," Tauber said.

"The Americans are no better than the British. Hypocrites all," Brauer said, a steely calm in his voice. "Perhaps you haven't heard, but their President Roosevelt called us the rattlesnakes of the Atlantic in his so-called fireside chat last month. And he said that 'when you see a rattlesnake poised to strike, you do not wait until he has struck before you crush him.' We will strike without warning, just like the American rattlesnakes. Is that understood?"

Tauber opened his mouth as if he wanted to protest but seemed to think better of it. He nodded to Radke, who leaned over the rail and, with the megaphone, shouted over the wind to the three gunners commanded by the Second Watch Officer. "Open fire."

The 8.8 cm gun lobbed one of its thirty-three-pound shells at the steamer about 1,000 meters away. It fell short, detonating in the ocean in a geyser of spray. A German War Ensign shot up the steamer's foremast, and its crew scrambled to remove the gun coverings. Stunned, both Tauber and Radke shouted and waved at the gunners to cease fire. After the shooting stopped, the fake *Peggy C* lowered a motorboat, and Dietz and two sailors sped over to the U-boat, climbing aboard with some difficulty in the rocky ocean.

Tauber, a cloud of cigarette smoke blowing around his face, watched from atop the conning tower as Brauer met on the upper deck with Dietz, who pointed at the leaping tiger on the conning tower. "Oberleutnant Brauer?" Dietz asked.

"Yes," Brauer snapped. "Why are you using that ship's name?"

"We got it from your Leutnant zur See Weber on the prize ship called *Pegasus* now," Dietz said.

"Weber's alive? On that ship? Where is it?"

"Just past Gibraltar heading to Tripoli."

"He wasn't heading to Tripoli. He's a prisoner. I—" Before Brauer could finish, a loud buzz made him turn abruptly and look up. A Walrus seaplane dropped out of the clouds and skimmed above their heads. "Idiot. They were following you."

"Alarm! Alarm! Aircraft at 180 degrees!" Tauber shouted, disappearing down the hatch.

Brauer, moving gingerly because of his injured back, followed Tauber into the submarine. The dive alarm blared. Dietz leaped into his boat and fled at top speed, bouncing high off the waves. The U-boat submerged, withdrawing from the scene with all the speed the small electric motors could muster.

Explosions rang out all around. Brauer raised the observation periscope inches above the surface. His view was obstructed by the enormous swells until a wave crested, revealing the fake *Peggy C* in a wall of flames and under savage bomb attack, its bridge already destroyed.

Suddenly, Brauer crashed against the steel floor, cutting his face on the periscope as he fell, lights flickering all around him, men opening their mouths in agonized shouts he couldn't hear; the taste of blood filled his mouth. What's that?

She calls him, again and again, her voice full of panic, tears welling in her eyes. "He's gone," she says. The body lay in the tiny hospital bed, so blue, so young, a victim of some disease Brauer could barely pronounce. "He's gone," echo the words in his brain. His wife cannot be consoled; he cannot weep. Well-meaning relatives say, "You can have another son." But he knows he won't, ever. Good things are not his lot in life. His Will be done.

A burst of icy water from a pipe shocked Brauer back into full consciousness with ears ringing and head throbbing, the vision haunting him still. He hadn't heard the explosion that damaged his ship. Tauber helped him to his feet with blood-covered hands, his left eye swollen.

Chief Engineer Schmitt rushed over to Brauer. "We're having trouble with the starboard engine. One of the explosions must have shaken something loose."

"Can you fix it, L.I.?" Brauer asked.

"I can jury-rig something, but I can't promise it will last long. We may need to return to base."

"There is no turning back. Do what you can," Brauer said, spitting out blood and a tooth as the Chief headed back into the engine room. "We must hunt them down, First Watch Officer."

"We told Dönitz that we were pursuing a convoy in the Western Approaches, Herr Oberleutnant," Tauber said, handing the captain a towel to wipe his face.

"I said we hunt them down!" Brauer shouted to be heard over the gushing water and screaming repair crews.

"Sir, I've trained in these waters, and I know that trying to make it through Gibraltar is practically suicidal. Even if we make it in, it is almost impossible to get out. A mousetrap—that's what I've heard Vizeadmiral Dönitz call it!" Tauber shouted back as much in frustration as to be heard. "The last I heard, nearly a dozen U-boats have gone in, and only U-26 has ever made it out of the Mediterranean, and that was two years ago."

"How would you know anything about that?"

"U-26 is the ship I trained on."

"Are you refusing to follow my orders?" Brauer took out two pills and raised them to his mouth. Tauber swatted them away.

"That is enough, Herr Oberleutnant. You need rest. You're not well. I am relieving you of command." Tauber waved at two sailors nearby in the control room. "Escort the captain to his quarters."

Brauer's vicious uppercut caught Tauber squarely on the bottom of his chin, snapping his head back and knocking him out cold. The two sailors summoned by Tauber gaped at Brauer in horror. It was unheard of for a U-Bootfahrer to question an officer's order or for one officer to strike another. They seemed at a loss at what to do. "Poor fellow's suffering from Blechkoller," Brauer said, referring to the "tin can disease" of irrational behavior that plagues U-boat crews during long missions. That seemed to assuage the reluctant sailors, who picked up the unconscious Tauber and carried him away. "Tie him up and put him in the aft head. And gag him. We don't want him to hurt himself." Brauer picked up the two pills and dry-swallowed them. "We will hunt them down."

CHAPTER 13

"Go back to Gibraltar cause we ain't taking this no more," Bosun demanded of Nidal, seated in the wheelhouse behind Cardoso at the wheel. Lonnie and Hywel stood at his side, defiant.

The *Peggy C* had idled for hours, anchored in the middle of the placid Mediterranean, waiting for someone to decide what to do—how to treat the wounded captain and where to seek help before it was too late. Nidal, as the First Mate, was in charge and should have been making these decisions. "There is no reward in Gibraltar, and there is no payment for the fuel there either," Nidal said. "Do you wish to give up all that money?"

Bosun hesitated, rubbing his cheek as if working out a problem in his mind.

"I will check on the captain," Nidal said. "I take my orders from him. You prepare the crew to weigh anchor."

"He's not even conscious, is what I hear," Bosun said. "We can't take no orders from a dead man."

"I will tell you what he says," Nidal said. He headed down the ladder to the captain's quarters and left the door ajar, knowing Bosun had followed him down and would be eavesdropping.

Inside, a distraught Miriam dabbed Rogers' sweaty head with a damp towel and checked his arm and leg bandages as he groaned in his bed and blood soaked through the sheets. Cookie and Obasi stood around the captain's bunk, watching with anxious faces. The rabbi rocked on the settee, praying.

"I cannot remove all the bullet fragments," Miriam said. "He will die without hospital."

"Stopping much longer would not be wise," Nidal said.

"What's the worry, mate?" Cookie chimed in. "Ain't no U-boat slipping through Gibraltar."

"I will ask the captain," Nidal said, raising a finger to his lips to stop anyone from protesting that the unconscious Rogers couldn't possibly hear him. "What's that you say, Captain?" Nidal said in a loud voice, leaning over the bed. "Where? Palm what?"

"Palma? Did he say Palma?" Cookie said, playing along. "We can make Majorca in a few hours. Hear they have a good hospital. Neutral country."

"Is that right, Captain?" Nidal said, hesitating as if listening to an answer. "That is where we will go. I will tell the crew they can abandon ship there if they are afraid. Leaves more money for the rest of us." Bosun slunk away.

———◆———

Down below in the locked secret compartment inside Hold Number One, Weber and two of his fellow prisoners played Skat, the popular German trick-taking card game, and smoked Woodbines, sweating in the heat. They were stripped down to their black underwear, which was standard issue for U-boat sailors designed to hide the dirt from weeks of wear without cleaning. The sailor Rogers shot had his foot in a large bundle of bloody rags; the sailor Obasi beat with a crowbar had his head wrapped in bandages, and apparently was unable to lift his chin off his chest or take his turn playing the three-handed card game. On the floor was a bucket for a toilet and another bucket half-filled with tepid drinking water. The secret door creaked open, and Hywel brought in tin bowls full of soup along with several loaves of bread. Behind him at the entrance, Lonnie held a submachine gun.

"Ah, Hywel, my favorite Welshman. What delicacy do you have for us today?" Weber asked.

"S-s-same as yesterday. S-s-soup."

"Delightful," Weber said as he passed along the handled bowls and bread to his men. When Weber took the last bowl, Hywel slipped him a note. It read: "How much for freedom?" Weber, still smiling jovially, glanced over Hywel's shoulder at Lonnie, who nodded. "Have you ever been to Tripoli, Hywel?"

"No."

"Well, let me tell you, it is a beautiful town full of beautiful women, bars, and restaurants and, they say, a place where a man such as yourself could quickly earn more than he could spend in a year or even two."

Hywel instinctively touched his forehead as if saluting the Leutnant. "S-s-sounds nice. I'll tell B-b-bosun about it."

"Yes, please do."

⟞⟩●⟨⟝

Brauer carried an empty vegetable crate to the aft head near the galley, opened the door, sat on the wooden box, and glared at Tauber seated on the toilet in the telephone booth-size closet, sweating amid stacks of cans. Gagged and tied to the toilet pump handle, Tauber stared right back with fierce, unblinking eyes. The captain took off his cap, revealing a large bandage around his head. Leaning toward Tauber, he spoke in a voice too soft to be overheard: "I owe you an apology."

He might as well have hit the First Watch Officer under the chin again. Tauber's head jerked back and his eyes widened in surprise at what, clearly, was the last thing he had expected to hear.

"You're right, First Watch Officer. I haven't been myself lately. Some of my decisions have been, well..." He searched for the right word: "rash, if you will. But my goal has always been consistent. Defeat the enemy and take care of my men. I realize now that you have been trying to do the exact same thing. You were only doing your duty. Now I'm going to ask something of you that

179

I've never asked of anyone."

He removed Tauber's cloth gag, reached behind him, and cut away the rope with his Bordmesser pocketknife, snapping the stainless-steel blade back into the handle opposite the marlinspike, a needle-like tool used by sailors for working with ropes.

"Ask me what?" Tauber said, rubbing his wrists and picking pieces of cloth off his tongue.

"Will you forgive me?" Brauer asked, stuffing the knife into his pants pocket. "Can you find it in your heart to do that and rejoin us as we seek our common goal? I know I never say it, but I do so value your partnership. What do you say?" He reached out his bruised right hand.

After regarding the hand for a moment and then examining Brauer's intense raccoon-like eyes, Tauber leaned back on his throne. "And the strait?"

"We, of course, must proceed," Brauer said, withdrawing his hand, his voice level, his face expressionless. "I believe it is our duty to rescue the men stolen from us, not to protect my honor, but all of ours—the crew's, the U-Bootwaffe's, the entire Third Reich's."

"That doesn't mean you can disobey orders," Tauber said. "What will you tell the BdU?"

"The truth."

"What?" Tauber sat up straight, looking confused.

"The truth. Mostly, anyway. We tell them we learned from Dietz about the re-named *Pegasus* heading in the Mediterranean to Tripoli with our sailors on board, all alive. So, we decided to go after them, danger be damned," Brauer said, toying with his hat. Tauber stayed silent, unconvinced. "Look, Vizeadmiral Dönitz told me he has been ordered to dispatch almost all of our U-boats to the Mediterranean. So, they won't ask questions, especially after we pull off such a daring rescue. We'll be heroes. Knights Crosses for the officers and fried eggs for the crew," he said, referring to the German Cross in Gold, which got its nickname from its starburst star centerpiece. "Believe me, the BdU will be happy to have us there."

"Herr Oberleutnant, even if all that's true, it is a hopeless mission. We'll never find that ship."

"Ah, that's where you're wrong. I would never risk my men on a wild goose chase. We have this." Brauer handed Tauber a note from the radio operator.

"Palma? How do we know this?"

"Weber. He now has help and is signaling us that the ship is heading to the hospital there. Seems Kapitänleutnant Dietz forgot to tell us he'd shot it up and wounded Captain Rogers," Brauer said, shaking his head in disgust. "At least he was good for something."

After considering what Brauer said for a moment, Tauber stood with difficulty on cramped legs and saluted. He shook Brauer's hands. "Ready to report for duty, sir."

"Good man," Brauer said. He took Tauber's arm and walked with him to the charts on a table in the control room. "Tell me what you know about Gibraltar."

They studied the map of the strait, which resembled the tip of a snapping turtle's mouth, stretching thirty-one nautical miles from the snout at the Atlantic to the open mouth in the Mediterranean, and around seven nautical miles wide at its narrowest point between Spain and Morocco. Tauber said it was a crowded place, with British destroyers and smaller corvettes listening for the slightest sound underwater with ASDIC (the early version of sonar); in the air, with Walrus seaplanes using searchlights and flares; underwater with submarines; and on land with lighthouses and human spotters scanning the waters day and night with spotlights and powerful binoculars.

"Even with only a quarter-moon, our damaged engine means the only way in is submerged," Tauber said. "We could try to ride the current with engines silent, but we'll have to pick precisely the right time for the tidal shift, and I don't know when that will be." He explained they would have to shoot a shallow, narrow gap because of the strait's rugged topography, unpredictable ridges, valleys, and rock outcroppings that limited maneuverability, and currents flowing both ways—the top 100 meters or so flowed east into the Mediterranean, and that limited their ability to maneuver even more.

"When the U-26 caught the current, it was moving at around two to three knots. So, it took us more than five hours to float through," he said. "But we had a hard time maintaining our depth, and we were almost forced to the surface at one point by what felt like underwater waves."

"So, it can be done," Brauer said.

"We'd be floating blind and helpless and, without engines, completely at the mercy of the currents," Tauber said. "But, yes, it can be done. If we're lucky."

"There is no luck, First Watch Officer. Only God's will."

It took only a couple of hours to prepare the crew, surfacing in the dark to dump the toilet buckets, shoot the stars with a sextant for their bearings, pump out the bilges, and recharge the 124 batteries under the metal floor planks as much as possible with the diesels. Fully charged, they would last around ten hours operating the twin electric motors. Brauer didn't have that much time. It was too dangerous to stay on the surface for very long, so he'd have to dive with the motors less than half-charged. They wouldn't last long enough for the passage. But his plan was to drift in the current and fire up the motors for a few minutes every half an hour to jump to seven knots, its maximum underwater speed. It was a risk; the slightest noise might attract attention, but with limited air and battery capacity, counting on an uncertain current speed to get them through was the greater risk.

As was his custom, Brauer knelt in prayer in his tiny quarters before taking command. When he did, the control room was illuminated by red lights used for nighttime surface travel to make it easier for sailors' eyes to adjust when they climbed onto the bridge. The same procedure was followed in the conning tower and control room when submerged at battle stations so the interior lights wouldn't shine through the periscopes.

The U-boat passed as close as possible to land on the surface around Cape Trafalgar and proceeded slowly past a towering lighthouse to avoid the sandbars and reefs that had been the downfall of many a ship. It submerged to fifty meters at the opening of the Strait of Gibraltar, the tide turning favorable on the cloudless night. The crew manned their stations in stocking feet, with their soiled mattresses on the floor.

"All ahead full for three minutes," Brauer whispered. The command was passed along in whispers to Chief Engineer Schmitt instead of by the noisy engine order telegraph. At Schmitt's signal, the Electric Motor Officer switched on the motors; they whined like a jet engine from a low to high pitch and then settled into a constant, soft hum. Their only guide going forward was the electric gyrocompass that could show true north, but not shorelines, ships in their path, or distance to the uneven and treacherous bottom.

The hills and valleys below were normally measured by an echo-sounding machine called a Fathometer, but the pings of the primitive sonar made too much noise to operate. They would have to thread the needle in the dark and silence. All in all, it was akin to walking blindfolded through a crowded train station full of winding hallways and stairs.

Schmitt and Stürkorl, the chief helmsman and navigator, each kept time, the chief engineer for his three minutes, and the chief helmsman for the duration of the trip. Stürkorl needed to calculate their location based on average speed. The rest of the crew sat at their stations or rested in their bunks, wide-eyed and straining to pick up any sound outside, trapped in a fetid coffin smelling of sweat and rotting food. Above them, the few remaining loaves of bread had turned into what the sailors called "rabbits" because they were covered with a white, fuzzy fungus. Brauer stood in the officers' quarters near the listening room, waiting for any signals. After three minutes, the motors kicked off, and they glided along using only blue emergency lights, which would help preserve the batteries.

After the first hour passed, Brauer was dripping in sweat. "Take us to periscope depth, L.I.," he whispered.

Schmitt coordinated with the two planesmen seated at their stations in the control room, keeping his eye on the Papenberg, a tall tube resembling an outdoor thermometer used to gauge the U-boat's relationship to the surface. On its side, there was a silhouette of a conning tower with an extended periscope. When the water inside, driven by the change in pressure, reached the desired location on the periscope—approximately fourteen meters—Schmitt nodded to Brauer.

"Up periscope," Brauer whispered. "First Watch Officer, see if you recognize any landmarks from your last trip to get our bearings."

"Aye, aye, Herr Oberleutnant," Tauber said. He pulled down the handles on each side of the observation periscope and pressed his face to the rubber eyepiece. He walked around slowly, pausing occasionally to get a better view of the land. "Spotlights everywhere make it difficult to see. But I think...yes, it's a lighthouse on the Moroccan side, some distance aft."

Tauber checked the map with Brauer and tapped on the Cape Malabata Lighthouse. "It's near Tangier, which means we haven't made much progress. At this rate, we won't make it through before daylight."

Brauer nodded at Stürkorl, the chief helmsman, listening nearby. "What do you think?"

"He's probably right, Herr Oberleutnant," Stürkorl said, after stepping over to look at the map. "We need more speed."

"L.I., start the motors and maintain them for five minutes this time," he said softly to Schmitt.

"Let me take a look," Stürkorl said. "That lighthouse is fifteen meters high, according to the map. I might be able to use that to get a better idea of how far along we really are. Up periscope." The chief helmsman studied the landmarks through the periscope, focusing on the rotating light of the lighthouse aft and another one, also on the Moroccan side, ahead. Suddenly, he pulled his head back. "Down periscope. Corvette approaching!"

"Cut the motors and the gyroscope compass. Absolute silence," Brauer whispered. The command was repeated quietly up and down the ship, making all the sailors freeze wherever they were, looking up, barely breathing and listening to the faint churn of propellers. Slowly, that sounds grew more distant, and there were no pings from an ASDIC.

Brauer looked over to the hydrophone operator, who shook his head and whispered, "It's heading west at top speed. Must be chasing something. No other ships close by."

"Good," Brauer said, wiping his face with a handkerchief. "L.I., resume all ahead full for five minutes. Set depth at fifty meters."

The next three hours passed without incident, and Stürkorl calculated they had maybe an hour left to escape the strait. Brauer gave the signal to start the electric motors once again, but as soon as they revved up, the hydrophone operator whispered: "Propellers approaching." The captain waved at Schmitt to stop, and the motors whined to a halt. Outside, the faint whir of high-speed propellers, the unique mark of a destroyer, got louder and louder. The tense crew looked up as if they could already see the sinking depth charges, although the worst damage almost always happened from explosions below the submarine.

The propellers thrashed directly overhead, and the *ping-ping* of the ASDIC echoed throughout the U-boat. Trapped at fifty meters, moving at three knots, tops, with no way to maneuver, they were the very definition of a sitting duck, one in full view of hunters in the duck blind. Crew members grabbed whatever they could to brace for the impending explosions. Brauer crossed his arms and gazed down the passageway, impassive, projecting a calm he did not feel, knowing in his heart that it was going to be bad. The pause between pings grew shorter and shorter as the hunter zeroed in for the kill.

There it was: the first wave of splashes, nine in all, appearing strangely distant, followed by the gurgling sounds usually indicative of oncoming depth charges. Brauer mentally counted down the time, calculating he had maybe ten seconds before the charges would reach his ship's shallow depth. The repeated blasts jarred the submarine, rattling pipes and men alike. Brauer swayed on his feet but didn't fall. Nothing broke. Nothing leaked. The second wave came as the propeller's egg-beater sounds grew more distant, and these exploding depth charges rattled Brauer and his men with less impact. Tauber gave Brauer a questioning look. The captain shrugged his shoulders and appeared as confused as the First Watch Officer.

The next explosions were louder, more violent, and much too long-lasting to be mere depth charges. And then it hit Brauer. His U-boat wasn't the target. Another U-boat had to be under attack, and not only had it taken direct hits, but it was being so ripped apart that not a single soul onboard would survive. The hydrophone operator hadn't picked up another submarine, so it must have been running silent, and Brauer's U-boat must have passed it, leaving a sonar trail of electric motor whines in its wake.

Since Brauer had not consulted the BdU before entering the strait, he had no idea what other U-boats were doing, and they had no idea of his presence. Tauber and the others in the control room listened in silent horror to the unmistakable wailing of a steel hull being crushed by the pressure as it sank to the bottom of the sea. They glared at Brauer with a mixture of disgust and anger, and Brauer knew why: They thought he had inadvertently led the destroyer to the unknown U-boat, and thus was responsible for the deaths of all those men, their brothers in arms. And even more sickening to think about, their deaths had provided Brauer cover for his escape because the British knew U-boats would never be foolish enough to travel in pairs on such a perilous mission.

Brauer could almost hear the crew cursing him for insisting on leaving Lorient on a Friday. They had had nothing but bad luck ever since. Brauer shuddered and prayed, then turned his attention above, listening for any approaching propellers as his ship drifted away without a sound on the tranquil current, and out of the strait to safety. His Will be done.

CHAPTER 14

Just after midnight, Brauer, Tauber, and two other sailors stood under a nearly full moon on their U-boat's wooden plank upper deck gazing across the mirror-smooth Mediterranean. Mostly they saw the reflection of lights from La Seur, the Gothic Roman Catholic cathedral towering over the harbor at Palma, the ancient capital city of the tiny Spanish island of Majorca, 140 nautical miles due west of mainland Spain. In the middle of the harbor, in front of the neat rows of small, white fishing boats, their sails stored away and their masters fast asleep, there sat the Germans' prey—the *Pegasus* (aka the *Peggy C)*—anchored with lights out. Trapped.

"You sure we can't wait for it to sail?" Tauber asked, taking deep breaths of the warm fresh air. It was as if, in between puffs on a cigarette, he was inhaling the bouquet of a fine wine. Waving the smoke out of his face, Brauer gave Tauber a disapproving glare.

"The waters are too shallow and clear for us to stay around for any length of time. This is the only way we can safely rescue the hostages," Brauer said, adding in a low voice, "after we've dealt with Captain Rogers." He caught the eye of Second Watch Officer Mueller on the conning tower bridge. "If we aren't back in four hours, go lie doggo on the bottom eight to ten nautical miles to the southwest, where it should be deep enough to hide from planes. Return tomorrow night as soon as the sun sets. Signal us when you're in position. Is that clear?"

"Aye, aye, Herr Oberleutnant," Mueller said. "What should we tell the BdU? They keep sending messages, asking for our location."

"Nothing," Brauer said firmly. "I will deal with them after our mission is complete." Exactly how he would do so wasn't clear. He knew his U-boat would have been listed as missing, and a red pin would have marked its last location on a map in Dönitz's Situation Room. Standard procedures called for the pin to be removed after seven days of radio silence, and for next of kin to be notified that the commander and his crew were missing and presumed dead. Brauer regretted the untold anguish this would cause all the families, including his own, but it couldn't be avoided, and whatever excuse he came up with later would be greeted with such joy and relief that a deep BdU probe was most unlikely.

Brauer snuck another Pervitin into his mouth and climbed down a rope ladder into a rubber dingy, followed by Tauber and the sailors, all of them armed with submachine guns and pistols, which they hid using the most unmilitary-style shirts they could find, sweat-stained shirts reeking of diesel fumes. Without their military hats and wearing borrowed gray-green denim trousers, they could pass for civilians, assuming no one paid heed to their seaboots.

"Funkmaat Vokel, starting to look familiar?" Brauer said to the radio petty officer as they paddled toward the beach.

"Yes, sir. I was just a kid when my family vacationed here," Vokel said. "Still, I should be able to find the hospital. My brother broke his arm, and we had to spend all day there."

"Good, good. And you, First Watch Officer? Any of your far-flung adventures bring you here?" Brauer asked in a chummy voice, a useful tool he had learned to fake over the years.

"No, Herr Oberleutnant," Tauber said. "We did travel quite a bit, and I even spent eight months in England at Oxford studying English. Have I ever told you about that?"

"Oh, yes, a few times," Brauer said with a thin smile, dabbing his sweat-drenched face with a handkerchief. "But tell us again. I'm sure everyone would enjoy a diversion. Not all of us were fortunate enough to have such a privileged upbringing. We can live vicariously, can't we, men?" The sailors nodded agreement as they continued to paddle with long, quiet strokes. Meanwhile, Brauer and his tiny crew scratched themselves almost non-stop. They were fighting the itchy skin caused by dried seawater, a consequence of being unable to wash with fresh water.

It took about half an hour to reach the dark, sandy beach near the piers. They dragged the dingy into a nearby dense grove of dwarf palms and covered it with leaves. They hid their submachine guns nearby for use later on the *Peggy C*, which was rocking in the bay a few hundred yards away. Vokel got his bearings and remembered enough to lead them on a somewhat winding path through the Old City toward their destination.

⸻➤●◄⸻

Not far from the harbor at the General Hospital, Rogers, in a hospital gown, was resting in one of a dozen occupied white-metal beds. The beds were lined up on both sides of a long ward with a tall ceiling and wide Palladian windows with cantilevered fanlights for circulation. It had taken almost five hours for surgeons to extract the bullets and dozens of bullet fragments from his right arm and leg, then to sew him back up, wrap him in bandages, and put a splint on his leg. After two days, he had gained some strength and was sitting up so Miriam could help him drink the water Obasi had brought him. A nurse in a white uniform, apron, and peaked cap checked Rogers' pulse and took his temperature. She wrote all that on a chart hooked onto the end of the bed, then moved on to the adjacent unconscious patient, whose labored breathing, ashen skin, and faintly putrid odor did not portend well for him.

Cookie rushed in, out of breath. "Germans are at the front asking about the captain."

"How did—?" Miriam asked. "It does not matter. We have to get him out of here."

"But how?" Cookie asked, his face anguished and red, still panting from the run up the stairs. He bent over his potbelly to catch his breath.

Miriam scurried over to the nurse and, in a mixture of French and broken Spanish, managed to explain their predicament. "Vienen conmigo, prisa, prisa," the nurse said, waving for them to follow her out of the ward and into a nearby utility room full of supplies and clean, folded medical garb where they could hide. Miriam tried to explain to the nurse that it was Rogers who was in trouble, but the nurse couldn't or wouldn't understand, threw up her hands, and left.

"What did she say?" Cookie asked.

"I am not sure. She did not seem to understand me," Miriam said. "We must hide Jake before the Germans find him."

"How?" Cookie asked. Miriam scoured the room, stumped and growing more anxious.

It took the Germans more than twenty minutes to search every ward before they reached the half-filled one on the third floor, its lights lowered to help patients sleep. Brauer examined each chart at the end of the beds for names until he made it halfway down the corridor to where a nurse, with her back to him, tended to a patient. He lifted the chart. "Captain Rogers," he said in English. "We meet at last."

"Shhh," said Miriam, dressed in a nurse's uniform and cap. "The captain just came out of surgery. He needs his rest."

Brauer scoffed and slid to the side of the bed. Putting his hands on the unconscious patient, he shook him until he moaned and coughed so hard, he choked and gasped for air. But he didn't wake.

"Please," Miriam said. "He is weak. You could kill him."

At Brauer's hand signal, the two German sailors dragged Miriam away. Rogers, in a bed further down the room, watched through half-closed eyelids, his head propped up on a pillow.

"Oh, I won't kill him...now," Brauer said. "I need him conscious so I can look him in the eyes and make him watch us execute his thieving crew."

"Oberleutnant Brauer!" Tauber exclaimed in a shocked voice. "We can't—"

"Enough!" Brauer snapped back and scooted up a chair. From his position, he could keep track of both the patient and the *Peggy C*'s dim silhouette in the harbor. "We have plenty of time." As he glanced at his watch, he noticed a patient's stare and pointed his pistol at him. "What do *you* want?"

Rogers rolled over on his side with his back to Brauer just as Cookie and Obasi, in poorly fitting orderly uniforms, rolled up with a rickety wheelchair, lifted Rogers off the bed, and started to roll him away with Miriam in tow.

"Wait," Brauer said.

They froze. Maintaining blank expressions, they glanced at one another through the corners of their eyes, trying to decide what to do. Cookie nudged Miriam, looked down without moving his head, and mouthed, "Your shoes." They were black; the real nurses wore white shoes. In a panic, Obasi reached for his knife, but Miriam pushed it back into the sheath. Taking a deep breath to calm her nerves, she turned to face the Germans.

"You forgot your stethoscope," Brauer said, holding it out for her.

"Thank you," Miriam said with a forced smile, snatching it from his hand, and leading the others out of the ward. Brauer sat and propped his feet up on the bed. Tauber and the two others set up chairs with their backs to the windows to stand guard.

Cookie and Obasi carried Rogers' wheelchair down the stairs and set him down just outside the hospital entrance. A moment later, Miriam followed in her own clothes. An orderly threw Cookie and Obasi their clothes, which they quickly donned. Miriam took some cash from Cookie and handed it to the young man, who slipped back inside. Obasi flung Rogers over his shoulder like a sack of potatoes, and they hustled to the harbor through deserted streets in the dead of night.

They were met at the *Peggy C* by Nidal and the Dogar brothers just coming off their watch. They helped lift Rogers onto the boat and set him down on the deck. The rabbi, barefoot in his pants and undershirt, shuffled over to help lift the captain and carry him to his cabin. Miriam walked along, speaking to the rabbi in Dutch. He wrinkled his brow in concern. The Dogar brothers exchanged questioning glances.

⟶➤●⥸⟵

A loud snort woke Brauer up. It was his own snore. Tauber, lighting a cigarette on the stub of another one, and the other two guards were awake but bleary-eyed. How long had he been asleep?

A worried doctor leaned over the patient next to Brauer, moving his stethoscope around his chest and shaking his head. With a sigh, he lifted the sheet over the man's head. Brauer, sweat dripping down his face, grabbed his arm. "What's happened to Captain Rogers?"

The doctor jerked away. "I do not know what happened to Captain Rogers. But Señor Garcia has passed away."

In a fury, Brauer ripped the charts off the other beds until he came to the one Rogers had actually occupied: "Garcia," it read. He threw the chart across the room, sped over to the window, and scanned the harbor, now bathed in the first rays of daylight. Gone. The silhouette wasn't there. The *Peggy C* had escaped—again. Glancing down at his watch, Brauer growled in anger. "Hurry, we have to get to the pier and hide before it's too bright."

The sailors raced into the hallway. Brauer tugged Tauber's arm and drew him aside, shouting to the others. "Go ahead; we'll meet you there! We have something to take care of first!" As they sprinted away, Brauer signaled for the First Watch Officer to follow him into an empty washroom. After checking under the stall doors to be sure no one was inside, Brauer leaned close to Tauber, wrinkling his nose at the ever-present stench of Trelacen hair lotion and cigarettes, and whispered in his ear. "You really should have learned to play chess, you disobedient, arrogant...heretic."

Tauber appeared shocked. As he stepped away, his face contorted in pain, he gaped down in horror at the black handle emblazoned with BUND sticking out of his chest. Blood was oozing out, and an odd wheezing sound was coming from between his pursed lips. He staggered and slipped to his knees and keeled over, his head hitting the tile floor with a loud thwack. With the cool indifference of a mortician, Brauer flipped the body over and slid out his pocket knife, wiping it clean on the body. After removing Tauber's pistol, he dragged the body into a utility closet. He cleaned up the trail of blood and strolled away as if he hadn't a care in the world, tossing the pistol into the ocean along the way.

When he caught up with his men, now hiding in the dwarf palms, Brauer was panting and red-faced, perspiration stains covering his shirt. "Tauber's been arrested. We have to stay hidden until dark."

"Arrested? For what?" Funkmaat Vokel asked.

"We were collecting medical supplies from different rooms when I saw the police grab Tauber and haul him away for stealing."

"Can't we get him released?"

"Not safe. I think they saw me. Can't have them arresting me, too," Brauer said. "We'll have to leave him here and get the consulate to take care of him when it's safe for us to message the BdU." He checked his watch. "We'll take shifts sleeping. You two first."

He knew his crew would never question his word. They obeyed orders. And he knew the BdU would believe him about everything because there would be no Tauber around to contradict him or to condemn him, just as Brauer had done to his previous commander.

Even if the Naval High Command made an official inquiry, Majorcan authorities would plead ignorance of any such arrest, as they would no matter the truth to avoid a diplomatic incident. By the same token, they wouldn't make any connection to a body found in the General Hospital dressed in British clothes and without any identification. It would be a mystery lost in some bureaucrat's files, and Tauber would be buried anonymously—just what Brauer thought he deserved.

CHAPTER 15

osun and Hywel brought the prisoners in Hold Number One a breakfast of porridge and tepid coffee. Obasi guarded them from the outside with a pistol. There would be no new escape attempt, or at least no successful one. Bosun took a bowl from Hywel and filled it from a large pot the Welshman was holding and kneeled down to hand it to Weber, who was sitting in his black underwear with his back to the wall.

The leutnant glanced outside to be sure Obasi couldn't hear. "Hywel, where's your one-handed friend?" He took the proffered bowl from Bosun. "And you, you're the bosun? Surprised they'd send you on such a lowly job."

"We's all pitchin' in," Bosun said, lowering his voice so Hywel and Obasi couldn't hear him. "Why didn't they show up?"

"Are you sure your radio operator sent the message with the location?" Weber said under his breath. Bosun nodded and reached for more bowls to hand the prisoners. He returned to Weber with a cup of coffee.

"Maybe they didn't get it," Weber said, "or got it too late, or couldn't make it through Gibraltar." He put the food down and stood on stiff legs, stretching and turning his back to the door. "Keep trying."

"I think the captain suspects something," Bosun said. "Ever since he got back, he's ordered radio silence, and he's making Sparks take watches at the helm."

Weber, with Bosun at his side, strolled around the tiny compartment, doing squats and leg stretches. "Why is the captain back? You saw what they did to him. He should still be in the hospital." Weber scooped up his bowl and gulped down the porridge with a loud slurp. "Unless he's afraid of something and had to leave in a hurry."

Bosun's eyes lit up. "They did bring him back in the middle of the night. Somethin' ain't right."

"Then help us take over the ship."

"Not enough of us yet. And the captain keeps all the weapons locked up in his dayroom cabinet." The other prisoners, having licked their bowls clean, held them out for a refill from Hywel, who waited for Bosun's approval. "Go ahead, Hywel, let's keep 'em fat and happy," Bosun said in a loud voice for Obasi's sake. He took Weber's bowl. "More?"

"Why, I believe I will," Weber said. "My compliments to the chef, Hywel. Please tell him this is the best shit we've ever eaten." Hywel laughed, joined by the other Germans—they knew enough English to understand what Weber meant.

Bosun handed the bowl back. "Once they see how little we get paid in Malta tomorrow, the others'll come around."

With a big grin on his bearded face, Weber downed the new bowl and burped. "Keep signaling," he whispered. "Brauer will never give up."

———— ⟫●⟪ ————

As the sun rose the next day, Rogers, with the rabbi on one side and Obasi on the other, made it up the ladder to the wheelhouse, though with considerable difficulty. His right arm was in blood-sprinkled wraps and his right leg in bandages and a splint. After Nidal rose, they settled Rogers in the tall captain's chair behind Helmsman Cardoso. The gray-haired Spaniard was chewing on his pipe and peering forward at the calm ocean and sunny sky through four windows—the other three shot-out windows were boarded up.

"Thanks, mates," Rogers said.

"Are you well enough for a watch?" Nidal asked, standing in the open door.

"Sure," Rogers said, waving him away. "Go get some chow. They'll come get you before we reach the harbor." Nidal closed the door behind him.

"Now what?" the rabbi asked.

"We'll be in Valletta soon and can hide there for a couple of days. We should get enough for the fuel to pay the men something and to replenish our supplies," Rogers said.

"And we'll be safe there?"

"Safe enough, although we won't be for long if I don't figure out how Brauer found us," Rogers said, squirming uncomfortably in his wooden chair. Obasi lifted the captain and moved him around until Rogers waved him off, irritated at his predicament. He did not like needing help.

"One of your men perhaps?" the rabbi asked.

"Could be, but he'd have to have Sparks' help. Or maybe the pirate ship somehow passed on word about us, or we were spotted by some other submarine. Could be a lot of things."

"That reminds me of a story about "

"You should be in bed," said Miriam, carrying Cookie's medicine bag as she jerked open the starboard door.

"I'm fine, thanks," he said with a grin that disappeared when a stern-faced Miriam did not seem amused.

"I will change your bandages here," she said. With the rabbi's help, she unwrapped the bandage on his right arm, cleaned the stitches with alcohol and sulfa powder, and then used a new roll of gauze to re-wrap the wound.

"There, look," Rogers said, using his left arm to point at a ship a few miles ahead. Clouds of smoke trailed from its funnel as it headed toward the growing outline of an island. "Welcome to Malta," Rogers said. "Just ahead of that tramp is the Grand Harbor and safety."

As an unsmiling Miriam opened her mouth to reply, an enormous explosion lifted the distant ship in a fountain of flames and debris, its bow buckling and thick black smoke shooting sky-high. Seconds later, shock waves from the blast rocked the *Peggy C* and rattled its windows. The vibrations almost knocked Rogers out of his chair. Obasi had to pull him back in. Cardoso bit off his pipe stem with a loud crack but never lost his firm grip of the wheel or looked away. The rabbi ducked and covered his head. Miriam didn't flinch.

"Full stop!" Rogers shouted.

"Full stop. Aye, aye, Captain," Cardoso said, spitting out pieces of pipe, rotating the engine order telegraph handles with a loud ring, and ending straight up at full stop.

Nidal burst through the door. "U-boat?"

"Unlikely this close to port. Too shallow and too many planes about," Rogers replied.

"The pirate ship?" Miriam blurted out.

"What? It's nowhere near here by now," Rogers said.

"What did they mean by dropping eggs at Valletta?"

Rogers turned to Nidal: "They did say *eggs*, Captain. I thought he used the wrong word."

"Oh my God," Rogers said. "Sound the general alarm, now!" Nidal lurched behind the captain's chair to pull the red-box switch on the wall, triggering a wailing alarm. "Obasi, go work with Bosun to drop anchor. Hurry." He ran off to man the donkey engine so the deck crew could get the anchors down as quickly as possible.

"What? Why?" Miriam asked.

"Mines," Nidal and Rogers said almost in unison, looking at each other.

"Right. What else could *eggs* be?" Rogers said. "We have to stop because I don't know if we're about to enter the minefield or if we're already in the chicken coop." The ship slowed, but Rogers knew it would take several more excruciating minutes for the steel hull to come to a complete stop unless he did something drastic.

"Full astern, until the anchor's lowered. Then full stop." Rogers said.

Cardoso gave him a questioning look before ringing the engine order telegraph. "Full astern. Aye, aye, Captain."

As the ship rattled from the sudden shift in direction, Rogers turned to Nidal, "See if any of the crew will volunteer to lead us out of here in the motorboat. And get the Germans out of the hold. Swing the lifeboats out on the davits and get everyone ready to abandon ship."

Obasi, of course, volunteered after lowering the anchor and joining the men assembled on the poop deck. Nidal declined the offer because he needed Obasi to guard the prisoners, tied up to the metal trunk-buckles connecting the stays from the mast to the deck. Obasi was the only one he trusted with a gun. When none of the other crew members stepped forward, Weber raised his one untied hand to volunteer. Nidal shook his head, unbelieving. "Are you all cowards? Even the Germans have more balls than you," Nidal said, raising his voice in a rare show of emotion. The crew members inspected their shoes or gazed at the sky. The Germans laughed

"I'll do it." Gaylord stepped forward, his proud British chin jutting out, half-raising his bandaged right arm out of the sling. "Someone needs to get us the bloody hell out of here."

"Let's go, then," Nidal said, surveying the crew with disgust on his face. "And he only has one good arm."

Obasi raised the anchor as the crew lowered the motorboat into the ocean with Nidal and Gaylord inside. They shoved away from the *Peggy C* with an eight-foot-long wooden boat hook. Nidal got the small outboard motor running and drove it to the stern, where Cookie waited on the poop deck with two red flags in his hands. Hywel, with his eyes on Cookie, stood on the monkey island atop the wheelhouse. Bosun positioned himself on the bridge in front of a window where the helmsman and Rogers could see him relaying the signals from the motorboat via Cookie and Hywel.

Obasi stood guard over the prisoners and was joined by other crew members not needed at their stations. Miriam stood on the poop deck with Truus, who sketched furiously in her notebook. The rabbi held Arie in his arms alongside Cookie. The two older boys, Julius and Wim, joined Hywel on the monkey island, wearing life jackets and using borrowed binoculars.

Pulling the stopper off the voice pipe, Rogers shouted to the engineers: "On my command, astern dead slow for thirty seconds and then full stop!" It was all a guess, and all Rogers could do was hope he was guessing right.

"Aye, aye, Captain!" Turani shouted back from the engine room. "On your command, astern dead slow for three-zero seconds and then full stop!"

Gaylord sat in the bow of the motorboat using his good arm and the wooden end of the boat hook to poke the water carefully. Nidal scoured the water on the sides as he inched the boat forward in tiny, zig-zagging increments as wide as the *Peggy C*, turning back to the ship often to maintain a straight line that retraced their way in. It was tedious and nerve-wracking; move ahead, stop, search, probe, and hope. Once the motorboat was a few hundred yards behind the *Peggy C*, Nidal waved a white flag at Cookie, who waved the white flag back and then signaled behind him at Hywel, who shouted "all clear" to Bosun. Bosun relayed the message into the wheelhouse. Rogers nodded at Cardoso, who yanked the engine order telegraph to "astern dead slow."

The *Peggy C* shuddered to life, and Rogers counted to thirty before nodding to the helmsman to ring the telegraph, pointing the arrow to "stop." There was no perceptible change in the ship's slow movement backward. He watched through the windows, waiting for any sign of trouble or success, but Bosun didn't take his attention off Hywel above.

On the poop deck, Cookie lowered his flag. Miriam stood by him, shaking. "Nothing to worry about, ma'am," Cookie said. "The safest way out is the way we came in."

"But will the mines not blow up the motorboat?"

"Most of 'em are magnetic charges," he said. "The motorboat's wood."

"*Most of them?*" Miriam hugged Truus with one hand and shaded her eyes with the other as the ship glided to a stop.

The rabbi waved at the two boys to come down to the poop deck. "I want them within reach," he said to Miriam.

The motorboat resumed the search, Nidal revving the engine ever so slightly. With his left hand, Gaylord jabbed the long wooden handle into an ocean as smooth as a backyard pond. Sweat dripping off his forehead, he jerked his right hand up with a wince, signaling Nidal to stop the engine. "Something's here," Gaylord said, leaning over the bow to get a better view. His pole hit something again: a large spherical ball with pointy metal horns suspended on a chain just under the surface. "Mine, Mr. Nidal," he said, his voice taut and frightened. Nidal reversed the motor, backed off, and waved two red flags at Cookie. The moored contact mine, loaded with hundreds of pounds of explosives, could blow a crater on land 460 feet wide and twenty feet deep.

Rogers shook his head when the signal reached him, knowing he'd have to wait for Nidal to reposition the motorboat to find a clear course. After a few minutes, Bosun signaled one point starboard astern. Cardoso made the adjustment and signaled for dead slow to the engineers. After thirty seconds, he signaled stop. For four terrifying hours, they repeated the pattern until Nidal and Gaylord determined no more mines were in their way. Now signaling with two white flags, they headed back to the ship.

"All clear!" Cookie shouted and signaled Hywel. "Sweet Jesus, Mary, and Joseph...Uh, sorry, ma'am."

"Do not worry," Miriam said, breaking into a warm smile of relief and patting his arm. "Good Jews all, and like us, fleeing persecution."

Cookie scrambled down from the poop deck and waved for the two boys to follow him. "Come on, mates. Help me lower the Jacob's ladder for 'em."

"Aye, aye, Mister Cookie," Wim said, saluting.

Julius seemed confused and gawked at his older brother. "Is Jacob coming to take us to heaven?"

"Julius," an exasperated Wim said and dragged him by the hand to the bulwark next to Cookie.

Later, as the sun was beginning to set and everyone was back on board and at their duty stations, Rogers and Nidal conferred over a map in the chartroom. Gaylord, Miriam, and the rabbi stood nearby.

"We'll have to try to trade the fuel in Palestine for the Suez pass," Rogers said.

"I have already set the course for Haifa. But the crew will not be happy," Nidal said. "They were expecting to be paid in Gibraltar, and then again in Valletta. And now, the food is running low."

"What are they going to do?" Rogers asked in a weak voice. "We can't pay them until—" Without warning, he slumped over the table, dragging the maps down with him to the floor, unconscious.

Miriam knelt quickly, felt his pulse, and checked his bandages. Red splotches were growing. "He is bleeding again. Help me get him back to bed."

Nidal and Gaylord lifted him by his feet and shoulders. "All ahead full," Nidal said to Cardoso before closing the door.

"Aye, aye, Mr. Nidal. All ahead full," the Spanish helmsman repeated, chomping on the stub of his pipe stem and muttering to himself, "Oh, we'll get paid, all right. Bosun'll see to that."

CHAPTER 16

The crew, exhausted by hours of fear and tension, went back to work without enthusiasm, going through the motions while grumbling about the constant state of danger Rogers had put them in. Bosun, of course, fanned those flames in a *tour de force* of sabotage that never quite crossed the line from bellyaching to mutiny.

"We ain't never gonna get paid," he whined to Hywel, scraping paint off the foredeck on his knees.

"You s-s-ure the k-k-kraut will pay us?" Hywel asked, torn between greed and fear.

"Sure, mate," Bosun replied with bravado. "And a lot more than the Jews, I bet. Now, you with me?"

"I don't know, boyo. Got to t-t-think it over."

"Tripoli's not that far, you know," Bosun said as he headed off to talk to the firemen.

He opened the fiddley door to an alleyway covered by a grate for ventilation and climbed down the iron ladder to the "Glory Hole," as some sailors called the stokehold, jumping off before the last rung onto a steel deck called "The Plates." He found the Dogar brothers in the eerie glow of coal-dust-covered light bulbs. Sweating profusely even with their shirts off, sweat rags tied around their necks, they held wet cloths in their mouths to keep from inhaling noxious fumes when they shoveled coal into the open furnace doors. Two Scotch boilers produced enough steam to power the *Peggy C's* engine. Larger ships, such as the *Titanic*, had as many as twenty-nine boilers.

Bosun tried a different tactic with the brothers, making his point as quickly as possible to get out of the burning-hot ninth level of hell. "The food's only gonna get worse, 'cause I seen Cookie washing the meat with Condy's Fluid, and you know what that means." They shook their heads. "It's a disinfectant; that's what it is. Meat's goin' bad. Everything's getting moldy. And, you know why Cookie's stopped making fresh bread?"

"No," the brothers said, leaning on their "banjos"—long-handled shovels shaped like the musical instrument—listening closely over the banging and scraping of the engines in the next room and the hissing of the boilers behind them. Their faces tensed up in concern, eyes darting from Bosun to steam gauges to be sure the pressure didn't drop too low.

"The captain told him there wasn't no money to buy supplies, and then the pirates stole a load, so he's to put us all on rations. And that includes water, I bet." The brothers perked up at that. Because of the oppressive heat and hard labor they had to endure, the firemen always got a quart more water each day than the rest of the crew. It wasn't a luxury; it was a necessity. "And soon alls we'll have to eat is that pork they have in cans," Bosun said innocently.

He left the brothers shouting at one another in a language he couldn't understand as Shakir returned to raking the boilers clean of clinker, glassy-looking waste from the burning coal. Amar picked up a thick, six-foot-long slice bar and used its wedge-shape end to poke and lift the clinker from the back of the boiler to provide better ventilation for the fire.

Bosun tried similar arguments with the young helmsman McAllister but got nowhere. "The captain's always been good to me," McAllister said, making it clear he didn't want to hear any more complaints. "I owe him."

Bosun dropped the subject and moved on to one of the bigger question marks: Seamus. He had been on the *Peggy C* for some time but did not seem all that happy now. When Bosun finally found him alone, Seamus was at the stern painting hatch coamings—raised deck-plating that kept water from getting into the holds. Bosun told him to take a break and tapped out a cigarette from a John Player and Sons packet labeled as "manufactured from rich, cool Navy cut tobacco." Bosun handed it to Seamus and stuck one in his own mouth, lighting them with a box of matches he pulled from his pocket as they both sat on the deck.

"Why you think they brought the captain back to the ship so soon?" Bosun asked between puffs. Seamus shrugged. "Seems strange to me, is all. He sure was shot up. Seems like he needed more time in the hospital, don't you think?"

"I haven't a baldy notion," Seamus said, blowing smoke rings. "I ain't no doctor, mate."

"And in the middle of the night, like they was runnin' from somethin'. You don't suppose the Germans found us, do you?"

Seamus' head jerked up. He stood and stamped out the cigarette. "Hadn't thought of that, matey, but they did leave in a hurry," he said and went back to painting.

"Sure does make you wonder," Bosun said, walking away with a smirk on his face. After two days, Bosun had most of the men riled up.

⟫●⟪

Gaylord was oblivious to the problem as he strolled along the deck in the cool night air, smoking a cigarette and admiring the vast mosaic of stars shining down on him. Around the corner, on the aft well deck behind the superstructure, angry voices competed for attention in stage whispers. Gaylord stopped and peeked around the edge. Bosun, Seamus, Lonnie, Hywel, and Cardoso gathered in a tight group with Sparks and the two firemen brothers, Shakir and Amar. Nidal stood in front of them, arms crossed. Gaylord could pick up only a few words and couldn't understand what Nidal said at all because he had his back turned.

"Enough's enough," Lonnie said, pointing his hook at Nidal's face.

"Yeah," Seamus said. "Where's our money?"

"In Haifa, as the captain told you," Nidal said.

"If that reward even exists," Bosun said. Nidal glared at him, his cheek muscles flinching. Bosun took a step back. "Look here. I'm not saying the captain's lying. It's just—"

"Just what?" Nidal said, staring down Bosun.

"It's just, just that, how's he knows them Jews is telling the truth. They don't seem all that rich to me," Bosun said. "Why take that chance when we could go to Tripoli and give the Germans the fuel and the prisoners? They'll reward us plenty." The crew members nodded to one another, murmuring in approval.

Nidal stroked his goatee and studied their faces as if searching for an ally amid a snarling pack of hyenas. "How do you know the Germans will not slaughter the lot of you?"

"That German officer Weber. He says he'll vouch for us, that's how."

"And you trust the word of a Nazi?"

"He ain't no Nazi," Bosun said, waving his arm around to make sure the men got his point. "He's a sailor, same as us, and sailors take care of sailors. Ain't that right, mates?" The crew mumbled "yeah" and "right you are" and nodded in agreement.

"And I'll bet that U-boat's on our tail, ain't it?" Seamus said.

The other crew members turned to Seamus with looks of sudden understanding on their faces—looks that turned threatening as the men's focus returned to Nidal, standing silent as a statue, unafraid and unmoved.

"Why'd we leave Majorca all panicky when the captain's not half-fit? Must've been that the Germans knew where we was," Seamus continued. Bosun signaled with his eyes for the radio operator to keep his mouth shut.

"The captain wanted to leave," Nidal said.

"Germans?" said Shakir, the elder of the Dogar brothers. "I heard that Jew lady tell the rabbi that Moffen were at the hospital." All the men's heads spun around, looking confused. "Moffen, you know—the Dutch nickname for Duitsers, uh, for Germans."

"You speak Dutch?" Bosun asked, incredulous.

"I told you before, my brother and I served on the *Beschermer*."

Bosun raised his hands in frustration, "So what?"

"It's a Dutch merchant. We were on it for a year before the Germans sank it," Shakir said.

"And," Amar said, "we have been on many ships and have learned the word 'Germans' in many languages—Alemanes, Tyskere, Tedeschi—"

"Why the hell didn't you say something before?" Bosun said sharply, cutting Amar off in mid-sentence.

"Why would I?" Shakir asked. "Germans are everywhere. Is this of significance?"

"It means the U-boat's done found us!" Lonnie shouted, his ordinarily soft southern drawl rising in panic as he pointed his hooked hand at the stern for emphasis. "We can't outrun no damn U-boat, ya'll. It can cruise nigh on twice as fast as this rust bucket. We don't stand no chance, I say."

"My brother and I have been sunk once. We do not wish to suffer through days in a lifeboat again, or worse," Amar said. "We must accept the German's offer." Grumbles of approval swept over the assembled crew.

"The Mediterranean is very large," Nidal said, holding his hands up in a futile attempt to calm everyone down.

"That didn't stop the U-boat from finding us in Majorca, now did it?" Seamus said, pulling on his suspenders with his thumbs like a folksy lawyer making his case in front of a jury. "You're in charge now, matey. Just give the word."

At that, Gaylord tried to sneak away but tripped over a bucket, causing a loud crash. The bucket went rolling and clanking across the deck just as the Brit stumbled into view of the startled sailors. "Lovely evening for a stroll, don't you think, chaps?" he said, quickly gaining his composure. The crew watched him with suspicion written all over their faces. "See that dazzling star?" Gaylord said, pointing up. "That's Sirius in the constellation of Orion, I believe. Wait, no, Canis Major. That's right. Dog Star and the Greater Dog. Always the brightest in the sky."

The crew members stopped talking and drifted away, leaving Gaylord staring at the stars.

Bosun and Hywel snuck into Hold Number One and let Weber know what they had heard.

"I told you Brauer would never give up," Weber said, rubbing his hands together in glee. "You must find a way to get our weapons and take over the ship, soon."

"What's the hurry?"

"Do you know why they call him Bloody Brauer?"

"He sinks neutrals without warning, they say," Bosun said.

"He sinks everything without warning," Weber said. "He won't care that his own men are aboard. He will torpedo us first and rescue us later, if we're not dead. And if we are killed, he will consider us unfortunate casualties of war. Now, has your Sparks been sending out our location?"

"He did right after we left Malta, but he can't get to the radio shack very often. And, when he does, there's lots of traffic, so he can't be sure anyone picks up the messages."

"Here's what I want you to do," Weber said. "Use the radio silence time to send our coordinates and this message on the 600-meter band over and over: 'To Viktor with love. Peggy of Haifa.'"

Scheduled radio silences came about after the *Titanic* sank in 1912. No ships came to help in time to save all the *Titanic* passengers because the nearest vessel didn't have a radio operator on duty, and other nearby ships either didn't hear or understand the distress signals. Since then, all ships had been required to monitor their radios twenty-four hours a day and cease transmissions for three minutes twice every hour for urgent telegraph signals on the 600-meter band, and another three minutes twice for voice messages. Those radio silence times were to be used only for emergencies, and every radio room was equipped with a clock showing in red the time blocks for telegraphs and in green for voice transmissions.

Bosun slipped the message to Sparks and made sure disgruntled crew members still on the fence knew how much danger they were in if they didn't act soon. He didn't mention who was putting them in danger.

⸺⸺⸺⸺

Brauer and the watch crew on the bridge scoured the horizon as the U-boat cut through the Mediterranean under a full moon, heading east, looking for a needle in a haystack. To establish their own location, Stürkorl shot a fix from the stars with his C. Plath sextant. "Made in Hamburg, you know," Brauer said to the chief helmsman and navigator, indicating the sextant painted flat black with an engraved eagle holding a swastika. "All the best things are."

"Aye, Herr Oberleutnant," Stürkorl said in a soft voice, as if afraid to offend his fidgety, overwrought commander who, of late, had been muttering loudly to himself, asking crew members the same questions over and over, and greeting the answers with surprise, saying, "Yes, of course. That's right."

Funkmaat Vockel, the radio operator, crawled up from the conning tower and handed the captain a note. Brauer, reading the paper as it flapped in the breeze, erupted in laughter, such a rare occurrence that Vockel and the four lookouts held still to avoid drawing the captain's inevitable angry attention. "Apparently, I have a girlfriend in Haifa," Brauer said, laughing so hard he had to take off his hat and bend over to grab his knees. The crew members glanced at one another and joined in with weak chuckles, as if unsure what the joke was.

Brauer signaled for the navigator to follow him as he nudged Vockel aside and slid down the ladder to the control room, all in one quick swoop, like a fireman sliding down a fire pole. Stürkorl scrambled down and followed the captain to the chart table, where they were joined by Mueller, the Second Watch Officer whom Brauer had elevated to First Watch Officer after Tauber's "arrest." The three men studied the charts. "These coordinates show them here," Brauer said, pointing to a spot in the ocean about halfway between Malta and Palestine.

"The fastest a tramp like that can move is nine to ten knots, assuming her engine is in perfect shape, and she has a full crew of firemen to shovel the coal as quickly as possible," Mueller said. "Which is very unlikely."

"Exactly. Stürkorl, plot a course to intercept them in no less than twenty-four hours somewhere around here," Brauer said, drawing a circle with his finger on the map a day's distance off the coast from Haifa.

"It'll be close, Herr Oberleutnant," Stürkorl said. "L.I. says the starboard engine is still acting up, and we'll only be able to do twelve knots, at most, during the night."

"Now, now. Don't make me late for my date. I'm so looking forward to it," Brauer said, guffawing and rubbing tears from his sunken eyes. All the sailors in the control room ducked their heads in awkward silence and went about their business as if nothing unusual was happening.

———⊳●⊲———

In the captain's quarters on the *Peggy C*, a ghostly pale Rogers was awake and fighting to sit up in his bed, something made more difficult by the bandages and splint. The rabbi read the Hebrew Bible on the settee; Arie slept on his lap, and Truus stretched out on the floor, drawing pictures on her pad.

"You praying for me?" Rogers asked with a dry, croaky voice.

Surprised, the rabbi jumped up, brought Rogers a glass of water, and helped him get more comfortable. "Reading the book of Judges about Samson. God gave him the strength to overcome his wounds and destroy the Philistines."

"Didn't Samson die?" Rogers asked.

"Afraid so," the rabbi said with a wry smile.

"How long have I been out?"

"Nearly two days." The rabbi took the glass from Rogers and placed it on the side table.

The door creaked open. When Miriam stepped in with the medicine kit, Rogers tried to rise, but she promptly eased him back down. Gaylord slipped in behind her and closed the door. "Hold still," she said, inspecting bandages dappled with blood. "You have lost much blood. You need rest."

Gaylord cleared his throat. "May I have a word, Captain?"

"We can't let you go," Rogers said.

"It's not about that. I believe you are in grave danger."

Rogers guffawed. "You're just noticing that?"

"Please, Captain. I just heard your crew talking mutiny," Gaylord said. "I don't particularly like you or the Jews. But mutiny is beyond the pale."

"He is too weak," Miriam said. "Cannot Mr. Nidal deal with this?"

"He may be the ringleader," Gaylord said, leaning in closer and lowering his voice so the children couldn't hear. "There was talk of taking us to Tripoli for a reward from the Germans. Nidal just stood there and did nothing. Damn nasty business this."

"What should we do?" the rabbi asked with a worried glance at the children.

"Nothing for now," Rogers said. "It sounds like it's just talk, and they have no weapons. But tomorrow, we'll see if we can't force their hands. As the saying goes: 'The expert in battle moves the enemy and is not moved by him.'"

"Sun Tzu?" Gaylord asked. "Is there nothing you haven't read?"

Rogers waved at the shelves of books all around his cabin. "Miriam, would you please bring me the pistols in my desk? And, Gaylord, go find Obasi and tell him I need him now."

"Right-o, Captain," Gaylord said, opening the door to leave.

"Hey, Gaylord!" Rogers called out. The Brit glanced over his shoulder. "Thanks." Gaylord saluted with a grin from ear to ear.

"Now you must rest," Miriam said, setting down on the bed Rogers' Colt and Weber's Mauser, and pulling up the covers.

"Yes, rest," the rabbi said as he picked up Arie and nudged Truus to follow. The young girl stopped at Rogers' bedside on her way out.

"I finished something for you to help you get all better," Truus said, handing the captain a stack of drawings tied together by a string. The cover sheet showed a remarkable likeness of Rogers and the words: "Get Well Soon."

"Thanks, sweetie," Rogers said in delight. He flipped through the detailed drawings of his ship and crew with admiration. Miriam gathered up the medicine kit to follow her family out.

"You'll need this," Rogers said, setting aside the drawings to pick up the Mauser. Shaking her head "no," Miriam opened the door to leave. "You must," Rogers said, his voice cracking in desperation. "If something happened to you, I'd—"

"Run out of entertainment?" Miriam said, keeping her back to him.

"What? Oh, hell," Rogers said. "You heard? It wasn't true. I don't care about the reward. I care about you."

"Why did you lie, then? Why did you make me sound like a *slet*? I mean a bad girl, uh, tart?" she said, looking over her shoulder.

"Don't you see? I had to convince them that all I wanted was money, that I had no feelings for your family, or for you, which," he paused to gulp some water, "which isn't true at all. Please believe me. I've never felt this way about any woman before." Dumbfounded, Miriam sat on the bed. "I'm too weak now to protect you," Rogers said. "Some knight in shining armor I turned out to be."

She took the Mauser and stuffed it in her belt, tears rolling down her face as she kissed his cheeks, his forehead, and his lips. As much as Rogers enjoyed the reconciliation, he couldn't help but worry that he had brought all this trouble on himself, and now he didn't know who he could trust.

Cookie and Turani had been with him for years and should be reliable; all the others were unknowns, except for Nidal. He had seemed on Rogers' side until recently, when the derisive nicknames and constant disagreements had started. Perhaps he had had enough. Maybe it was one gamble too many, one fueled by visions of all his heroes in those damn books. Maybe he should have folded long ago. All he could do was wait, tossing and turning, until morning, and hope his plan worked. He probably wouldn't get a second chance.

CHAPTER 17

Early the following day, Gaylord closed the door to Rogers' cabin and joined the captain, Miriam, and the rabbi around the bed. Obasi sat nearby holding the Colt.

"We don't know who or when, so we have to force them to make the first move," Rogers said, fully dressed, his feet dangling over the bed.

"Mr. Nidal is the ringleader, yes?" Miriam asked.

"That's hard for me to believe," Rogers said, shaking his head. "Still, he didn't come talk to me about the meeting. We just have to assume the worst. Who else was at the meeting?"

"I'm not sure, really," Gaylord said. "It was dark."

"Can you describe them?" Gaylord shrugged in frustration.

"Wait," Miriam said. She handed Gaylord the get-well book of Truus' drawings and watched him thumb through it with Rogers.

"That one for sure and maybe that one. Yes, he was in the front," Gaylord said, tapping a picture of a bent-over Bosun picking up some rope and looking over his shoulder. "He did a lot of the talking." He moved on to other drawings.

"Wait a minute. Go back," Rogers said. Gaylord flipped the pages back to the likeness of Bosun. "Look at that," Rogers said, putting his finger on a Luger handle sticking out of Bosun's shirt at his belt. "Where in the hell did he get that? Obasi, were the other guns in the case?" Obasi nodded his head yes. "Now, we have our bell cow."

"A bell what?" Miriam asked.

"The cow other cows follow," Rogers said. "Obasi, go fetch Bosun at gunpoint. Gaylord, help him and go spread the word. Make a big deal out of it. Then pick up a can of cooking oil from the galley and bring it to me. Rabbi, you and the children hide in the galley and stay out of sight. You'll be out of harm's way, and they'll never think to look for you there."

"What about the others?" Gaylord said.

"Nidal, Cookie, and Turani should still be sleeping because they have seniority," Rogers said. "As for the others, who knows? Let's just hope they take the bait."

<hr/>

Gaylord took out a Woodbine and ambled onto the foredeck, where he found Bosun greasing the derrick wires in the bright sunshine. "I say, old chap, do you have a light?" Without a word, Bosun pulled out a box of matches and lit Gaylord's cigarette, stuffing the box back into his pocket. As he turned, he came face-to-face with a pistol Obasi was pointing at his head. "I'd hold still if I were you," Gaylord said. The two men patted down Bosun but didn't find the Luger. Obasi shoved his prisoner towards the captain's quarters.

Gaylord strolled off, puffing on his cigarette and smoothing down his mustache, a satisfied look on his face.

"Have you seen Wim?" the rabbi said, herding Truus, Arie, and Julius along the deck.

"No, sorry," Gaylord said.

The rabbi checked above and all around. With a sigh of exasperation, he led the children into the galley, closing the door behind him. Inside, he hid Truus and Arie in one floor cabinet and Julius in another. "Do not make noise or leave, no matter what. I must find Wim."

Gaylord sauntered to the aft deck, where he found Lonnie and Hywel chipping, scraping, and slopping gooey red paint onto the metal deck. "Wonder what your Bosun did?" Gaylord asked, the very picture of genuine concern.

"What do you mean?" Lonnie asked, setting down his paintbrush.

"The African marched him to the captain's quarters," Gaylord said. "And at gunpoint. Most peculiar." Lonnie and Hywel traded uneasy glances and scurried away. Gaylord went in pursuit of the cooking oil can.

———⟫•⟪———

Lonnie and Hywel roused Seamus from his bunk and galloped up the ladder to the wheelhouse, where they found Cardoso at the wheel and Sparks in the captain's chair on watch.

"They've taken Bosun," Seamus said. "We have to act now. Are you with us?"

"Aye," Cardoso and Sparks said in unison.

"Good," Seamus said. "Lonnie, you and Sparks head to engineering and overpower whoever is on duty and wait for the all-clear from us. We'll round up the others."

Cardoso tied a rope around the wheel to keep the ship moving in the current direction. Then he joined Seamus and Hywel as they ran into the captain's dayroom behind the wheelhouse. Seamus plucked a key from his pocket and dangled it in front of the others. "Lookie at what I got, mateys." He opened the cabinet, removed the Germans' three submachine guns, and handed one to Cardoso and one to Hywel. "Now, what do we have here?" Seamus said, wrapping his hand around the gold bar Miriam's father had given Rogers in Amsterdam. "The Old Man lied about having no money. We don't have to tell the others about this, now do we?" The other two nodded as he stuffed the bar in his pocket. He stuck his hand back in the cabinet and pulled out a bottle of Scotch. Opening it with his teeth, he took a long swig, sharing it with the others. "The girlfriend's mine...first." They snickered and each took another long drink. "Now, let's go see Mr. Nidal," Seamus said.

———⟫•⟪———

Below in the captain's quarters, Bosun sat on the floor, tied up and gagged. Rogers rested on the settee with Miriam at his side and Obasi standing in front.

"Didn't you find the Luger?" Rogers asked.

"No," Obasi said, handing Rogers the Colt and a matchbox. "Just this." He locked the cabin door and slipped into the adjacent office, leaving the door cracked open.

"He must have given it to someone else," Rogers said, pocketing the matchbook and eyeing Bosun, squirming against the ropes. "So, here we are again, Bosun. You. Me. Mister High and Mighty. The crew all riled up. Only this time, I've got a gun."

"Who is Mister High and Mighty?" Miriam asked.

"Me. Isn't that right, Bosun?" Rogers said with a sneer. "He gave me that nickname after I caught him stealing from the slop chest and turned him in to the captain."

"Slop chest?" Miriam said.

"Sorry. The ship's store where the crew can buy tobacco and toiletries and such, and alcohol, on occasion. Bosun would steal some of the stuff and sell it to the crew at a discount, telling the men the captain had been overcharging them. When I caught him, the captain cut off his supply and docked his pay. So, Bosun egged on the crew with more lies about the captain and me. We almost had a mutiny on our hands, all thanks to Able Seaman Critchfield, now Bosun."

The handle to the cabin's locked door jangled back and forth. Rogers calmly laid the Colt on his lap and crossed his arms; Miriam held her breath. The door, rattling like a shutter in a storm, burst open with a kick from the outside. Seamus, Cardoso, and Hywel rushed inside, swinging their submachine guns around. A bug-eyed Bosun struggled to speak through his gag.

"We're taking over this ship," Seamus said, a little wobbly from the Scotch.

"Really? Got a plan, do you?" Rogers said, reaching for the gun in his lap.

"I wouldn't do that, Captain," Seamus said. "We don't want to hurt nobody."

Rogers ignored the threat and put his hand on the pistol. "Sorry, matey," Seamus said, closing his eyes and pulling the trigger of his submachine gun. Nothing happened. Cardoso and Hywel pulled their triggers, also with no result. They shook their weapons, cocking them over and over and gawking at them in frustration. Obasi stepped into the room, a broad grin on his face, holding something in his outstretched hand.

"Firing pins, Seamus," Rogers said. "Didn't you ever wonder why I didn't take the guns out of the cabinet?"

Seamus spun around and dashed out the door into an oil can that Gaylord smashed into his face, knocking him back into the room, where he sprawled on the floor. The gold bar popped out of his pocket and slid over to Rogers, who picked it up. Obasi tied up Seamus and the other two prisoners, searching each one until he found a key in Seamus' pocket, which he tossed to Rogers.

"How'd you get Nidal's key to the cabinet?" Rogers asked Seamus, who glared back defiantly. Obasi pressed his knife against Seamus' neck until it drew a trickle of blood, but he wouldn't talk.

"You never told us about no gold," Seamus spat out.

"How long would you have let me live if I had?" Rogers asked, handing the cabinet key and gold bar to Obasi. "Besides, you would have gotten your share in Haifa."

As the tension rose, Gaylord held the submachine guns with his bad arm, and with military efficiency used his right hand to install the firing pins. He handed one weapon to Rogers and one to Obasi, keeping the third for himself. Seamus spat on the ground in defiance.

"Let's find Mr. Nidal," Rogers said. "Find him, and we find the Luger." Obasi and Miriam helped him get to his feet. "This is getting embarrassing," he said.

⟾►◄⟽

It was an ordeal, but they managed to lug Rogers to Nidal's cabin. It was empty, so they walked and half-carried Rogers into the empty wheelhouse, where they found the rope holding the wheel in place. Everyone moved fast to prepare the trap they had planned to bring the rest of the mutineers to them. Gaylord poured the cooking oil on the floor in front of both doors, and he slipped into the captain's dayroom to join Obasi, who was locking the gold bar back in the cabinet. Miriam ducked under the desk in the chartroom. Once everyone was in place, Rogers flipped the switch on the alarm box, setting off a loud wail that could be heard for miles.

Rogers hobbled to the engineer order telegraph and jerked the lever, ringing contradictory instructions. After untying the wheel, he turned it clockwise as far as it would go and secured it with the rope. He hid the submachine gun behind the wheel, and stuffing his pistol in his pants, lowered himself to the floor. He spread out, face down, as if knocked out. "Olly, Olly oxen free," he whispered.

Shouts and pounding footsteps rang out from the wheelhouse ladder. Shakir's face popped in and out of sight at the starboard door's window until he caught a glimpse of Rogers face down on the floor. The door flew open and Shakir burst in, waving a long slice bar from the stokehold, followed by his brother, who came armed with his banjo shovel. They skidded on the oil, flipped, and slammed into the floor with a thud. Rogers rolled over and raised his pistol. Obasi and Gaylord ran out, tiptoeing through the oil to grab the Dogar brothers. Gaylord held them at gunpoint while Obasi tied them up.

Miriam helped Rogers to his feet. He switched off the alarm and cut the rope from the wheel before plopping into the captain's chair. "That makes six," Miriam said.

"And we still don't know how many of the others are involved," Rogers said. "Somehow, we'll have to pick them off one by one. But Mr. Nidal is the key. Where is he?"

Obasi and Gaylord pushed the bound and gagged firemen into the dayroom and returned to Rogers, leaning back in the captain's chair.

"Now what's your plan?" Gaylord asked.

"Did you feel that?" Rogers said.

"I don't feel anything."

"That's just it. The engines have stopped," Rogers said. "They're in control of the ship. You and Obasi will have to take it back. They only have the Luger, so they're outgunned. But be careful. They're probably expecting you."

Obasi and Gaylord, submachine guns at the ready, made their way from the wheelhouse to the engine room door down below. The African pointed to himself and down the ladder, signaling Gaylord to stay as lookout. Obasi crept down until Gaylord lost sight of him. As he leaned over to get a better view, the butt of a gun whacked the back of his head. He slumped to the deck.

⟞➣●⟝⟞

In the engine room, Obasi glided past the line of stilled pistons and stumbled over the unconscious Assistant Engineer Dunawa, who was tied to the engine and gagged. Obasi set down his weapon to cut his crewmate loose, pausing when he heard a noise behind him. Scooping up his submachine gun, he spun around, but saw no one and didn't see Gaylord above. Lonnie smacked the back of Obasi's head with an oar; Sparks tackled him from behind, knocking the submachine gun out of his hands. Sparks snatched Obasi's knife from his belt and sliced the African's right arm. They rolled on the floor until Obasi managed to kick Sparks away long enough to regain his feet.

"What's the matter, boy? Can't fight without massa coming to save you?" Lonnie said with a sneer, swinging the oar with all his strength at Obasi's ribs. The African grabbed the oar, jerking it so hard that Lonnie flipped over. With Obasi's back to him, Sparks lunged with the knife. Obasi sidestepped him, deflected the blow, and used the oar to chop down on Sparks' wrist, dropping him screaming to the floor.

A woozy Lonnie charged, brandishing a large wrench. Obasi ducked, rolled on the deck, and snatched the submachine gun, turning to fire a salvo that ripped across Lonnie's chest. Picking up the knife with his one good hand, Sparks lunged at the back of the unsuspecting Obasi but tripped over an oar wielded by Dunawa, rope still dangling from his hands. The fall bloodied Sparks' nose, and Dunawa knocked him unconscious. Obasi gave Dunawa a head nod of thanks and indicated for him to tie Sparks up and hide.

Truus and Arie, curled up together in the louvered cabinet in the galley, jumped at the sound of the gunshots from below. A door creaked, followed by footsteps—lots of them. Cabinet doors were opened and shut with a bang. Truus held her hand over Arie's mouth.

"What have we here?" Weber said, pulling Julius from his hiding place and holding him by his shirt. "I don't recall your name. Wim? Arie? No, that's the little sick one. Julius. That's it, isn't it?"

"Leave the boy alone," the rabbi said, rushing through the door and grabbing Weber's arm.

"Get out of the way, Rabbi," Weber said. "We won't hurt our little hostage."

"No, no, no. Run, Julius!" the rabbi screamed, kicking and throwing wild punches. Weber let loose of the boy to deflect the blows, and Julius dashed toward the door, falling into the grasp of one of the other German sailors carrying Gaylord's submachine gun. The rabbi, refusing to back off, struck Weber. Weber drew Bosun's stolen Luger and shot the rabbi point-blank. He slumped to the ground, blood spreading over his shirt, his pallid face pointed toward Truus and Arie, who peeked out of their hiding place through the slats. The rabbi's eyes seemingly implored the children to keep quiet.

The three German sailors filed out of the galley, followed by Weber, who was holding Julius tightly by the hand. As the sailor with the bandaged head stepped into the light, he stopped with a suddenness that made the others crash together like train cars buckling in a wreck. He looked down and clutched at his chest, aghast to see Obasi's knife sticking out. The next sailor in line—the one with a wrapped foot from being shot by Rogers at the beginning of the voyage— shoved the stabbed sailor impatiently to keep moving, toppling him over onto the deck. Before the others could react, Obasi fired the submachine gun, blasting the German with the wounded foot backward into Weber and Julius and the fourth sailor. That paralyzed everyone for the briefest moment.

Obasi aimed the still-smoking submachine gun at the remaining Germans and pulled the trigger. A sickening single click followed because the gun was either out of ammunition or jammed. Obasi tried to clear the chamber as he dashed for cover. Submachine gunshots from the German sailor tore across the deck, hitting Obasi in the legs and back. He slid down unconscious, a pool of blood growing larger around him.

⟫●⟪

In the wheelhouse, Rogers and Miriam couldn't see what had happened. "Sneak out the starboard door and tell me what's going on," Rogers said, holding the Colt, the submachine gun resting at his side. Miriam crawled out of the door, peeked over the railing, and dashed back in.

"They shot Obasi," she said.

"Who? Nidal?"

"No, the Germans," she said. "Oh, my God. The children." She dashed by Rogers, snatching the submachine gun, and fleeing through the port door before Rogers could stop her. He rose and took a step to follow but was too weak and fell, clutching his pistol. As he fought to pick himself up, a creak on the ladder outside the starboard door gave him pause. He crawled up into his chair and listened, shifting his gaze from door to door in tense anticipation.

Outside, Miriam crouched as she snuck around the wheelhouse, the submachine gun leading the way. A sound caused her to raise the gun and aim, focusing all her attention ahead, so much so that she didn't notice the shadow coming up from behind or the swing of the submachine gun butt

223

that crashed down on her head, knocking her out. Weber's last German sailor kicked Miriam. Seeing no response, he took her submachine gun and padded up the ladder to the wheelhouse's port door.

Inside the wheelhouse, more footsteps on metal ladders seemed to come from outside both doors, muffled by the stiff wind and the creaking ship pitching and rolling in the waves. Weber looked through the starboard door and ducked. To Rogers' left, the German sailor flung open the door and crouched, holding the two submachine guns in his hands, hesitating at the sight of the oil on the floor. Rogers swung his pistol from door to door, uncertain how to escape the crossfire.

A heavy fire bucket full of sand from above clunked on top of the German sailor's head, stunning him just long enough for Rogers to fire a shot. The German collapsed, lifeless. Wim hung down from his hiding place on the monkey island above the wheelhouse and let go, hitting the deck with a clang, terror on his face. Rogers waved for him to flee, and he limped away. The starboard door inched open. Rogers pointed his gun, ready to fire, only to lower it when a terrified Julius stepped out. Weber was holding Bosun's Luger to the boy's head. "Drop your weapon, Captain," Weber said. "I will not hesitate to shoot you both."

Reluctantly, Rogers let the Colt slip from his hand. Weber pushed Julius, who slid on the oil and had to fight to keep his balance. Weber shook his head at Rogers in apparent amusement and negotiated the puddle of oil with cautious half-steps. When they reached the captain's chair, Weber slapped Rogers' head so hard with his pistol that he flew out of the chair. Releasing Julius, who cowered behind the wheel, Weber kicked Rogers' gun away and dragged him to the front window.

"It's all been a waste of time!" Weber shouted, spittle flying from his mouth. "You killed my men for nothing." He smashed Rogers' bleeding head on the glass. In the distance appeared the barest silhouette of a submarine. "Your Sparks has been most helpful sending our location since Gibraltar.

And I'm afraid Oberleutnant Brauer doesn't permit prisoners of war." Weber pressed the Luger to Rogers' temple.

"I thought you weren't like the Nazis. What about your honor?" Rogers said, gasping for breath.

"You Americans are such hypocrites," Weber said. "You don't know the meaning of honor. Tell your Indians about honor. Tell your Negroes about honor. Tell the Jews about honor. They stabbed us in the back during the war to end all wars. I don't make policy, Captain. I follow orders. No prisoners." Weber pushed Rogers to his knees, the gun still to his head.

Suddenly, several shots slammed into Weber, jolting him against the windows. He slid to the floor, blood spurting from his mouth and chest. A relieved Rogers jerked his head around toward the source of the shots. Miriam, leaning on Wim for support, pointed Weber's confiscated Mauser through the door. In shock, she dropped the weapon and stumbled over to Rogers, falling to her knees, retching, crying, looking with horror at Weber's lifeless eyes. "Close them, please. They are staring at me." Rogers brushed Weber's eyelids closed with his hand and wrapped his arms around Miriam. Wim grabbed Julius' hand and limped over to join them.

"That's OK. You're OK. You did the right thing," Rogers said, stroking Miriam's head.

Truus rushed through the open door. "They shot Uncle Levy."

"What? Where is he?" Miriam said. "And where is Arie?"

"Hiding in the galley, maybe," Truus said, bursting into tears. "I'm sorry. I ran and forgot him."

"Go get him," Rogers said to the still-shaking Miriam. "Bring me the submachine gun and help me out to the bridge wing. We'll cover you, won't we, kids? We still don't know who else is against us. Hurry." As soon as she got Rogers situated on the bridge, Miriam held the Mauser in front of her and snuck off for the galley. On the horizon to the west, the U-boat loomed larger.

CHAPTER 18

Miriam maneuvered around the bodies of the two German sailors and pushed open the galley door. She edged inside, swinging her gun barrel left and right. Quickly scanning the room, she crept over to the rabbi, who was lying on the floor. "Arie, come. It is safe." The young boy crawled out of his hiding place and scampered to Miriam, who was holding the rabbi's head in her lap.

"I'm sorry. I tried," the rabbi said in a shaky voice between coughs.

"You saved the children."

"No. You saved us all. Now look after them in the Promised Land."

"You will be there with us," Miriam said, tears welling in her eyes.

"In my coat pocket, there is an envelope," he said. "When you are safe, give it to Captain Rogers."

"The reward?"

The rabbi coughed violently, spitting up blood. His voice weakened. "There is no reward, dear."

"What? Then why did he—"

"Hear, O Israel," the rabbi mumbled in Hebrew. "Help me, Miriam."

"Hear, O Israel, the Lord is our God," they recited together in Hebrew. The rabbi choked, closed his eyes, and took his last breath, leaving Miriam to finish the prayer.

"The Lord is one," she said in English. Arie hugged her, overcome with grief, as they cried together.

A *thump, thump, thump* startled them. Miriam scoured the room with the pistol, moving Arie behind her for protection. More thumps and muffled voices. She stood and prowled around, stopping when she found a door in the floor and tugged it open. Looking up from the darkened cold storage room were Nidal, Gaylord, Cookie, Turani, and McAllister, all tied up and shivering.

After freeing the prisoners, Miriam and Aire filed out of the galley and made their way past the bodies. A tearful Miriam stared up at Rogers, shaking her head "no." "I found Mister Nidal!" she shouted. Nidal and the other survivors followed behind, patting themselves to get warm and still untying the ropes.

Rogers pointed to the U-boat on the horizon and shouted. "Our only hope is to make it to Haifa. Chief, give us flank speed." Turani saluted and rushed toward the engine room, then turned around and rushed back.

"And who's going to shovel the coal?" Turani shouted. "Can't make headway without a fireman or two, and trimmers."

That stumped Rogers for a moment. "The Dogar brothers are tied up in my dayroom. Use them and any of the other mutineers still alive, four hours on and four hours locked up in Hold Number One."

"What if they refuse? I can't be guarding them and watching over the engine at the same time, especially since I don't know where Dunawa is."

"Tell them their German buddies are dead, and the U-boat is on our tail. So, if they don't shovel with all their might, they will be blown sky-high just like the rest of us. And have the ones you don't need now soogee the blood off the deck and up here in the wheelhouse," he said, using the sailor's term for scrubbing down the ship with a strong cleaning product.

"Aye, aye, Captain," Turani said and dashed off.

"Wait!" Rogers yelled. "Not Bosun." But it was too late. The chief engineer didn't hear him as he ran down the ladder to the engineering room.

"What do you want done with him, Captain?" Cookie shouted. "Throw him overboard, perhaps?"

"Unfortunately, no. Just lock him up, away from the others."

"Let's see how he likes the cooler," Cookie said with a self-satisfied chuckle.

"Before you do that, tend to the bodies. Gaylord, you can help Cookie. Nidal and McAllister, I need you up here." They jumped up the ladder, two steps at a time.

Gaylord and Cookie lifted Obasi's limp and bleeding body. "Captain, he's still breathing!" Gaylord shouted. Miriam sprinted over to help.

"What do you want done with the bodies?" Nidal asked, his lips blue and slightly out of breath, beating his arms to get warm.

"Toss them overboard and let Neptune deal with them." Nidal gave him a surprised look. "There's no time for ceremony, Mr. Nidal."

"The rabbi, too?"

"No, no...not the rabbi," Rogers said, his voice drifting off. "Is he really dead?" When Nidal nodded, Rogers sighed. "We'll have to ask Miriam what to do."

Down below, Dunawa stepped out of the engineering room into the light on the deck.

"Dunawa!" Rogers shouted. "Thank God you're alive. Don't you know how to operate the radio?"

"I trained on it a long time ago, sir. But why not use Sparks?"

"Sparks? Where is he?" Rogers said in surprise.

"I tied him up down under after he and Lonnie tried to kill us. I will bring him to the radio room."

"Good, just have him turn it on the right frequency, and then you tap *dit-dit-dit*, wait, then *dit-dit-dit*, wait, then *dit-dit-dit* and count to ten and repeat until your fingers bleed. Understand?"

"Aye, aye, Captain. And, Captain, Lonnie didn't make it," he said, ducking back into the engine room and dragging Sparks up the ladder to the radio room to send the S-S-S warning of merchant ship under U-boat attack.

"Even if the British can figure out where we're located, they're very unlikely to reach us in time," Nidal said in his usual flat tone.

"That's why McAllister will run us in a zig-zag pattern at flank speed, right, Helmsman?" Rogers said. The young Scot tapped his head as if saluting and hurried over to the wheel. "That should buy us a couple of hours." It didn't take that long. The *Peggy C* was traveling in a major shipping lane heavily patrolled by British warships and planes.

Just before noon, a Sunderland bomber buzzed over the ship, diving at the U-boat, which crash-dived under the surface as bombs exploded all around it, shooting geysers of spray and smoke dozens of feet high.

Watching, slumped in his captain's chair, Rogers said to Nidal standing next to him, "Turani assures me we can hit ten knots for short periods. U-boats can only do seven knots underwater, I hear. That is after it's finished hiding from the beating it's taking."

"But once the sun sets in a few hours..." Nidal said, his voice drifting off.

"I know," Rogers said. "It can do seventeen knots." After a long, awkward pause, Rogers cleared his throat. "You know, I'm sorry. I should have, uh—"

"I thought I had them under control," Nidal said.

"I should have trusted you—"

"You were wounded. I did what I thought best," Nidal said. "So did you."

Rogers, touched and speechless, looked up in relief as Miriam came in with cups of hot coffee. "I'm so sorry about your uncle," Rogers said. "He was a good, brave man."

"We must bury him soon. Jewish tradition says it must be done within one day. But I cannot do Taharah, the purification. Only a man can do that."

"Talk to Cookie. He'll know what to do."

She handed out the coffee, holding back her tears, and headed down the ladder.

In the galley, after being instructed by Miriam about how to perform the purification ceremony, a distraught Cookie used a long board to help her lift the rabbi's body off the deck and onto a table. They removed his clothes and covered the body with a sheet.

"You must wash the body. But you must show respect and not reach over it or remove the blood," Miriam said, taking off the rabbi's glasses and wedding ring.

"Don't hardly seem right to bury a man all bloody," Cookie said.

"We believe that a person's blood is as important as his life and should be preserved," she said. As Miriam recited prayers and Psalms, Cookie followed her instructions by lifting the sheet a corner at a time and carefully washing the body in this order: the head and neck, the right side of the body, the left side, and finally the back. When he was done, Miriam handed him a glass of water. "Traditionally, the water would be poured over his body from head to toe nine times," she said. "But we cannot disturb the wounds. So, please, pour it nine times on his head." He followed her instructions and then toweled off the body.

With Miriam's help, he tightly wrapped the sheet around the rabbi like a shroud. They lifted the body off the table with the board and placed it next to a large piece of canvas Cookie had spread on the floor. Once the rabbi was folded inside the canvas, Miriam stuffed his bloody clothes inside, and Cookie stuck a heavy fire bar—one of the replaceable cast-iron bars that forms the base of the furnaces—inside at the feet to weigh down the body.

"You can help with this, right?" Cookie asked. Miriam nodded. He handed her a large needle with thick thread and showed her how to sew the canvas closed. "Lord knows I've had to do this too many times," he said. Miriam's shaky fingers struggled to punch the needle through the thick canvas for a few stitches. So, with his calloused hands, Cookie gently guided her hand to get a better angle and a tighter pattern. "We normally try to do eight stitches per inch, but don't worry, lass. One or two is fine. Never had a customer come back to complain."

Miriam smiled weakly and patted Cookie's back in appreciation, her tears splattering on the shroud. "Thank you."

—◦◦◦◦—

By necessity, the burial was short—the *Peggy C* couldn't be slowed down. Nidal and Cookie carried the rabbi's canvas-wrapped body on the board and perched one end on the starboard railing. Everyone not locked up or manning his station gathered around with hats off and heads bowed in sorrow as puffy clouds drifted by. The rabbi's three sons stood slightly apart from the others, their shirts torn on the left side near their hearts, a sign of the *Kriah*, a ritual rending of the garments by close family members of the deceased.

Speaking English so everyone could understand, Miriam recited the short *Hashkavah*, a traditional Sephardic prayer for the dead that called for God to "provide a sure rest on the wings of the Divine Presence." She concluded with, "Therefore, the Merciful One will protect him forever in the hiding of his wings, and will tie his soul with the rope of life. The Everlasting is his heritage, and he shall rest peacefully at his lying place, and let us say: Amen."

As everyone replied, "Amen," Truus clutched Miriam, who looked over at Rogers, held steady on his wounded leg by Turani. Rogers seemed stunned, head down and holding a well-worn book in his shaky hand—a book he had found years ago at Amsterdam's Scheltema bookshop. It was a copy of a poetry collection his mother had given him with her handwritten commentary throughout—notes he had tried to remember and re-enter over the years. It was his turn to speak, but Rogers couldn't find the words. Memories of the rabbi, his lost friend, flooded his mind, the corny stories so full of wisdom, warmth, and understanding. Also, his devotion to faith and family, and his basic decency.

It was almost like losing a father. "Family is everything" had never felt so real.

And the wings. The prayer had overwhelmed him, triggering visions of Pegasus, the winged horse they were riding to safety, the one whose name was inspired by the rabbi's story. Was it coincidence or fate that they were hiding in the wings of Pegasus?

"Captain," Nidal called out softly.

"I'm sorry, I don't know any prayers," Rogers said in a trembling voice. "But I think the rabbi would understand and appreciate this." He opened the book and read aloud *Crossing the Bar* by Alfred Lord Tennyson. "Sunset and evening star / And one clear call for me! / And may there be no moaning of the bar, / When I put out to sea." He recited the other three stanzas from memory without taking his watery eyes off the shroud, stumbling only when he came to the line, "And may there be no sadness of farewell, / When I embark." He closed the book and signaled for Nidal and Cookie to proceed. They lifted the end of the board, allowing the body to slide into the sea and sink below the undulating blue waves.

Rogers bowed his head and covered his face with his hands, his shoulders shaking. Truus pulled free of Miriam's hand, wrapped her arms around Rogers, and would not let him go. The boys joined her, patting him on the back and hugging him, seemingly forgetting their own sorrow to comfort a friend. The gesture made Miriam smile.

———⸺⸺———

Later that evening, Rogers manned his watch in the captain's chair, with Nidal next to him and McAllister at the wheel. Miriam opened the starboard door and stepped in, trailed by all four children carrying blankets and their life jackets. "They are afraid to sleep anywhere else," Miriam said. "Does that meet with your approval?"

"Sure, let's have a slumber party in the wheelhouse. Mr. Nidal and I do it all the time." Nidal fought a smile.

"How is Obasi?"

"He is doing well. The bullets did not strike bones or organs. He is resting. You need rest, too."

"She's right, Captain," Nidal said, helping Rogers out of the chair. Miriam had made a blanket bed for him in the dayroom. She and Rogers sat together on the floor, leaning against each other. The children crowded all around them.

"I am so sorry, Jake," Miriam whispered so as not to disturb the children as they drifted off to sleep.

"What for?"

"For getting you into jam. You did not have to do this."

"Not my smartest move, was it? But for once, the admiral would approve."

Miriam sat up, "The admiral? In the picture?"

"My grandfather—my mother's father," Rogers said.

"So, that is where your name came from?"

"Had to change it," Rogers said. "I told your uncle I didn't know the admiral until the night he got me out of jail, put me on the *Peggy C,* and said I could never return because—" Miriam pressed a finger on his lips.

"I do not care what you did in America." She kissed him and rested her head on his shoulder.

"I guess you're right," Rogers said, wrapping his arm around Miriam's shoulder. "Doesn't really matter now that I've led us into another losing battle...like your Deborah."

"She did not lose."

"But you said..."

"The Israelites faced impossible odds. That is true," Miriam said, snuggling his neck. "The Canaanites had 900 chariots of iron and wore armor. But on Mount Tabor, Deborah could see a storm coming and had General Barak lure them into battle on the plain below."

"How would rain stop an army?"

"Mud," she said, letting him think about it before continuing. "The chariots got stuck, and the stream Kishon overflowed. The Canaanites could not move in their heavy armor. What was once their strength led to their slaughter." They continued talking well past sunset, for a moment forgetting about the U-boat, only having eyes and ears for one another.

All lights on the ship were switched off to make the *Peggy C* harder to find, and the open cabin doors were covered with blackout curtains. The only light in the dayroom was a red 40-watt bulb covered by an empty can with a hole in the bottom for the socket.

———⟫●⟨———

Brauer's U-boat, surfacing as soon as the sun set, plowed through the smooth Mediterranean Sea as fast as its damaged engines would allow. White foam parted over the sharp prow like a train through a snowbank, its wake trailing behind to the horizon. With his four-man watch crew nervously scanning through the dark in all directions, Brauer paced the bridge, stopping abruptly to pull the plug out of the speaking tube.

"Bridge to L.I.," he said.

"L.I. here," Schmitt replied.

"Can't we go any faster?"

"We're straining to maintain twelve knots, Herr Oberleutnant."

"Let your old donkeys run themselves hard."

"Herr Oberleutnant, any moment now, the cylinder heads are going to blow clean out through the pressure hull."

Brauer, who could feel the bridge vibrating from the strain of the engines, looked around in frustration. "L.I. to the bridge."

"Aye, aye, Herr Oberleutnant."

When Schmitt ascended the ladder from the control room to the bridge, he carried two cups of hot coffee. "Smutje thought you could use this."

An unsmiling Brauer greeted him. Barely concealing his fury, a maniacal glint in his bloodshot eyes, he took the coffee without a word of thanks. "I need more speed, L.I. We'll never catch them in time at only twelve knots."

"I'm sorry, Herr Oberleutnant, but we need—"

"Max," he said, a faint smile on his face to match his forced casual tone. "Once they are in range of Palestine, we'll be a sitting duck. All of this would have been for nothing. Isn't there anything you can do?"

Schmitt took a long sip of coffee and nodded, apparently mulling over an idea. "Well, there is one thing we haven't tried."

"And that is...?"

"I could connect the electric motors to the diesels and run them together."

"Max! You genius! How long will it take to rig up?"

"Oh, I can do it in a matter of minutes, but I don't think you really want me to do it."

"Why on Earth not?"

"After an hour, the batteries will run out of juice." Schmitt didn't blink, apparently waiting for Brauer to realize what was causing his concern. After a moment, Brauer's shoulders sank.

"No batteries, no electricity, no diving," Brauer said, lowering his head in disappointment.

"Correct. If we are spotted, we won't be a sitting duck. We'll be a dead duck with no place to hide."

"We have no choice, L.I.," Brauer said, lifting his head and putting his hand on Schmitt's shoulder. "Give me the speed, and we'll leave the rest to God."

<hr />

Turani, nudging Rogers awake at daybreak, waved for him to follow. With a gentle touch, Rogers lowered Miriam's head onto the pillow and, with Turani's help, struggled to stand. They walked past Cookie at the wheel and outside to the bridge. Nidal tightly gripped binoculars facing the stern. Gaylord stood behind him. "It is gaining," Nidal said, pointing at the distant blot on the horizon, its outline too low-slung to be anything but a U-boat. "I'm surprised it has taken this long."

"Doesn't matter," Turani said. "At this speed, we'll be in range before noon."

"Can't you go faster?" Rogers asked.

"Captain, I can't even maintain *this* speed much longer."

"Why not send out the distress signal again?" Gaylord said.

"We're too far away from land," Rogers said. "The U-boat will be on top of us before any plane can reach us. And the Germans will hear our message and know they'll have to make quick work of us."

"What are your orders then, Captain?" Nidal asked.

Rogers paced along the bridge and tugged on his lower lip, torn about what to do next until he glanced through the window and saw Miriam sleeping like an angel with the children. "We stop."

"We cannot give up!" Nidal said, shock and anger in his voice.

"After all we've been through?" Gaylord said, raising his voice. "How dare you sacrifice all these people? How dare you surrender—"

"I didn't say *surrender*," Rogers said. He scanned the clear, blue sky of a new day. "Looks like rain."

As one, Turani, Nidal, and Gaylord gaped at Rogers like he had lost his mind.

CHAPTER 19

Miriam, the children, Nidal, Gaylord, Cookie, Turani, and Dunawa—all in life jackets—gathered in front of Rogers in his captain's chair. McAllister manned the wheel. "You all have to do exactly what I say," Rogers said. "Chief, slow down and blow smoke."

"Aye, aye, Captain," Turani, wearing a German sailor's jacket and forage cap, said before heading down the ladder.

"Gaylord, you and McAllister carry Obasi to the lifeboat," Rogers said.

McAllister hesitated, "Captain, you're in no shape to do this alone. I'll stay."

"Thanks, son, but no."

"Sir, at least let me help you down the ladder. Then I'll leave."

Rogers nodded. "First help carry Obasi, then come back up. But you get back on the motorboat the second my foot hits the deck. Do you hear me, sailor?"

"Aye, aye, Captain." He and Gaylord went below and carried out the unconscious African, his body wrapped in bloody bandages.

"Mr. Nidal, give me time to close. Cookie, keep the *Peggy C* between the lifeboats and the U-boat until you hear the alarm, then row like hell."

"But Captain—" Gaylord began.

"No arguments. I got us into this mess, so it's up to me to get us out of it. I can move well enough," Rogers said. "Dunawa, make Sparks send this message, word-for-word, then help Cookie and Gaylord get the prisoners into the lifeboats. Everybody understand?"

With worried looks but no questions, they all filed out of the wheelhouse. Rogers stood on shaky legs at the wheel and rotated it to starboard, heading dead toward the looming U-boat.

———⟫●⟪———

Brauer saw the maneuver through his binoculars on the conning tower. The *Peggy C* was within range, and now was getting even closer, although its prow made for a thin and difficult target. "What do you think they're doing, First Watch Officer?"

"They are blowing a lot of smoke. Must have engine problems," Mueller said. "Look, they are raising a flag." It was the blue flag with a white "X" signaling that the ship was stopping.

"Herr Oberleutnant, we have a message from Leutnant Weber," Funkmaat Vockel said, sticking his arm up through the hatch and handing Brauer a note. He read it with a look of grim satisfaction on his face.

"Weber says he has taken control of the ship and asks us to board to deal with the wounded and the prisoners," Brauer said. He inspected the distant ship with his binoculars as it slowed, blew its whistle three times, and turned to present a broadside—all clear signs of submission.

"Look, a couple of our men are waving from the deck," Mueller said.

"We don't have time to send over a dingy," Brauer said, scanning the sky with a worried look on his face. "Pull alongside and tether us as close as you can, First Watch Officer. "I want you to cover me and the boarding party with as many guns as you can fit on the upper deck."

———⟫●⟪———

Out of Brauer's sight on the other side of the *Peggy C*, Miriam, the children, and Obasi waited in a lifeboat that Cookie rowed further away, making sure to stay hidden from the U-boat. In another lifeboat next to them steered by Dunawa, Gaylord guarded six bound and gagged mutineers. A motorized lifeboat rocked alongside the *Peggy C*, roped to the Jacob's ladder.

In Hold Number Four at the stern of the *Peggy C*, Nidal, wearing a bloody German jacket full of bullet holes and a cap, tied a rope hanging from a boom on the deck to one of the dozens of fuel drums jammed together. He used a wrench to pop off the top of the drum and opened a second drum, turning it over to spill the green-dyed fuel all over the floor. He held his nose and bolted up the ladder. Once outside, Nidal cranked a winch and raised the rope from the hatch until the attached fuel drum reached deck level.

Turani joined him from the engine room, looking up in admiration at the billowing black smoke streaming from the funnel even though the engines were now at full stop. Together, they quickly lowered the anchors and scurried around the wheelhouse, making sure the crew cramming the deck of the fast approaching U-boat saw them but not their faces. They then continued around to the other side, where they climbed down the Jacob's ladder into the motorboat and waited for Rogers.

As the *Peggy C*'s alarm wailed, McAllister helped Rogers make his painful way down the ladder to the deck and out of sight of the U-boat. They shuffled toward the stern with the captain holding onto the wall for balance. Rogers, a wistful smile on his face, briefly stopped to pat the faint outline of the name *Peggy C*. "Good-bye, old girl," he whispered.

With his arm over McAllister's shoulder, Rogers tottered on the splint to the hanging drum. "Now, go. And tell them to keep pulling the rowboats out as far as they can."

"Aye, aye, sir. Good luck." He headed to the Jacob's ladder, stopping before disappearing over the rail. "And, Captain, thank you."

Rogers waved him off, pulled out a box of matches, and prepared to strike one, but then he spotted the two lifeboats. He counted the passengers to himself, repeatedly, concern growing on his face. He examined the matchbook: it was Bosun's.

"Light it! Jump! Now!" Nidal shouted from the motorboat as it slowly pulled away. "It's the smart move, damn it. Yalla, yalla."

Rogers, his shoulders slumped, lowered his head. "Tuan Jake, my ass." He dragged his wounded leg around the superstructure and toward the galley but stopped with another realization: the gold bar was still locked in the dayroom cabinet. He hesitated, looking up the three flights of stairs, trying to decide whether he could get up and back in time to release Bosun and spring the trap on the approaching U-boat.

He shook his head, ducked into the galley, and opened the hatch to the cold storage. Bosun, still tied up and shivering, bounded up the ladder. Rogers found a kitchen knife and cut the ropes. "If you want to live, follow me and don't do anything stupid."

Bosun shoved Rogers away and dashed out. Shaking his head, Rogers snuck out, heading for the stern. At the bow, Bosun waved at the U-boat, now practically on top of him, and threw a thick line to the German sailors. As soon as they secured the rope, the Germans opened fire, cutting down Bosun.

Rogers heard the shots as he fought, over and over, to get a match to light. Finally, one ignited, and he set on fire the rope holding the open drum, which he cranked high above the hold and away from fumes starting to drift out of it. As the rope smoldered, he backed away, tripping over a mop and falling to the deck. He labored to regain his feet, but the splint made it almost impossible. In utter frustration, he kicked the mop, snapping the handle, and used it as a lever to pull himself up. With the mop as his cane, Rogers hobbled to the Jacob's ladder and leaned over the bulkhead to wave at Nidal. "Further out, further out."

Nidal tossed out a roped life ring, revved up the engine, and backed away, reeling out the rope for more than a hundred meters so the life ring stayed near the ship for Rogers to grab. But Rogers wasn't sure how to escape, deciding the only thing to do was to roll over the side.

A gun cocked behind him. "Where are my men?" Rogers spun around and came face-to-face with Brauer holding a Mauser, his bandaged head covered by his white cap. Several armed German sailors scurried around the deck, searching for their comrades, the hostage-takers, and food.

"In hell...where you'll be shortly, Brauer."

"I have the gun," Brauer said, almost amused. "And it is Oberleutnant Brauer, Captain Rogers." He pressed the pistol against Rogers' head. "You have created many...difficulties for me." He lowered the gun to Rogers' heart, then his belly. "For that, I should kill you slowly—"

"Alarm! Alarm!" the other sailors shrieked. Confused, Brauer turned. His panicked men were scrambling to the bow and the U-boat. Some dove into the ocean. Brauer searched the sky to find the plane causing the panic, but the sky was empty.

Rogers slammed the mop handle onto Brauer's hand, knocking away the pistol. Shouting in pain, Brauer threw a round-house punch that Rodgers deflected. Grabbing the German's sleeve, Rogers pulled them both to the deck, where they rolled around and threw wild punches, kicking each other, fighting to reach the gun first. Brauer screamed at the pain shooting through his back and shoved the weakened Rogers far enough off of him to get his right hand on the Mauser.

Swinging the mop handle in desperation, Rogers again knocked the gun away. Brauer kicked him, rolled over, and crawled on his hands and knees to the gun, picking it up and turning to fire. But before Brauer could pull the trigger, Rogers stabbed his right leg with the broken end of the mop handle. The German screamed and dropped the weapon, clutching his leg to stanch the spurting blood and rolling onto his back.

Rogers crawled on top of him and flailed away, landing punch after punch to his head, bloodying his nose, knocking out teeth. In a blind rage, Rogers clutched Brauer's collar and lifted his head up. He cocked his right arm like a pile driver to deliver the final blow. Brauer, helpless and bleeding profusely, showed no fear, only resignation, as if to say, "Go ahead, get it over with." But the hatred and anger in his eyes made Rogers stop in mid-swing. He flung Brauer's head to the deck.

Panting and shaky, Rogers rolled off Brauer and hauled himself to his feet on the rail. As he got his legs over the railing, he glowered at Brauer. "Now you can look me in the eyes," he said in disgust and slid over the rail into the ocean. He held tight to the life ring and waved. Nidal fired up the motorboat engine and dragged Rogers slowly away from the ship.

Brauer grabbed his gun, fought to his knees and, standing on wobbly legs, clutched his aching back. He leaned over the bulwark and aimed at Rogers. Smoke curled around his face. He crinkled his nose and sniffed, looking in every direction until he saw at the stern exactly why his men had fled: the oil drum hanging from the flaming rope was ablaze, cords crackling and popping. Brauer, his face contorted and red, screamed and started shooting at Rogers as he scooted along the ocean some distance behind the motorboat.

The rope snapped with a crack, and the flaming drum plummeted into the hold. The ear-shattering explosion of the BAM-100 fuel sent shock waves and flaming debris hundreds of feet into the air. Walls of orange flames and black smoke engulfed the German sailors desperately climbing the scrambling nets on the U-boat's side or still swimming away from the *Peggy C*, incinerating them and scattering their remains like fiery grains of sand in a windstorm.

Inside Brauer's tethered U-boat, the unsuspecting men stood no chance, either. Before they even heard the blast, it ripped apart the hull of the 220-foot-long vessel from stem to stern, catapulting it out of the water in a hail of molten chunks of steel and body parts. Torpedoes in the U-boat exploded in rapid succession like a string of firecrackers, adding tentacles of red, orange, white, and blue flames to a mile-high mushroom cloud reeking of cordite and smoldering flesh.

The *Peggy C,* having done her duty, was pulverized out of existence.

Rogers' eyes fluttered open, but he was having trouble adjusting to the daylight. After a minute or two, he was able to focus on the rows of hospital beds, passing nurses, and bandages on his arms and legs. His head throbbed, and his skin stung all over. Miriam sat next to him in a chair, reading one of the red *Ivanhoe* volumes, apparently the only thing she had managed to grab before abandoning ship.

"Don't tell me I'm still in Majorca," he whispered, his throat dry and sore.

Looking surprised and pleased, Miriam leaned over and grabbed his hand. "No. Haifa. A British destroyer rescued us a few days ago."

"The others?" Rogers asked weakly.

"All safe. But we do not know if the authorities will let us stay."

Gaylord snuck up on them in time to overhear her. "Not to worry, my dear," Gaylord said. He threw down a newspaper on the bed. The headline read: "REFUGEES SINK U-BOAT." "You're heroes now. They wouldn't dare deport you. I've seen to that."

Miriam picked up the paper and gasped, "You are royalty?"

"Third cousin to His Majesty, actually," he said, smoothing down his mustache with both his index fingers now that he was free of his sling. "Helped get the attention of the local Fleet Street boys. There's even talk of awarding us all the George Cross."

Rogers gave him a look of disapproval.

"Right," Gaylord said with a cough. "I'm sure it's just talk."

"How can we thank you?" said Miriam, overcome and near tears as the months of worry and terror seemed to slip away.

"No need. You saved my life," Gaylord said. "Twice." He picked up *Ivanhoe* and turned it over in his hands. "Lovely book. Perhaps I should give it another read...Maybe learn something about your tribe." He set down the book and pumped Miriam's hand. "I am delighted to have met you. Both of you." He saluted and spun around to leave, almost banging into Nidal, Cookie, McAllister, Dunawa, and Turani, the latter of whom was pushing Obasi in a wheelchair.

With Miriam's help, Rogers scooted to sit up. "Guess you've come for the reward."

"Never crossed our minds," Nidal said. "We are just happy you are alive."

"So, how do I say this?" Rogers said. Apparently suspecting what was coming next, the men started arguing loudly, speaking over one another about the reward and how they deserved it, and how could Rogers have deceived them so.

Miriam stood and tore off a patch of cloth sewn inside her blouse, pulling out a diamond necklace and earrings and held them up, shouting for attention. "Here is your reward!" The crew members stopped screaming and gawked in amazement. She set the jewelry down on the bed. "My father wanted us to have it, but you have earned it and need it more than we do. We have family here to look after us." She handed the rabbi's note to Rogers. "This is from Uncle Levy."

Rogers read the note, his face turning in a matter of seconds from grim to surprised to amused. And then he roared with laughter. "Congratulations, boys. We're rich." He looked at Miriam. "Did you know your father owned the *Peggy C*?"

"No. Uncle Levy must not have known either. He said there was no reward."

"Well, he's deeded it to us in recognition of...what's a mitzvah?"

"A good deed," she said.

"I just wish we could have pulled it off without sacrificing the *Peggy C*," Rogers said, his eyes suddenly sad and misty. "She has been—uh, had been—my only home for a lot of years. I'm really going to miss her."

Before the captain could get too sentimental, Nidal scooped up the jewelry. "Your share will be waiting for you when you get out of here."

"My share? I don't deserve any," Rogers said, stopping to think over what he was going to say next. "Tell you what: Give me fare home, and we'll call it even."

Nidal checked with the other men. "Fair enough. We must go get our visas. Get well...Jake."

After they were out of earshot, Miriam turned in obvious agony to Rogers. "Home?"

"Sorry. I have to make things right."

"I told you I do not care what you did in America."

"I do. They say I killed somebody at the Academy. Truth is, I'm not sure. I thought it was self-defense. The admiral said one of the midshipmen who jumped me wasn't expected to live, and there was no way I'd get a fair trial because of who his family was. But now it's time to stop running. I can't keep living this way."

"We could build a life together here," she said.

"You could come with me."

"I have the children to look after. Besides, Jews are never truly home in other countries."

"America's different."

"Do they now allow in Jews from Europe? They did not when the ship named *St. Louis* brought hundreds of Jewish refugees from Germany."

Deflated, Rogers shook his head, paused as if in thought, and then perked up. "I know a good smuggler," he said.

Laughing and crying at the same time, Miriam laid down next to Rogers. "We have time. We must spend it well, yes?"

Rogers, smiling broadly, hugged her. "Yes, indeed."

In the hospital lobby, Nidal and the other crew members lined up at a table to get their visas from British soldiers. Cheers and shouts of glee caught them by surprise. As they turned, Truus, Wim, and Julius ran over to hug them all. Behind them, Arie hung on the hands of an elderly couple before shaking loose and running over to join in the joyous reunion. Even Nidal's hardened face broke out into a smile, and he warmly reciprocated the hugs. Truus handed each man a drawing of himself, signed by all the children with messages of thanks and squiggled stick people by Arie.

As the children headed into the hospital to visit Rogers, Wim called out: "Mr. Cookie!" All the sailors turned toward Wim, who stood with Julius, both at attention and saluting. "Farewell, matey," they said in unison. The boys grinned and sped off to catch up with the rest of the family. Cookie teared up.

"What's wrong with your eyes, Cookie?" Nidal asked.

"Nothing. Got a spec of something in 'em is all," he said, keeping his face turned away. Still sniffling, he rubbed his eyes and blew his nose in a handkerchief. Once composed, he looked at his colleagues. "Now, where to, mates?"

"The nearest bar," Turani said. "Then we find work on a ship heading to the States. At least the Americans have enough sense to stay out of this damn war."

As Turani spoke, one of the soldiers stamped his visa: "DECEMBER 7, 1941."

BIBLIOGRAPHY

Blair, Clay. 2010. *Hitler's U-Boat War: The Hunters 1939-42 (Modern Library War Book 1)*. New York: Random House Publishing Group. Kindle Edition.

Bunker, John. 1995. *Heroes in Dungarees*. Annapolis, MD: Naval Institute Press. Kindle Edition.

Busch, Harald. 1955. *U-boats at War: German Submarines in Action 1939-1945*. New York: Ballantine Books.

Cooper, Harry. 2010. *U-Boat!: The U-Boat War by the Men Who Lived It. Volumes 1-4*. Hernando, FL: Kindle Edition.

Doenitz, Karl. 2012. *Memoirs: Ten Years and Twenty Days*. South Yorkshire, England: Pen & Sword Books. Kindle Edition.

Duffy, James P. 2001. *Hitler's Secret Pirate Fleet: The Deadliest Ships of World War II*. Westport, CT: Praeger Publishers. Kindle Edition.

Gallery, Daniel V. 2018. *Twenty Million Tons Under the Sea: The Daring Capture of the U-505*. Laticlave Press. Kindle Edition.

Gasaway, E. B. 2014. *Grey Wolf, Grey Sea: Aboard the German Submarine U-124 in World War II*. New York: Open Road Media. Kindle Edition.

Goebeler, Hans, and John Vanzo. 2008. *Steel Boat Iron Hearts: A U-boat Crewman's Life Aboard U-505*. New York: Savas Beatie. Kindle Edition.

Gunn, George. 1999. *Tramp Steamers at War*. Llandysul, Ceredigion, Wales: Gomer Press.

Konstam, Angus, and Jak Mallman Showell. 2003. "7th U-boat Flotilla: Dönitz's Atlantic Wolves." *Slideshare*. Ian Allan Publishing. Accessed December 2020. https://www.slideshare.net/PeterPieters1/dnitz-atlantic-wolves.

Lee, Christopher. 2012. *Eight Bells and Top Masts: Diaries from a Tramp Steamer*. London: Faber & Faber, Kindle Edition.

Mulligan, Timothy. 1999. *Neither Sharks Nor Wolves*. Annapolis, MD: Naval Institute Press. Kindle Edition.

Padfield, Peter. 2020. *War Beneath the Sea: Submarine conflict during World War II*. London: Lume Books. Kindle Edition.

Paterson, Lawrence. 2003. *Second U-Boat Flotilla*. South Yorkshire, UK: Pen & Sword Books Ltd. Google Edition.

—. 2004. *U-Boat War Patrol: The Hidden Photographic Diary of U-564*. S. Yorkshire, UK: Pen & Sword Books. Kindle Edition.

Shuren, Teddy. 2011. *Teddy Suhren, Ace of Aces*. South Yorkshire, England: Pen & Sword Books. Kindle Edition.

n.d. www.u-boat.net.

van Kuilenburg, Hans Moederzoon. 2013. *The Silent Heroes: A Memoir of Holland During WWII*. Houston TX: Strategic Book Publishing and Rights Co. Kindle Edition.

Vause, Jordan. 1990. *U-Boat Ace*. Annapolis, MD: Bluejacket Books, Naval Institute Press. Kindle Edition.

Whitehead, Edward "Ted" Jones. 2018. *Down Below: Reminiscences of a World War II Engine Room Merchant Seaman*. USA: Self-published. Kindle Edition.

Wiggins, Melanie. 1999. *U-Boat Adventures: Firsthand Accounts from World War II*. Annapolis: Naval Institute Press.

Woodman, Richard. 2011. *The Real Cruel Sea: The Merchant Navy in the Battle of the Atlantic, 1939–1943*. Barnsley, South Yorkshire, United Kingdom: Pen & Sword Books. Kindle Edition .

Workman, Charlie. 2010. *From Hardships to Steamships: Memoirs of a Merchant Seaman During World War II*. Ailsa, Castle Gate, Penzance, Cornwall, United Kingdom: United Writers Publications Ltd. Kindle Edition.

PRIMARY WEB SITES

u-boat.net: https://www.uboat.net/

u-boataces.com: https://www.uboataces.com

U-Boat Archive: http://www.uboatarchive.net/

Wikipedia: https://en.wikipedia.org/wiki/Main_Page

Youtube.com

ACKNOWLEDGEMENTS

Writing this novel was a lifelong dream that took many years and many forms and a fleet of mates to bring to life. When I retired from journalism the first time, I had a dream—literally. When I awoke, I knew the first scene, the last scene, and the ship's name for a screenplay. That was it.

I have no idea what inspired the dream, except perhaps all the times I spent watching bad movies with my wife Margo and our daughter Allison (now a screenwriter, actress, and director) and thinking, "I know I can write a better screenplay then that." So, I wrote the screenplay, re-wrote it, re-wrote it again, and pitched it in Hollywood to some positive reviews but no sale.

Then came the Covid-19 pandemic. Being stuck at home for months, what else could I do but turn the screenplay into a novel? After all, I had gotten into journalism because I wanted to write the great American novel, only I had no idea how to write a novel and no death-defying experiences to write about. I still haven't written the great American novel, but at least I've taken the initial step thanks to many special people.

First, I need to thank my late parents, Pat and Harry B. Miller Jr., who imbued me with a love of reading, storytelling, and poetry. Some of my father's real-life experiences appear in this novel, as well as the poetry book his mother Ann Walcutt Winn gave him with her notes scribbled in pencil. She always had a book in her hand as she curled up in her favorite green over-stuffed living room chair, drinking Coke from a silver julep cup and puffing on a cigarette. She was full of stories, especially about her grandfather, John Macy Walcutt, a U.S. Naval Academy graduate who made his fortune before the Civil War as a sea captain working for the Delano family (as in Franklin Delano Roosevelt) in the opium trade with China.

She also loved to tell us about her other grandfather, Thomas Henry

Hines, a Confederate cavalry captain and spy who engineered a clever prison escape for fellow inmate Gen. John Hunt Morgan and other officers. So, I have storytelling in my blood.

But writing a novel is a whole different animal from writing a news story or even a screenplay. For that, I needed help. I especially need to thank fellow writer Chris Evans, my development editor, whose eagle eye and great suggestions made this so much better than I ever could have done by myself.

I also want to thank writer Matt Zullo, a former submarine petty officer, and my college roommate Dr. Joe Holmes, a Navy vet, for making sure I didn't screw up all the nautical terms and descriptions because I have never been on a tramp steamer or a U-boat. Likewise, I want to thank Matthew Adler, a Ph.D. student in the Department of War Studies at King's College London, for fact-checking my work.

Several friends have also been nice enough to read my manuscript and offer suggestions or corrections. These include Ron Mitchell, my first editor on the student paper and current tennis partner, and Jonathan Miller, my cousin and a non-fiction author.

I also want to thank Lisa Haneberg for her excellent workshop on novel writing and her encouragement.

This book wouldn't have been possible with such useful websites as uboat.net, uboatarchive.net, uboataces.com, and especially Wikipedia, to which I make frequent donations and encourage others to support.

I also owe a debt of gratitude to Bancroft Press publisher Bruce Bortz and editor Elizabeth Redmond for having faith in me and working such magic with my prose.

Finally, I want to thank my lovely wife Margo for her encouragement, for reading and re-reading the screenplay and manuscript, for offering good suggestions and critiques, and for her meticulous editing.

And for putting up with me for more than four decades of rambling around the world.

ABOUT THE AUTHOR

John Winn Miller is an award-winning investigative reporter, foreign correspondent, editor, newspaper publisher, screenwriter, movie producer, and now a novelist.

As a foreign correspondent for The Associated Press, Miller covered wars in Beirut, Chad, and Eritrea. He traveled with Pope John Paul II and covered such varied stories as the hijacking of the *Achille Lauro*, Mafia busts, and terrorist attacks around the Mediterranean. He briefly served as Rome bureau chief of the Wall Street Journal/Europe before returning to his hometown to work for the Lexington (Ky.) Herald-Leader.

In Lexington, Miller was part of a team of reporters that wrote a series that helped trigger educational reform in Kentucky. The series won the 1990 public service award from the Society of Professional Journalists, top honors from Investigative Reporters and Editors, the $25,000 Selden Ring award, and was a Pulitzer Prize finalist.

He was named executive editor of the Centre Daily Times (State College, Pa.) in 1996 and executive editor of the Tallahassee Democrat (a Knight Ridder newspaper like the Herald-Leader and the Centre Daily Times) in 1999. When

Knight-Ridder traded papers with Gannett in 2005, Miller was named publisher of one of the newly acquired papers, The Olympian in Olympia, WA.

After McClatchy acquired Knight Ridder, Miller helped merge most of his paper's operations with The Tacoma News-Tribune and then took early retirement in 2009.

He returned to Lexington, where he wrote screenplays and TV shows and partnered in a social media marking startup called Friends2Follow.

Miller also helped produce four independent feature films: *Hitting the Cycle* with Bruce Dern; *Armed Response*, starring Ethan Evans and Michael Gladis and three generations of Arkins—Adam, Alan, and Ayote; *Band of Robbers*, written and directed by Adam and Aaron Nee, and *Ghost in the Family*.

In September 2010, Miller was hired as publisher of the Concord (N.H.) Monitor. Two years later, he was elected to The Associated Press board of directors, and selected as a juror for the Pulitzer Prizes for the second year in a row.

He retired again the next year to return home to Lexington, where he taught journalism at The University of Kentucky and Transylvania University.

Born and raised in Lexington KY, he attended Emory University in Atlanta before graduating from The University of Kentucky.

He lives in Lexington with his wife Margo, a potter and former college English teacher. Their daughter Allison Miller is an actress-screenwriter-director currently starring on the ABC series *A Million Little Things*.

This is Miller's first novel.